Forbidden Magic

Andrea A James

Published by Whispering Hearts publishing, 2024.

This is a work of fiction. Similarities to real people, places, or events are entirely coincidental.

FORBIDDEN MAGIC

First edition. December 5, 2024.

ISBN: 979-8230480655

Written by Andrea A James.

Also by Andrea A James

Hearts Entwined
Forbidden Magic
Mistletoe Magic
Fae and Flame

To my soul sisters, Iris and Cibele, for always being there, no matter the miles between us—your friendship knows no borders.

To Greg, my rock, my parents and sister, my gran who now watches over us from heaven—I hope to make you proud.

To my wonderful aunts Tie and Bernie, Uncle Gideon, and Aunty Jenny, for your endless encouragement.

And to my new friends from work, for bringing light and laughter to this chapter of my life.

This is for all of you, with love and gratitude.

Prologue

In a distant time lost to history's fog, the French Quarter's cobblestone streets echoed jazz melodies, and magnolia scents lingered like cherished memories. Amongst this rich blend of culture and mystery, a coven's ancient magic intertwined with the city's soul, its roots delving deep into the essence of New Orleans.

As fate guided them forward, the coven's path shifted towards Tridion, a land brimming with magic and mystery. Amidst this growing enchantment, they formed new bonds and created a haven in the city's core. Still, traces of their New Orleans roots lingered, a poignant reminder of where they began.

Now living in the lively streets of New Orleans, the Johnston family's roots extend to Tridion's magical forests and high mountains. Eighteen-year-old identical twins Amy and Annie Johnston resided with their parents, Michelle and Craig, in a mysterious mansion, part of a coven with centuries-old connections.

Amy's hazel eyes sparkled with curiosity in this world of abundant magic, her captivating charm enchanting all who met her. Damien LaStat, with his blue eyes and magnetic charisma, couldn't help.

Annie exuded quiet strength by her side, with her hazel eyes reflecting her sister's and her braided hair symbolizing resilience. Lucian Ravenshaw, with his captivating emerald eyes and enigmatic presence, sensed an inexplicable connection with her; their fates entwined in ways that defied comprehension. Their home in Tridion wasn't just a house; it was a sanctuary for a diverse group of friends and family. As Amy, Annie, and their friends explored the intricacies of Tridion, their connections grew more muscular, fueled by the magic within them. But shadows loomed beneath the surface of peace, suggesting hidden dangers and undiscovered truths waiting to be uncovered. Despite facing many challenges, the coven and their allies were unprepared for the trials that awaited them. But be drawn to her, his heart stirred by her presence. Annie exuded quiet strength by her side, her hazel eyes reflecting her sister's, her braided hair symbolizing resilience. And Lucian Ravenshaw, with his piercing emerald gaze and mysterious aura, felt an unexplainable bond with her, their destinies intertwined in ways beyond understanding. Their home in Tridion wasn't just a house; it was a sanctuary for a diverse group of friends and family.

As Amy, Annie, and their friends explored the intricacies of Tridion, their connections grew more muscular, fuelled by the magic within them. But shadows loomed beneath the surface of peace, suggesting hidden dangers and undiscovered truths waiting to be uncovered. Despite facing many challenges, the coven and their allies were unprepared for the trials that awaited them.

As hardship hit, their once-stable world spiraled into chaos. Betrayal seeped from within their circle, putting their lives and the entire coven's existence at risk. With the need for reinforcements dire, Gregory and Lucian stepped up, leading their allies in combat and tapping into the power of their dragons. Amid the turmoil, doubts arose—was their enemy truly who they believed, or was a darker threat hiding in the shadows? The sting of betrayal cut deep, testing the very core of their trust.

They are seeking help from their cousin Liam, the alpha of his pack, as Lucian and Gregory prepare for a showdown that could determine their very survival. Will the coven and their allies possess the strength to overcome this pivotal clash?

During the chaos, Amy felt drawn to the realm of literature, eager to capture her world's essence within the pages of books while safeguarding its secrets to avoid conflicts with the Elders. Meanwhile, Annie nurtured dreams of pursuing journalism. Will each sister achieve her aspirations, or will destiny interweave unexpected turns into the fabric of their lives?

Will they ever experience normalcy? Discover soulmates, build families, explore the world? Or will they be condemned to perpetual fear, constantly wary of lurking danger? Will their magical abilities forever pose a threat? Can they safeguard themselves and their loved ones? Or will the cycle of reincarnation forever bind them to their fate?

Chapter 1

The evening of our eighteenth birthday arrived with a sense of expectation that neither Annie nor I could ignore. The house was filled with the aroma of fresh pastries and the buzz of excitement as our parents, Michelle and Craig, made sure every detail was perfect. The anticipation in the air was almost tangible, but there was something heavier, something unspoken, that made the evening feel different.

"Girls, come sit down," Dad said, his voice holding a rare note of seriousness that cut through the festive clamor. He was carrying a small, ornate box—one of those things that seemed to promise secrets wrapped in velvet.

Annie and I exchanged glances, the same unease mirrored in our hazel eyes. We took our seats around the dining room table, which was set with candles and crystal goblets, a stark contrast to the lively chaos that filled the rest of the house.

"Is something wrong?" I asked, trying to keep my voice steady. I had always felt the weight of unspoken truths, especially with the recurring nightmares Annie and I shared, but tonight was different.

Mom took a deep breath, her eyes soft yet resolute. "There's something important we need to tell you, something we've kept hidden until now."

I could feel a shiver run through me, a mix of dread and excitement. "What do you mean?" Annie asked, her voice barely above a whisper.

Dad placed the box on the table and nodded. "Tonight, as you turn eighteen, you step into a new chapter of your lives. This is the moment we reveal what has been a part of our family's legacy for generations."

I swallowed hard, my curiosity flaring despite my anxiety. "What kind of legacy?"

Mom looked at us with a sadness that made my heart ache. "You are witches, born into a family with a history that stretches back to the French Quarter of the 1920s. Your gifts are not just magical—they are part of a lineage that carries both great power and great responsibility."

Annie's eyes widened. "But... what kind of gifts?"

Dad's gaze was steady. "Amy, you have the gift of telepathy. You can communicate thoughts, influence minds, and see beyond the surface of things. Annie, your gift is a bit different. You have telekinesis, divination, and the ability to transmute objects."

I felt a rush of confusion and awe. "So, what does all this mean for us? What are we supposed to do with these abilities?"

Mom's expression grew solemn. "One of you will be chosen to become the next Supreme Witch of the Crescent City Coven. It's a role that carries immense power but also great danger."

Annie and I exchanged a look, our minds racing. "And if one of us fails?" I asked.

Mom's voice was heavy. "If one of you dies, the cycle of reincarnation will begin anew. You will be reborn, and I will have to endure the pain of losing you all over again."

I shivered, trying to process the enormity of what she had just revealed. "We've been through this before?"

"Yes," Mom said softly. "You have lived many lives, each tied to the fate of the coven. The memories fade with each rebirth, but they will come back in dreams and visions."

Annie's brow furrowed. "And we've never lived past twenty-three?"

"That's right," Dad confirmed. "But each lifetime is a chance to break the cycle, to change your fate."

The weight of their words settled on us like a leaden blanket. I glanced around, looking for something to anchor me to the present. The doorbell rang, cutting through the tense silence.

"Your guests are here," Dad said, standing up to answer the door. "Let's not keep them waiting."

As Dad went to greet our friends, I caught Annie's eye. "We'll talk more about this later, okay?"

She nodded, her expression mirroring my own turmoil. "Yeah, let's get through tonight."

The house was now filled with the laughter and chatter of our friends. I looked around at the familiar faces—Grayson and Christian Cole, our best friends from New Orleans, along with the rest of our tight-knit group of fourteen. We had been inseparable since kindergarten, but now there was a new layer of mystery between us that I couldn't ignore.

"Wow, look at all the people," Annie said, her eyes scanning the crowd.

"Yeah, it's bigger than I expected," I replied, trying to keep my composure. I had hoped this night would be about celebration, not revelation, but the two were now tangled together.

Grayson approached, a grin on his face. "Hey, Amy, what's got you so lost in thought?"

I tried to smile, though I could feel my nerves fluttering. "Just thinking about how strange everything feels tonight."

Grayson's grin widened. "Sounds like you've got something on your mind."

I hesitated, then decided to test my new abilities. "Hey, Grayson, do you want to come upstairs with me? I need to talk to you about something."

I watched him closely, but he didn't react. His attention was caught by someone else, and my message seemed to fade into the background.

"Hey, Amy, you okay?" Annie's voice pulled me from my thoughts.

"Yeah, I'm fine," I said, trying to shake off the unease. "Grayson didn't seem to catch my message. I was just wondering if I might have a stronger connection with someone else."

Before I could say more, Christian appeared beside us, a mischievous glint in his eyes. "I heard you trying to reach Grayson. What's up?"

I looked at him, sensing an opportunity. "Christian, can we talk in private for a moment?"

Christian followed me upstairs, his curiosity evident. "What was that back there? I felt like you were speaking to me without saying a word."

I took a deep breath, deciding to trust him. "I'm not entirely sure what's happening, but I think I might be able to connect with people telepathically."

Christian's eyes widened. "That's insane! Are we like... telepathic now?"

I nodded slowly. "It seems that way. But I tried to reach Grayson and it didn't work. I'm not sure why."

Christian looked thoughtful. "Maybe there's something special about our connection?"

I wasn't sure, but something in Christian's words resonated. "Maybe you're right. I have to keep this a secret, though. If my parents find out..."

"Don't worry," Christian said, his eyes serious. "Our secret is safe with me."

As we returned downstairs, I tried to push away the anxiety about what lay ahead. It was my birthday, and despite everything, I wanted to enjoy it. The room was filled with music and laughter, a temporary escape from the weight of what we had learned.

Annie and I would face this new chapter of our lives together, no matter how daunting it might be. For now, we were surrounded by friends and celebration, and I intended to savor it while it lasted.

The night wore on with dancing and laughter, a fleeting moment of normalcy before the unknown journey that lay ahead.

As I looked around at the faces of my friends and felt the warmth of their presence, I allowed myself a brief moment of hope. Maybe the future held more than just the shadows of our past lives. Maybe we could find our own path amid the magic and mystery.

And as the music played and the party continued, I promised myself that I would not let fear dictate my future. For tonight, I was going to celebrate being eighteen and embrace whatever came next.

Chapter 2

The hazy echoes of last night's party drifted through my mind as I sat at the kitchen table. Sunlight streamed through the windows, warming the room as if trying to soothe my nerves. The smell of bacon and eggs filled the air, wrapping around me like a comforting blanket. It was just another breakfast, but today was different. My parents had promised to share something important, and my gut was twisted with a mix of excitement and dread.

Mom placed a plate of toast in front of me, her usual morning routine, but her eyes were fixed on me and Annie with a gravity I hadn't seen before.

"Alright, girls," she said, her tone serious but laced with a trace of hesitation, "Your father and I have decided it's time you knew more about our family history."

I looked up from my plate, a forkful of eggs halfway to my mouth. "What do you mean? We know about the coven."

Dad leaned forward, his face shadowed by the morning light. "We've kept a lot from you. But it's time you understood the true nature of our legacy."

My heart skipped a beat. "Is there something more to it?"

Mom exchanged a glance with Dad, then took a deep breath. "We're part of the New Orleans Crescent Coven. It's more than just tradition—it's a legacy that's been with us for generations. But with that legacy comes danger. You know how our friends are also descendants of the coven? Their fates are intertwined with ours."

Annie's eyes widened. "You mean, we're not just living normal lives?"

"Far from it," Dad said. "There are witch hunters in New Orleans who have been trying to dismantle us for centuries. We must keep our existence a secret from them."

A shiver ran down my spine. "So, you're saying our nightmares... they're real?"

Mom's gaze was solemn. "Yes, they're echoes from our past lives. We need to be vigilant."

I took a deep breath, steeling myself. "Okay. So, what does this have to do with Christian?"

Mom's eyes softened. "Christian is your soulmate, Amy. But there's more you should know."

"What is it?" I asked, leaning in, my heart racing.

She hesitated, then said, "There's a vampire named Damien LaStat. He's been a thorn in our side for centuries."

The name struck me like a cold wind. "Damien LaStat? Is he... the cause of our suffering?"

Mom nodded gravely. "He's caused many tragedies over the years. He's a master of manipulation and has a dark history with our coven."

My resolve hardened. "I won't let him win."

Mom gave a sad smile. "Be cautious. He has a way of charming you, drawing you in until you're lost."

I nodded, my mind racing. "I understand. I'll wait until the others are ready to join us before I take any action."

Mom and Dad exchanged a look of approval before Mom handed us the box from last night. "This is for you. It's our family's spell book and some of the ingredients we'll need."

Annie and I opened the box, revealing the Book of Shadows and jars of magical ingredients, each meticulously labeled. There was also a rainbow of candles, hinting at the potential spells we could cast.

"Everything you need is here," Mom said. "But remember, magic is dangerous. We will guide you through it."

Excitement buzzed in my chest. "Thank you. We'll be careful."

Dad cleared his throat. "There's one more thing we want to show you."

He led us upstairs to a hidden chamber we had never seen before. The room was lined with portraits of our ancestors, and shelves overflowed with ancient books and mysterious jars.

"Wow," I breathed. "This is incredible."

Mom's expression was stern. "This room is off-limits unless your father or I are with you. You must earn the right to explore these secrets."

Annie and I nodded, absorbing the weight of her words.

Dad gestured to a large table with a grand cauldron. "This is where we've practiced magic for centuries."

Mom took out a few ingredients and began a demonstration. The cauldron bubbled, releasing a swirl of colors and enchanting scents.

Weeks passed, and as our friends turned eighteen, I felt the time was right for our next step. I gathered everyone and showed them an old map from one of the books—a guide to the French Quarter, where our ancestors once practiced magic.

"Let's explore this place," I said. "We have one weekend to uncover what we can."

We ventured into the French Quarter, the streets alive with an eerie magic of their own. Supernatural shops and whispers of dark secrets greeted us as we followed the map to an old, crumbling building.

Inside, the air was thick with the weight of history. We found a room with bookshelves and a pentagram carved into the floor.

"It looks like we're in the right place," I said, glancing around.

We split up to search for clues. Hours passed, and we found nothing until a loud rumbling shook the building.

I turned to see a strikingly handsome man standing in the shadows. His presence was commanding, his French accent smooth and dangerous.

"Greetings, Amy," he said, his voice dripping with charm. "I've been waiting for this moment."

"Damien LaStat," I said, trying to keep my voice steady. "I've been preparing for this."

Damien's smile was a mask of menace. "Ah, so you've learned about our past. How delightful."

Before he could approach, I pushed him away, and the coven formed a protective circle around us. Damien's smile only grew as he vanished into thin air.

"Whoa," Christian said, his eyes wide. "Who was that?"

I took a deep breath. "That was Damien LaStat, a vampire who's been causing us trouble for centuries. Our parents told us about him. Every twenty-three years, he's been the reason for our downfall."

A hush fell over the group as the weight of my words sank in. "We have to break the cycle. We need to find out more about our past to stop him."

Milo's eyes were full of shock. "What do we do now?"

"We need to investigate further," I said, scanning the room. "There might be more clues here."

As we searched, I found a hidden grimoire. "I think I've found something."

The grimoire was filled with dark spells, one of which promised to reveal the past.

"We should try this spell," I suggested.

We chanted the incantation, but it failed to work.

Grayson took charge. “Let’s head back to the hotel and see if we can find a way to clear this blockage. We’ll try the spell again after that.”

We left the building, the night closing in around us. Our mission was far from over, and the path ahead was shrouded in shadows and uncertainty.

But as we walked back, I felt a flicker of hope. We were on the right path, and together, we’d face whatever came next.

Chapter 3

We staggered back to the hotel as the clock blinked 2:00 AM in bright red digits. I felt like we were walking out of one world and back into another, like the French Quarter had been a shadow realm where time forgot itself.

"Man, that place was weird," Christian said as we dropped our bags in the hotel lobby. "Did it seem like time was off to you guys?"

“Yeah, it was like we were caught in a time loop or something,” I said, rubbing my tired eyes. “Like we’re still there, even though we’ve left.”

We shuffled into our room, the flickering light from the lamp stretching our shadows long and eerie on the walls. The grimoire lay open on the table, pages sprawled across like a cryptic map we hoped would lead us somewhere—anywhere.

“Why is this so hard?” Milo mumbled, thumbing through the ancient text. “There’s got to be something we’re missing.”

We pored over the grimoire for hours, the silence only broken by the occasional sigh or frustrated groan. By 5:00 AM, the grimoire had become our only friend in the dark. We exchanged glances, exhausted but resolute.

“We need to sleep,” Annie finally said, rubbing her eyes. “We can’t solve this on no sleep.”

I sighed and closed the book. "Yeah, let's get some rest. We can't be late getting back to our parents. They have no idea we've been running around the French Quarter."

I could barely keep my eyes open as I climbed into bed, but sleep was elusive. Instead, nightmares swept me away into a world overrun by supernatural chaos. Shadows of creatures I couldn't recognize crept through the streets, and I was there, fighting alongside the coven to protect a world that didn't even know it was in danger.

I woke up with my heart pounding, the images still fresh in my mind. The dreams were always the same—our coven battling an endless darkness while the mundane world remained blissfully unaware of the horrors that lurked just out of sight.

"Another rough night?" Annie's voice jolted me from my thoughts. She sat on the edge of my bed, her expression a mix of worry and curiosity.

"Yeah," I said, rubbing my temples. "I keep dreaming about battles and evil forces. It's like the past lives are trying to tell me something."

We decided to grab breakfast at a nearby café. The French Quarter was waking up around us, the city's charm a stark contrast to the unease that gripped me. We passed by St. Louis Cemetery No. One, the final resting place of Marie Laveau, her grave adorned with tokens and prayers from the faithful.

"Look at this," Annie said, kneeling beside the tombstone. "All these offerings. It's like people are still trying to connect with her."

"Yeah," I said, glancing around. "It's like the French Quarter holds onto its magic, even when the rest of the world moves on."

As we walked back to the hotel, I couldn't shake the feeling that we were being followed. I glanced over my shoulder, half expecting to see shadows lurking in the alleys.

"Amy, you okay?" Milo asked, noticing my unease.

"Yeah, I just—" Before I could finish, I felt a sharp tug on my arm. I spun around, but the figure was already gone, leaving a cold imprint on my skin.

"What happened?" Annie's voice was tense.

"Someone grabbed me," I said, showing them the red marks. "But they vanished before I could see who it was."

We hurried back to the hotel, a sense of urgency fueling our steps.

"Alright, let's get inside," Christian said, his voice steady despite the tension. "We need to figure out what's going on."

Once we were in the room, Annie's questions came fast and furious. "Who was that? What do we do now? Damien couldn't have been involved, right?"

"Daylight vampires are a bit of a stretch," Milo said, trying to lighten the mood. "But who else would have been out there?"

"I don't know," I said, grabbing the grimoire. "But we need answers. If someone's after us, we need to figure out why."

I flipped through the pages, frustration bubbling up. "We need to find a spell or something, but everything feels so out of reach."

"I'm starving," Christian said, breaking the tense silence. "Should we order food? We've wasted the whole day."

"Yeah, let's do that," I said, grateful for the distraction. "Order something, and we'll figure out our next steps."

As Christian ordered food, the weight of our situation settled on us again.

"Are we doing the right thing?" Annie's voice trembled. "I mean, if anything happens, Mom and Dad will go ballistic."

"We've come too far to turn back now," I said, though my own doubts gnawed at me. "We just need to grab some food and rest. We'll tackle this after a good night's sleep."

With food ordered, we settled outside on the hotel's veranda, trying to ignore the looming presence of our upcoming finals and the endless mysteries that awaited us.

"That grimoire is starting to feel like a weight on my shoulders," Christian said, staring into the street.

"I know," I said. "We'll get through this. After exams, we'll dive back into the past and figure out what we need to know. For now, let's focus on the present."

As we ate, the conversation drifted from the supernatural to our everyday lives, but the undercurrent of our shared mission remained.

Just then, my phone buzzed with a call from an unknown number. I glanced at Annie, her eyes wide with concern.

"Answer it," she urged. "It might be important."

I hesitated but finally picked up. "Hello?"

"Well, hello, my love," Damien's voice dripped with dark charm. "Did you think you could hide from me forever? I know you have questions about your past lives. We need to meet. I hold the answers you seek."

My heart raced, but I managed to keep my voice steady. "Where do you want to meet?"

"I'll send you the details," Damien said. "But come alone. I'm not worried about your coven; I'm worried about your safety."

As the call ended, a shiver ran down my spine. I had just agreed to meet Damien again, and the weight of that decision pressed on me.

"What did he say?" Annie asked, her eyes sharp.

"He wants to meet tonight," I said, voice shaky. "He says he has answers about my past lives and warns me about Christian."

Annie's eyes widened. "What are we going to do?"

"We need to be careful," I said. "I don't know if Damien can be trusted, but we need to find out what he knows."

I turned to Christian, who was already on his phone. "We need to gather the coven. We have to prepare for whatever happens tonight."

Christian quickly rallied the others, and within minutes, we were huddled together, ready to face whatever came next.

"Thank you all for coming," I began, trying to sound confident despite the storm in my mind. "Damien has contacted me and wants to meet tonight. He claims to have information about my past lives and warns that Christian might be a threat. We need to go to the French Quarter and find out what he knows. But we need to be careful—he's warned me that we should come alone, but we can't trust him."

I gestured to the grimoire. "We're going to cast a cloaking spell so he doesn't sense us coming. Everyone, repeat after me."

Together, we chanted the spell, and soon a ping on my phone told us where to meet: *The French Quarter's oldest vampire bar*.

As we walked through the bustling streets, Damien's charm and dark allure hung in the air like a thick fog. I tried to ignore the pull of his presence, focusing instead on the task at hand.

When Damien appeared, he was as captivating as ever, his eyes glinting with secrets. "Ah, Amy, you've come," he said, his voice smooth like velvet. "Have you tried to recall anything from your past lives?"

Before I could respond, he began recounting a story of our past. "It began one fateful night when you confided in me about your burdens and dreams," he said, eyes locked on mine. "We defied the coven and the world, creating a love story as tragic as it was beautiful."

His words wove a complex tapestry of our past lives, each detail pulling me deeper into the enigma of our shared history.

I was captivated but wary, trying to balance the allure of his presence with the knowledge that he was both a source of answers and danger.

"Damien, this is a lot to take in," I said as he finished. "But I need more than stories. I need to know how to move forward."

"Patience, my love," he said, his eyes intense. "In time, the truth will unfold."

As he left, I felt a mix of hope and dread. There was so much more to uncover, but I knew this was only the beginning of a much larger journey.

I glanced at my coven members, their faces a mirror of my own conflicted emotions. "Let's go," I said. "We have a lot to think about, and it's time to get ready for what comes next."

As we made our way back to the hotel, my thoughts were a tangled mess of past lives and future challenges. But through the uncertainty, one thing was clear: our journey was far from over.

Chapter 4

After our final exams wrapped up, we packed our bags and geared up for our long-awaited trip to the French Quarter. It was like a mix of excitement and dread, and I couldn't shake off the feeling that we were on the brink of something monumental.

The morning was a blur of energy and nerves. Christian and Grayson were the first to arrive, buzzing with anticipation.

"Good morning! Is everyone ready?" Christian asked, his eyes sparkling with that familiar determination. "Milo and Mason are picking up Arielle and Gwen, while Andy, Meghan, Gabriella, and Nancy are carpooling over. Dylan and Richard will catch up with us later."

"Almost," I replied, grabbing a cooler from the kitchen. "Annie's still upstairs, lost in her own world. Grayson, could you see if she's, okay?"

Grayson gave me a quick nod and headed up the stairs, leaving Christian and me alone in the living room. The tension between us was palpable, like the air before a storm.

"Amy," Christian began, breaking the silence, "I keep thinking about what we learned about our past lives. How did we get to that dark place where we betrayed each other? It's haunting me. We were meant to be together, right? So why did we end up so twisted?"

"I wish I had answers for you," I said, my voice heavy. "It's like I'm hitting a wall every time I try to dig deeper. I've scoured the grimoire and tried spells, but it's like something's blocking me from seeing the full picture. It feels like we're stuck in a cycle of secrets and lies. We have to go back to the French Quarter, where we might find something, our parents never told us. There's this dark force from our past, and it's been gnawing at me. I don't know what we unleashed, but the nightmares have been relentless."

Christian's face grew somber. "I haven't had those nightmares, but I believe you. Maybe this trip will give us some answers."

Before we could dive into more theories, my phone buzzed with yet another anonymous call. I glanced at Christian, my unease evident.

"Should I answer it?" I asked, my hand shaking slightly.

"Yeah, put it on speaker," Christian said, trying to sound calm.

I hesitated for a moment before pressing the button. The line was filled with the sound of heavy breathing, like someone was standing right behind us but refusing to speak. Then a voice broke through the static, low and menacing.

"Stay away from the French Quarter if you know what's good for you," the voice said before the call ended abruptly.

Christian's eyes widened. "What the hell? Someone doesn't want us poking around."

"This isn't the first call I've gotten," I said, my voice trembling. "Earlier, it was just breathing. But this time, they made a threat. We have to keep this to ourselves for now. We can't let anyone get scared and back out."

Christian nodded, though his concern was evident. "How can we be sure it's Damien? And how did he touch you in the alley? It didn't seem like a normal touch."

"I'm not entirely sure it was Damien," I admitted. "But for now, we can treat it like it is him. If it's someone else from our past, they'll have to deal with us. We have to stay focused on our mission."

Christian extended his pinky finger towards me, a grin spreading across his face. "Pinky swear? Just like when we were kids?"

I laughed, taking his pinky in mine. "Pinky swear. We won't let anyone scare us away."

Just then, Annie and Grayson came downstairs. Their eyes widened as they took in the sight of Christian and me in such a serious moment.

"What's going on here?" Annie asked, raising an eyebrow.

"Nothing much," I said, shrugging. "Just a little pre-trip pep talk."

Annie smirked. "You two look like you're about to take on the world. Did something happen?"

"Just a bit of tension about our past lives," Christian said, glancing at me with a reassuring smile.

As we piled into the car and drove towards the French Quarter, the air was thick with anticipation. It felt like we were heading into a storm, and no matter how much I tried to shake it, the sense of impending discovery was almost overwhelming.

Once we arrived and settled into our old, creaky building, the weight of our task pressed on us. I took a deep breath and took out my spell book.

"Alright," I said, trying to sound confident, "I'm going to use a spell to light up this place. It's not too complicated, but it might help us see what we're dealing with."

I chanted the spell, and a soft glow filled the room. My friends stared at the light as if they'd just witnessed magic for the first time.

"How did you do that?" Grayson asked, his eyes wide.

"I'll teach you later," I promised. "For now, let's focus on finding what we came here for."

As we began exploring the building, Milo suddenly shouted from the corner of the room.

"Guys, come check this out!" he called excitement in his voice.

We rushed over to him, and he held up an old, dusty grimoire with a familiar symbol on the cover—a pentagram encircled.

"This has to be it!" I said, taking the book from Milo. I opened it, and my eyes widened as I saw the contents. This wasn't just any grimoire. An Elder wrote it of our coven, and the pages were filled with dark magic.

"Look at this," I said, pointing to a spell at the bottom of a page. "It's a time manipulation spell, but there's a warning: *'DANGEROUS, USE WITH CAUTION.'*"

The coven gathered around, their faces a mix of awe and fear.

"This is what we've been searching for," Annie said, her voice trembling slightly.

We flipped through the pages, finding spells of immense power, including one for assuming different identities. It was clear that this grimoire held secrets meant for those who were ready to face them.

Suddenly, a strange sound came from a wall in the far corner of the room. We froze, staring at the spot where the noise was coming from.

"What is that?" I asked, my voice barely above a whisper. "Is anyone else hearing this?"

As we watched, a figure began to materialize from the shadows. I could barely breathe as the figure took shape, revealing a man with an air of eerie familiarity.

"Hello, Amy. It's been centuries," the man said, his voice smooth and chilling. "You haven't changed a bit."

"Who are you?" I managed to ask, though my voice was shaky.

"Lucian Ravenshaw," he said, his grin revealing sharp, predatory teeth. "I've been waiting for this moment."

Annie gasped and collapsed to her knees, her face ashen. My heart pounded in my chest as the pieces of a forgotten past fell into place. Lucian wasn't just a name from a history book—he was a force from our past.

"Lucian Ravenshaw?" I whispered, barely able to comprehend. "Why are you here?"

Lucian's eyes gleamed with dark amusement. "I've come to see what you've been up to, Amy. And to see if you're ready to face the shadows of your past."

The room was thick with tension, and my thoughts swirled with memories of battles and betrayals. I couldn't shake the feeling that Lucian's arrival was just the beginning of a new chapter in our story.

In the chaos, my thoughts drifted back to Damien LaStat. Despite the danger, I couldn't completely push aside the memories of our past. But for now, the focus was on Lucian and the revelations he might bring.

With our path ahead shrouded in uncertainty, one thing was clear: we had to confront whatever came our way. We wouldn't leave the French Quarter until we had uncovered every secret it held.

Chapter 5

Following Lucian's sudden disappearance, we scrambled to search for any hidden entrances or passages. If Lucian could vanish like that, there had to be a way he came in.

"Guys, check this out!" Mayson's shout cut through the tension, making my heart race.

We crowded around him as he pointed at a faintly glowing door set into the wall. The energy that rippled around it was almost tangible.

"What the heck is this?" Grayson asked, peering at the door.

"I don't know, but we need to find out," I said, trying to ignore the way my pulse quickened. "Are we ready?"

"Let's do this," Christian said, his gaze steady despite the danger.

One by one, we stepped through the door. Each of us blinked out of existence on one side and reappeared on the other in a shadowy, damp corridor. The flickering candlelight on the walls cast eerie shadows that seemed to writhe and twist as we moved.

"This place is seriously freaky," Annie whispered, looking around with wide eyes.

Christian took the lead, his flashlight cutting through the gloom. "Stay close. We don't know what's waiting for us."

The corridor felt endless, and the air was thick with the smell of mildew and wet fur. Strange noises came from behind the heavy doors that lined the passage.

"Can you hear that?" I asked, my voice low.

"Yeah," said Mayson, his eyes darting nervously. "What is it?"

"Probably just echoes or something," Christian said, though he didn't sound convinced.

We pressed on, our footsteps echoing off the stone walls. The deeper we went, the more the corridor seemed to close in on us. I felt a chill, not from the cold, but from the overwhelming sense of doom.

Suddenly, a blinding flash of light exploded in front of us. I barely had time to shield my eyes before we were hurled into a chaotic battlefield.

"What the—" Christian started, but his words were swallowed by the roar of combat.

The scene was a surreal nightmare. Soldiers clashed with monstrous beasts, their cries of battle mingling with the roar of flames and the clash of steel.

"Get back!" I yelled, grabbing Annie's arm and pulling her into a nearby alcove.

From our sheltered spot, we watched in horror as the chaos unfolded. Above us, a massive, fiery dragon soared through the sky, its scales glowing like molten lava.

"Infernus..." I said, my voice trembling. The name was a whisper of dread that seemed to make the very air around us vibrate.

Annie clung to me, her eyes wide with fear. "Is that really Infernus the Firestorm?"

"Yeah," Christian said, staring up at the dragon. "We need to get out of here. Fast."

Infernus's roar shook the ground, and the heat from its breath was intense even from where we hid. The dragon's wings cast a shadow that darkened the entire battlefield, and its fiery breath turned the land into a raging inferno.

"Does it ever end?" Mayson asked, his voice barely audible over the din.

"Nope," I said, trying to sound more confident than I felt. "But we need to find a way out of this mess."

Christian nodded. "There's no way we can fight that thing. We need to get back to the corridor and regroup."

"Agreed," I said. "But we also need to think about who could help us here."

A thought hit me like a lightning bolt. "Damien."

Christian and Grayson exchanged uneasy glances. "Are you sure?" Christian asked. "We don't exactly have a good history with him."

"It's him or nothing," I said, feeling a strange pull towards the idea. "He's the only one who knows anything about these realms."

Grayson ran a hand through his hair. "Alright. Let's try it."

We headed back to the door, and I took a deep breath. I pulled out the spell book and recited the incantation for summoning Damien.

A moment later, Damien appeared with his usual cocky grin. "What's up, kiddos? Need a hand in the middle of a dragon's banquet?"

"Damien," I said, forcing a smile. "We need your help. We're way out of our depth here."

Damien raised an eyebrow. "Oh? And why would I help you?"

"Because you're our only option," I said, trying to sound persuasive. "We need to find our way through this place and avoid getting turned into dragon food. We're desperate."

Damien's grin widened. "Well, if you're begging, I guess I have to help. But you should know, this isn't going to be a walk in the park."

"What do we need to know?" Christian asked, his tone steady despite the situation.

Damien's eyes glinted with mischief. "Tridion is a land of illusions. Your memories might warp, and what you see might not be the truth. Stay sharp and don't let your guard down. And I'm not doing this for free, you know."

"We know," I said, gritting my teeth. "What's the cost?"

Damien shrugged. "Just a chance to prove that I'm not the villain you think I am. You're going to need more than just magic to survive this."

I took a deep breath. "Alright, let's get started. We need to figure out how to get through this place without getting ourselves killed."

"Sounds good," Damien said. "But first, let's talk about your strategy. You've got to be prepared for anything. This place will test you."

As we huddled together, Damien laid out some ground rules for dealing with Tridion.

"First off," he said, "keep your eyes open and your wits about you. Second, expect the unexpected. Third, trust your instincts, but don't close off the possibilities."

"We'll keep that in mind," Christian said, nodding.

"Good," Damien said. "Now, you have a decision to make. Do you want to dive straight into this mess, or do you want to be prepared?"

"We want to be prepared," I said. "But we also need to make sure we don't get stuck in this world for too long. Time works differently here."

Damien's eyes sparkled with amusement. "Ah, you're a clever one. There's a spell in that grimoire of yours that can stop time in your world. You might want to use it to avoid missing out on your mundane life."

We pulled out the grimoire and flipped through the pages. My heart skipped a beat when I saw the section labeled **Forbidden Spells**.

"Should we really use these?" Mayson asked, peering over my shoulder.

"We don't have a choice," I said. "We need to find a way to manage time."

Christian read the spell aloud, his voice steady despite the warning in the grimoire. "This spell requires a feather and our combined focus."

I gathered us into a circle, holding out a feather from my bag. "Alright, let's do this. Hold hands and focus on stretching time."

We began the chant, our voices blending into a rhythmic chant. The words felt powerful, almost alive as they left our mouths.

As we finished, the world outside the building fell silent. Grayson peeked out the window and his eyes went wide.

"We did it! Time is frozen!" he exclaimed, his excitement barely contained.

"And not a moment too soon," Damien said with a grin. "Nice work. You guys are starting to look like real witches."

I let out a relieved laugh. "We're doing it, guys. We're making it through this."

"Let's keep moving," Damien said, eyes scanning the dark corridor. "We've got a lot more to face before this journey is over."

With renewed determination, we stepped forward into the unknown, ready to face whatever came next.—

Chapter 6

As we walked through the shifting shadows of Tridion, the weight of Damien's story seemed to press down on us, heavy as the fog curling through the streets.

Damien glanced over his shoulder at us, his eyes glinting in the dim light. "So, where do I start? I guess I should give you the full picture."

Grayson, always curious, piped up, "Yeah, lay it on us. We need to know what we're dealing with."

Damien began walking again, his stride measured. "Alright. I was born in 1825, in a place that's nothing like your world. My father was a vampire, and my mother was a witch. I grew up navigating the delicate balance between those two worlds. Imagine being a vampire who can survive on blood and mundane food alike—it's like having two identities and trying to keep them from crashing into each other."

As we moved through the cold, desolate streets of Tridion, the sound of distant whispers and the flicker of torches added to the eerie atmosphere.

"Five years old, and I was already fully grown," Damien continued, his tone somber. "Legends called me a 'demon child,' a future king of Tridion destined for greatness or disaster. I was supposed to take over as ruler, but in 1935, my uncle—the king—was killed by a dragon."

I shivered at the mention of dragons. “So, what did you do?”

Damien’s gaze was distant. “I fled to the mundane world, hoping to escape my fate. But every twenty-three years, this pull, this sense of destiny, draws me back to Tridion. I’m searching for a witch who’s meant to be my queen.”

Annie raised an eyebrow. “A queen? You mean you’re looking for a partner to share the throne?”

Damien nodded. “Exactly. She’s supposed to be the one who completes the prophecy.”

“So, you think my mom might be tied to our coven here?” I asked, my voice trembling slightly.

Damien met my eyes with a knowing look. “You’re right to wonder. My mother was incredibly clever and manipulative. It wouldn’t surprise me if she’s been working behind the scenes in your world.”

Annie’s face went pale. “If she’s in our coven, then we’ve been dealing with her all along?”

Damien’s expression darkened. “It’s a real possibility. And if that’s true, we need to be on high alert. My mother has always been a formidable enemy and underestimating her could be disastrous.”

A silence fell over us, heavy with the weight of Damien’s words. I took a deep breath, trying to steady my nerves. “We must come up with a plan. We need to find out if there’s a traitor among us and make sure we’re ready for whatever she throws at us.”

Damien gave a faint smile. “You’re already thinking like a leader. We need to stay focused, but let’s not get ahead of ourselves. Let’s start by finding a safe place to regroup and strategize.”

I nodded, though a small voice in the back of my mind questioned the limits of our strength. “What do you suggest we do?”

Damien gestured ahead. “There’s a village nearby where we can meet with Lucian and his pack. They can offer us shelter and information.”

As we approached the village, I couldn't help but notice how different it was from New Orleans. The air was colder, the snow falling in soft, silent flakes. The village itself looked like something out of a dark fairy tale, its buildings huddled together against the cold.

Then I saw him. Lucian stood at the edge of the village, waiting for us. His presence was both majestic and intimidating, his fur bristling in the cold wind.

Annie's eyes widened. "That's Lucian?"

Damien nodded. "Yes. He's been the Alpha of his pack for years now. He's loyal, but he's also very serious about his role."

As we approached, Lucian greeted us with a nod. "Welcome to Tridion. I assume Damien has filled you in on what's going on?"

Christian gave a tight smile. "We've heard the basics. We're ready to help in any way we can."

Lucian's gaze lingered on Annie. "You've been missing from Tridion for a long time. It's good to see you again."

Annie's face was a mix of relief and tension. "I didn't expect to see you like this. What brought you to the mundane world?"

Lucian's expression grew pensive. "I had to see it for myself. I needed to make sure you were safe."

Annie's eyes flashed with concern. "But you put yourself in danger to do that. Why?"

Lucian's eyes hardened. "Damien's mother took everything from me. I needed to confront her and make sure she'd pay for what she did."

Annie took a step closer, her voice gentle. "We understand your pain, Lucian. But we need you here with us, not risking your life for vengeance."

Lucian's shoulders slumped slightly. "I know. I was reckless. I just couldn't let her get away with it."

Annie reached out and took his hand, squeezing it reassuringly. "We need you with us, Lucian. We're all in this together."

He looked at her, a small, sad smile forming. "Together," he echoed, a glimmer of hope in his eyes.

Damien watched their exchange, a faint smile on his lips. "You two are always so emotional. But we can't afford to be distracted right now."

Annie shot Damien a skeptical look. "We need to focus on our mission. No more secrets."

Damien met her gaze with a nod. "Agreed. Let's go inside and meet the pack. We can talk more there."

The inside of the building was warm and inviting, a stark contrast to the cold outside. A Christmas tree stood in the corner, decorated with handmade ornaments. It was a cozy, almost surreal setting for the conversations we were about to have.

I felt a pang of nostalgia as I looked around. The room reminded me of past holidays, of laughter and joy I had lost. Tears stung my eyes.

Damien noticed my reaction and approached. "Are you okay, Amy?"

I wiped my tears away, my voice catching. "It just reminds me of... times I had with my daughter, Kaitlin. I miss her."

Damien's face softened with empathy. "I'm sorry, Amy. I can't imagine what you're going through."

Annie stepped in, wrapping me in a comforting embrace. "We're here for you, Amy. You don't have to face this alone."

I leaned into her, grateful for the support. "Thank you, Annie."

Damien gently put a hand on my shoulder. "We'll get through this. We have to."

As we settled into the room, Lucian began introducing the pack members, though their names blurred together in a rush of unfamiliar sounds. My head spun as I tried to keep up, the sheer number of faces overwhelming.

"Meet Adam, Seth, Angel, Pamela, Tina, Tinker, Isabella, Jennifer, Adam Jr., Seth Jr.," Lucian said, listing names one after another.

I tried to focus but felt a wave of dizziness. "This is... a lot," I managed to say, trying not to let my anxiety show.

Damien looked at me with concern. "Are you alright?"

I nodded, though I felt faint. "Just a bit overwhelmed. It's a lot to take in."

Lucian's eyes softened. "Let's sit down. We'll make sure you're comfortable."

As we sat, I took a deep breath, trying to steady myself. The room was filled with warmth, but my thoughts were tangled in the revelations of the day.

A child from the pack came over with a plate of food. "Welcome! I'm Adam Jr.," he said, offering a friendly smile.

I managed a smile back. "Thank you, Adam Jr."

Damien glanced around the room. "Let's eat and then talk strategy. We have a lot ahead of us."

As we started to eat, I looked around at the faces of the pack. Despite the strange setting and the weight of our mission, I felt a glimmer of hope. We were here together, facing an unknown future, but we had each other to rely on.

I turned to Damien. "What's next? How do we start preparing for the battle ahead?"

Damien took a sip of his drink, his eyes serious. "We need to uncover any hidden threats, strengthen our defenses, and find clues about my mother's plans."

I nodded, feeling the weight of responsibility on my shoulders. "We'll find a way. Together, we can overcome this."

With those words, we prepared ourselves for the challenges to come, the warmth of the room and the presence of our allies offering a fleeting sense of comfort in the face of the darkness that lay ahead.

Chapter 7

I woke up in a room that felt like home, a room that belonged to a past life I'd forgotten. My eyes slowly adjusted to the soft light filtering through a large window. For a moment, I could almost believe I was back in New Orleans, surrounded by the familiar sights of my old life. But the laughter drifting from the corner of the room was a stark reminder that this was Tridion.

"Hey there, sleepyhead," Annie's voice cut through my thoughts. She was curled up in a rocking chair, her eyes sparkling with relief. Lucian was beside her, his intense gaze softened by a rare, warm smile. Their laughter was an odd comfort, like a flicker of light in a storm.

I blinked, trying to shake off the fog of sleep. "Where are we? I thought... I thought I was back in New Orleans."

Annie laughed softly; her voice laced with a teasing note. "Well, you're not dreaming. We're still in Tridion. You fainted, remember?"

My hand went to my head, which throbbed like a war drum. "Yeah, I remember that part. But how did I end up here? Did Damien carry me or something?"

Lucian chuckled. "You bet he did. And now you're awake, so I guess the plan worked."

I propped myself up on my elbows, glancing around the room. It was decorated with familiar touches—ancient tapestries, mystical symbols etched into the woodwork, and the scent of old parchment mixed with incense. It was a strange juxtaposition of home and otherworldly mystery.

"So, how long was I out?" I asked, trying to ignore the pounding in my head.

Annie tilted her head thoughtfully. "Just a few hours. We've been talking with the pack downstairs, trying to figure out our next move."

I sighed, trying to steady my thoughts. "Something doesn't feel right. Ever since we got here, I've been bombarded with memories and questions. This place... it's like it's alive with secrets."

Lucian leaned forward, his eyes steady on mine. "You're not alone in that feeling. This house has a way of stirring up the past. It's seen joy and tragedy alike."

My eyes met his. "Do you think there's something we're missing? A part of our past we haven't uncovered yet?"

Annie reached out, squeezing my hand. "Maybe we're just overwhelmed. Tridion is where we belong, but we're still getting used to it. We must focus on why we're here and not get lost in doubts."

I wasn't sure if her optimism was helping or just a distraction from the gnawing uncertainty in my gut. "I hope you're right, Annie. But right now, I can't shake the feeling that there's some enchantment at play, something we don't fully understand."

Annie gave me a reassuring smile. "We'll figure it out. For now, let's focus on what we can do. We need to find out more about our past lives and why we were brought back here."

Before I could respond, Damien appeared at the door, a smirk playing on his lips. "Ah, the sleeping beauty awakens. I trust you're feeling better?"

I shot him a tired smile. "Better than when I hit the floor. But I could use something for this headache. Got any aspirin, or do you have some ancient remedy that'll do the trick?"

Damien raised an eyebrow, his smirk widening. "Aspirin? In Tridion, we have far more effective remedies. But since you're so insistent, I suppose I could get you something."

Lucian stood up with a slight bow. "I'll fetch it, Damien. Consider it my pleasure to assist the future Queen of Tridion."

Damien shot a glance at Lucian, then turned back to me with a wink. "While Lucian is off to get what you need, perhaps we can discuss what's troubling you?"

I tried to keep my voice steady. "What I need right now is a moment to think. And maybe some clarity on what's happening around us."

Annie squeezed my hand again. "We'll have time for that later. For now, we should focus on our mission."

"Right," I said, though my mind was still swirling with questions. "But first, I need to know where everyone else is."

"They're downstairs with the pack," Annie said, her eyes steady. "We have time to talk before we join them."

"Good," I said, leaning back against the pillows. "We need to address the weirdness that's been going on since we arrived."

Annie looked thoughtful. "I think we might be overthinking things. Yes, there's a lot we don't know, but we're here to uncover the truth. We should trust that we're in the right place."

"I want to trust that," I said, trying to believe her. "But something feels off. The way everyone is so accommodating, it feels almost... too perfect."

Annie tilted her head, her eyes searching mine. "Maybe it's just the shock of everything hitting you at once. We're in a new world, dealing with old emotions and memories. It's a lot to process."

I nodded, though doubts still lingered. "I suppose you're right. It's just hard to ignore the feeling that there's something more we need to uncover."

Annie's eyes were steady and kind. "We will uncover it, Amy. We have to focus on what we can control. Our parents' choices might have been misguided, but we have the chance to make things right now."

Her words were like a warm blanket against the chill of uncertainty. I took a deep breath, trying to let her optimism wash over me.

"Alright," I said, forcing a smile. "Let's get through this. We have to find out what's hidden in our past and use it to our advantage."

Annie's smile was bright. "Exactly. We have a future to look forward to, and it starts here."

As if on cue, Damien and Lucian returned, each holding a potion in hand. Damien handed one to me with a flourish. "For the mighty witch's headache. I trust it will suffice?"

I took the potion, eyeing it warily. "I hope this doesn't turn out to be some elaborate joke."

Damien's grin widened. "I assure you, it's very effective."

I took a sip, the liquid surprisingly cool and soothing. "Well, that's not half bad."

Lucian chuckled, his eyes sparkling. "Glad to hear it. Now that you're feeling better, let's join the others and get to work."

As we left the room, the weight of the task ahead hung heavy in the air. But with Annie and Lucian by my side and the promise of answers in the depths of Tridion, I tried to hold on to that glimmer of hope.

Chapter 8

Annie and I sat on the edge of the bed, listening to the distant hum of the coven's revelry below. The laughter and chatter mingled with the low glow of the TV—or whatever their version of television was. I'd half-expected the setting here to be purely medieval, but the modern touches threw me off. Dragons and Fae might be real, but there was electricity, and that was just strange.

Damien and Lucian's voices drifted up the stairs, filled with the kind of easygoing banter that only came from long friendships. "We're back! Did you miss us?" Damien called, his voice carrying a teasing note.

I heard Lucian's chuckle. "Sorry for the delay. We got caught up watching Christian and Grayson take on Angelo and David in some kind of epic video game showdown. I didn't know werewolves had such game skills."

Annie laughed. "Sounds like a good time. I hope you're not too tired from the excitement?"

"Not at all," Damien said, walking in with Lucian. They were carrying a couple of glasses filled with a potion that looked more like a science experiment than a remedy. "I hope you're ready for a night of fun. We have quite the feast downstairs."

I took the glass from Damien, peering at the swirling contents with a hint of skepticism. "Thanks. I could use something for this headache."

Lucian grinned, his eyes sparkling with mischief. "Just don't expect it to be a miracle cure. This stuff might taste terrible, but it should do the trick."

I took a sip, wincing at the bitter taste. But almost immediately, a soothing wave of relief washed over me. "Wow, this stuff really works fast."

Damien raised an eyebrow. "Well, you did create a powerful potion back in the day. Seems like you had a knack for it."

"Wait, I did?" I asked, genuinely surprised.

"Yes," Damien said, sitting down beside us. "You were the Supreme Witch. You had powers that went beyond the ordinary. Remember how you used to cast spells to protect this place from unwanted visitors like dragons and Fae?"

"Dragons and Fae are real?" I said, trying to wrap my head around it.

Damien nodded. "Oh, yes. This realm is full of beings you only heard of in myths before. The Fae, for example, love a good party, but they rarely cross us. They're more trouble than dangerous."

"And you're telling me that I had to hide the house from them?" I asked, trying to recall something I couldn't quite reach.

"Exactly," Damien said, leaning back with a grin. "You were quite the witch in your time. You cast a spell to make the house seem mundane to anyone who might stumble across it. It was one of the many ways you kept us safe."

Annie looked between us, her brow furrowed. "What's this about you dying first, Amy? Damien mentioned it earlier, but you didn't catch it."

"Ah, yes." Damien's eyes grew serious. "I had a vision before you fainted. I assumed you saw it too?"

"No, I didn't see anything. Is there a way you could've shielded that vision from me?" I asked, feeling a mix of frustration and curiosity.

Damien's gaze was steady. "The visions are unpredictable. It's better if you discover them on your own. We didn't want to push you into remembering things too fast. These experiences need to come naturally, even though it might feel like a maze."

"I wish you'd warned us about this earlier," I said, trying to keep my voice calm.

Damien sighed. "We couldn't rush you or force it. The visions are part of the process, and pushing too hard could be dangerous."

Annie placed a hand on my arm. "They're trying to protect us, Amy. We have to trust them, even if it's hard."

I nodded slowly, though my doubts still lingered. "Alright, I guess we should put this aside for now. What's the plan for tonight?"

Damien's eyes sparkled. "We're going to enjoy ourselves. Drinks, dancing, and a little romance if you're up for it. We've set up a barbecue, and after that, we have a little surprise for you."

"That sounds good," I said, forcing a smile. "But first, I hope you've got something delicious for us. I'm starving."

"Of course!" Damien said, his dimples flashing. "We've prepared all your favorites. Ribs, salad, and rolls. It's all waiting for you downstairs."

As we followed Damien and Lucian down to the main floor, I tried to shake off my unease. The house was alive with the sounds of the coven celebrating. I poured myself a drink, eyeing the feast laid out on the long table. The food smelled incredible, and despite everything, I found myself looking forward to the meal.

After we ate, Damien and Lucian led us out into the woods. The night was cool and crisp, and the forest seemed to whisper with secrets. I noticed Annie and I exchanged glances, sensing that this was more than just a casual walk.

We walked for what felt like hours, the forest growing thicker and more familiar with each step. "Are we there yet?" I finally asked, trying to break the silence.

Lucian smiled. "Just a bit further. I think you'll like what's waiting for you."

When we emerged from the trees, the sight before us took my breath away. The moonlight shimmered on the ocean, casting a silvery glow over the waves. The beach stretched out before us, peaceful and serene.

"This place is beautiful," Annie said, her eyes wide with wonder.

We kicked off our shoes and walked along the shore, letting the cool sand slip between our toes. The water was too cold for a swim, but the tranquil beauty of the scene was enough.

As we strolled, I spotted the stables back by the edge of the forest. My heart leaped. "Are those our horses?" I asked Damien, hurrying over to the stables.

Damien followed with a knowing smile. "Yes, they're the horses you rode into battle. Yours is the white one with the black nose, and Annie's is the black one with the brown nose."

I approached the white horse, my fingers brushing its soft coat. "I remember now. We rode these into battle. We fought monsters together."

Damien nodded. "You did. And yes, I'm wearing a ring that protects me from the sun. It's something you made centuries ago."

"And what else could I do?" I asked, eager to know more.

Damien's eyes grew serious. "Some things you'll have to rediscover on your own. It's part of the journey."

I sighed, accepting his answer. "Fine. I guess we should head back now."

As we walked back to Lucian's house, the excitement of the night's surprise kept me on edge. We entered the house, and the coven and pack were still celebrating. The energy was high, and I couldn't help but be caught up in the joy of the moment.

Despite the looming uncertainties, I took a deep breath and tried to enjoy this rare, peaceful moment. For now, we would be "normal" and embrace the chance for a little happiness before the weight of our mission pressed down on us again.

Chapter 9

I gathered the coven around the old oak table in the dimly lit room. The flickering candlelight cast long shadows on the walls, adding a touch of drama to the moment. I took a deep breath, trying to shake off the anxiety that had been building up for days.

"Hey, everyone," I began, trying to sound confident. "We need to talk. Our current magical strength isn't going to be enough for the fight against Damien's mother. We need to step up our game."

Annie's eyes met mine, her usual bright demeanor replaced by a serious resolve. "Absolutely, Amy. If we're going to face her, we need to be stronger. We need a plan."

Mayson was hunched over the grimoire, flipping through its yellowed pages. "There's got to be something in here that can help us. I just need to find it."

Gabriella, her eyes shining with determination, spoke up. "What if we combine our magic? We could merge our abilities to create something more powerful."

A spark of hope ignited in me. "Yes! That's it, Gabriella. If we join our powers, we might be able to unlock new abilities. Mayson, is there a spell in the grimoire for merging our magic?"

Mayson looked up from the book, his brow furrowed. "Let me see. I think I remember seeing something about merging spells earlier."

Annie put a hand on my shoulder, her touch warm and comforting. "Amy, you've been the one holding us together. Imagine how strong we'll be if we all work together."

Her words gave me a boost. "You're right. We're stronger together. Let's do this. Mayson, find that spell and let's make it happen."

Mayson nodded and went back to the grimoire. After a few tense moments, he pointed to a passage. "I think this is it. The spell for merging our magic."

"Great," I said. "Everyone, gather around and join hands. Let's cast this spell together."

We formed a circle around the table, our hands clasped in a chain of unity. I took a deep breath and began reciting the incantation from the grimoire. "By the power of moon and earth, we unite our strength. Merge our magic to forge a bond of might."

As we spoke the words, a brilliant flash of light erupted from our joined hands. The ground beneath us seemed to tremble, and for a moment, it felt like the entire room was shaking.

"Are we okay? Do you all feel anything different?" I asked, trying to keep my voice steady as I looked around.

"I feel amazing!" Annie said, her face lit up with excitement. "This spell really worked! I've never felt so strong!"

"I feel it too," Mayson agreed, glancing at the others with a mix of awe and satisfaction. "We've definitely tapped into something big here."

"That's good to hear," I said, trying to hide my relief. "So, we're all on the same page that the spell has boosted our power?"

"Yes, but it looks like we might have aged a little," Mayson said, examining his hands. "I think we might have gained an extra year or two."

"Wait, aging? I didn't expect that," I said, my eyes widening. "It must be a side effect of the spell. It could be draining our life force."

"Regardless," Damien interjected, a confident smile on his face, "we've got the power we need now. We're ready for what's coming."

"We can't get too cocky," I said, feeling the weight of our mission pressing on me. "We need to practice and prepare. The battle ahead won't be easy."

Mayson nodded. "We need to hone our skills together. And Amy, you're right about being cautious. We should also know how to reverse the spell if things go wrong."

"Good point," I said, turning to Mayson. "Is there a reversal spell in the grimoire?"

Mayson started flipping through the pages again. "Yeah, there is. It's just the incantation in reverse. It should be straightforward to perform."

"Thanks, Mayson. We need to remember that in case we need it," I said.

Annie gave me a knowing smile. "Always the practical one, Amy. What would we do without you?"

"I guess that's part of my job," I replied, trying to smile. "I'm a bit older, so I have to be the responsible one."

Damien smirked. "Not older than me, though."

"True," I said with a teasing grin. "But you're not exactly part of the coven. You're a bit of an outsider here."

Damien rolled his eyes. "Still, after all these years, you still doubt me?"

"It's not about doubting you, Damien," I said, trying to keep my tone even. "It's about understanding where you come from. We need to know more about your background, especially if we're going to work together."

Mayson nodded. "She's right. We need to understand each other's strengths and weaknesses."

Damien sighed and leaned against the wall; arms crossed. "Fine. What do you want to know?"

"For starters," I said, "how did you discover you were half witch, half vampire? Was it something you figured out on your own or did someone tell you?"

Damien's eyes softened as he spoke. "It was a mix of both. My mother told me about my heritage when I was young, but I had to figure out the details and learn to control my powers on my own."

"And your father?" Mayson asked. "Was he the vampire?"

Damien's expression darkened. "Yes. He left when I was a child. I barely remember him. My mother raised me by herself."

"I'm sorry, Damien," I said gently. "I didn't mean to bring up painful memories."

He shrugged. "It's fine. I've come to terms with it. What matters now is that we're a team and we need to focus on that."

"Exactly," Mayson said. "But we still need to know more about your powers. Have you tried tracing them back to a source?"

Damien considered this. "I could look through some old family journals. They might have some information."

"That sounds like a good plan," I said. "In the meantime, let's keep practicing. We need to be ready for whatever comes next."

Damien nodded. "Agreed. I'll start on those journals. For the coven."

"For the coven," Mayson echoed, a determined smile on his face.

"For the coven," I said, feeling a renewed sense of unity among us as we prepared for the challenges ahead.

∞

By the time we reached the stables, the sky had darkened into a deep shade of twilight. Our horses waited for us, their soft snorts and shifting hooves a welcome distraction from the tension of the evening.

We mounted our steeds and began the ride toward the castle. The chill in the air was invigorating, and the rhythmic sound of hooves against the cobblestone streets was almost soothing.

Annie looked up at the dark silhouette of the castle in the distance. "Is that it? The castle?"

"That's the one," Damien confirmed, scanning the sky for any signs of danger. "We'll need to be ready for anything. My mother's dragons will have informed her of our approach."

Annie glanced at the dragons circling above us. "I still don't get how she controls them. What's the deal with that?"

"Powerful beings like her can bond with dragons," Damien explained. "She probably forced their allegiance. But with our new powers, we might stand a chance."

As we approached the castle gates, I took in the sight of the ogre and werewolf guards stationed there. Their armor clinked ominously in the dim light, and their eyes glinted with suspicion.

"We should have brought more of our pack with us," Annie said, her voice laced with concern.

Damien shook his head. "It's too late for that now. Let's just stick to the plan."

I stepped forward, casting a quick protection spell around us. "Let's be ready. We must be cautious."

The ogres approached their heavy steps echoing in the quiet night. "Which one of you is Damien?" one of them growled.

Damien stepped forward, his face set with determination. "That would be me."

The ogres seized him roughly and dragged him toward the castle. One of them turned to us, eyes narrowing. "You're coming too. Move it!"

We followed, the oppressive presence of the castle growing with each step. Inside, the grand chandelier above us cast eerie shadows on the stone walls.

At the end of the hall, Damien's mother sat on a throne made of blackthorns, her dark beauty, and sharp gaze sending a chill down my spine.

She looked at Damien, a cruel smile on her lips. "Welcome back, my son. I've been waiting for this reunion."

Damien glared at her. "You've betrayed everything we stood for. How could you align yourself with her after all we've been through?"

She raised a hand, silencing him. "Enough of your defiance. You and your friends are here to face the consequences of your choices."

Her eyes turned to me. "And you, Amy. Still clinging to my son? What is it that you want from me?"

I squared my shoulders, trying to hide my nerves. "I'm here because Damien and I are bound by fate. Your schemes can't change that."

Her laughter was cold and sharp. "

You think you can defy me? I'll show you just how powerless you are."

She began to cast a spell, but the protective barrier around us held firm, her magic bouncing harmlessly off it.

"What have you done?" she hissed, fury and surprise mixing in her voice. "Why are you immune to my magic?"

"Maybe you should have read your own grimoire more closely," I said, bracing myself for what was to come.

Her eyes blazed with rage. "You will regret this insolence."

I took a deep breath, ready to face whatever came next.

Chapter 10

Around eight in the evening, we walked away from Lucian's home, the weight of our mission pressing on us like the chill in the night air. The sky was a canvas of deep blues and purples, the first stars peeking through the darkness as we headed for the stables. Our destination was the castle, looming ahead in the distance like a dark promise. Our loyal pack of twenty fighters followed behind us, their presence a comforting reminder of our strength.

I mounted my black stallion, the familiar feel of the leather reins in my hands evoking memories of battles long past. The metal of my armor felt cool against my skin, a stark contrast to the warmth of my memories—Damien beside me, his eyes reflecting the same resolve that I carried now.

Damien, riding at the head of our group, glanced up at the sky where dragons circled like menacing sentinels. "They know we're coming," he said, his voice steady but with an edge of apprehension. "My mother's dragons will have informed her of our approach. I hoped we might catch her off guard."

Annie squinted up at the dragons, her brow furrowed. "Dragons are not exactly the kind of welcome wagon I was expecting. How does she communicate with them?"

"I know it's unsettling," Damien admitted, his gaze following the dragons as they dipped and soared. "Communing with dragons isn't unheard of. In her case, she probably coerced them or bound them through dark magic."

"That's reassuring," Annie said, though her tone was anything but. "Are we ready for whatever's waiting for us there?"

"We are," Damien said with more confidence than he felt. "Our combined powers give us an edge. She won't be prepared for our united front."

"Still," I said, a hint of worry in my voice, "it wouldn't hurt to have a little extra protection."

Damien looked at me with a hopeful expression. "Could you cast a protection spell for us, Amy? Something quick and effective?"

I stopped my stallion, pulling out my grimoire. "Alright, give me a moment." I flipped through the pages, scanning for a spell that could offer us some temporary shielding. "Got it. This one should do the trick."

I began the incantation, my voice steady despite the unease bubbling beneath my calm facade. "By the ancient forces of earth and sky, protect us now from harm's cruel eye."

As the last syllables left my lips, a shimmering barrier wrapped around us, casting a faint blue glow that danced in the twilight.

"Can you feel it, Damien?" I asked, my eyes scanning his face for a sign of reassurance.

"Yes, it's perfect," Damien said, his relief evident. "Thanks for pulling that out of the grimoire so quickly."

"As the head witch of the coven, it's my job to keep these spells ready," I said, trying to sound more confident than I felt. "Part of my role is to have the right spell for any situation."

"Lucky for us that you're so diligent," Damien said with a grateful smile. "Let's keep moving."

As we approached the castle gates, the sight of the ogres and werewolves on guard sent a shiver down my spine. The ogres were hulking figures, their armor scratched and dented from countless battles. The werewolves, their fur bristling and eyes gleaming with hostility, stood at attention beside them.

"Damien, what's the deal with the werewolves?" I asked, my voice low. "I thought they were loyal to our cause."

"I didn't know there were other werewolf factions," Damien said, his expression troubled. "We should have brought more of our pack with us."

Lucian stepped forward, his eyes scanning the guards. "We might have underestimated the situation. Our twenty fighters might not be enough against this."

"Let's not panic," Damien said. "Amy, can you come up with another spell, just in case we need it?"

I took a deep breath, feeling the pressure mount. "I'll see what I can do."

I thought quickly and came up with a minor enchantment to boost our strength. "This should help a bit. Just a little extra power for when we need it."

I spoke the words of the spell, and a faint golden aura enveloped us. "There we go. A little extra boost."

"Thanks, Amy," Damien said. "Let's hope this keeps us going."

We approached the gates, the ominous silence of the castle greeting us. The ogres eyed us with suspicion as the werewolves moved to flank us.

"Which one of you is Damien?" one of the ogres growled.

Damien stepped forward, releasing my hand—a gesture I hadn't realized we'd been holding until it was gone. The ogres seized him, dragging him toward the castle entrance.

"What are you waiting for? An invitation?" one of the ogres sneered at us.

We followed, the castle's towering silhouette growing darker and more menacing against the backdrop of the night. The flickering glow of the chandeliers inside cast eerie shadows on the walls as we walked through the grand hall.

Inside, the corridors were dimly lit, the oppressive darkness giving way to a grand chamber at the end. Damien's mother sat on a throne of twisted blackthorns, her presence exuding both elegance and malice. Her eyes locked onto Damien, a cruel smile playing on her lips.

"Well, if it isn't my son," she said, her voice dripping with mock affection. "How lovely to see you again. I feared I'd never have the pleasure of this reunion."

Damien's eyes were cold, but his voice held a note of frustration. "Vivian, you've chosen a path of darkness. You know where your true loyalties should lie."

Vivian's eyes flashed with anger. "Enough. You are still my children, and you will face the consequences of your defiance."

She turned to me, her eyes narrowing with disdain. "And you, Amy. Still clinging to my son? How many times must I rid myself of you?"

I stood tall despite the fear gnawing at me. "I'm sorry if my existence bothers you, Your Majesty. But you must understand that Damien and I are bound together by a curse that neither of us can escape. Our love is beyond your control."

Her laugh was a harsh, cruel sound that filled the chamber. "You think you can defy me? I've tried countless times to remove you from Damien's life, but you always return. It's infuriating!"

"Your Majesty," I said, my voice steady, "you can't break us. We are destined to be together, no matter your schemes. Damien has chosen his path, and you need to accept that."

Vivian's eyes sparked with fury; her hands raised to cast a spell. But the protective barrier around us held firm, the magic bouncing harmlessly off.

"What kind of sorcery is this?" she demanded, her voice a mixture of rage and disbelief.

"It's called preparation," I said, trying to keep my voice steady. "You should have expected us to come prepared."

Vivian's frustration only grew, her spells fizzling against our shield. "You and your coven are more troublesome than I anticipated. But this is just the beginning."

I braced myself for whatever came next, the weight of our fight against Vivian settling on my shoulders.

This battle was far from over, and the darkness that awaited us was only beginning to reveal itself.

Chapter 11

"Apologies if this disappoints you, but we're currently shielded from harm," I said, my voice steady as I faced Queen Vivian. "If you could explain your intentions, we'd be happy to get on with our packed schedule. We don't have time for your games."

Vivian's eyes narrowed, her fury building. "How dare you speak to me like that! I am your Queen!" She snapped her fingers, and the ogres lumbered toward us, their expressions menacing.

I didn't flinch. "As I said, no one can touch us." The moment the ogres reached out, a crackling wave of sparks surged from our barrier, sending them stumbling back with yelps of surprise.

The Queen's eyes widened. "How is this possible? Why weren't you so powerful before?"

"Times change," I said, with a calm that didn't match the storm of thoughts in my head. "We've grown stronger, and your magic can't break through. If you want to continue this fight, be prepared for consequences."

Vivian's anger turned to confusion as she struggled to grasp what was happening. "You've never had this kind of power. Why are you so different now?"

"Growth happens," I said, meeting her gaze without flinching. "And our coven is more united than ever. We won't be easily defeated."

I looked back at the coven, the resolve in their eyes matching my own. "Ready, everyone? Let's start the incantation."

We began the chant together, our voices rising in a unified hum. The words of the spell filled the room, and Vivian's form started to shimmer and then solidify into stone. She tried to fight it, but it was too late; her body turned to cold, gray rock.

"Perfect," I said, relieved as the final words of the spell settled into place. "We did it. Vivian is now a statue."

Damien stepped forward, looking at the stone likeness of his mother. "What do we do with her now? We need a place to keep her safe."

"The bell tower should work," Damien said. "I'll find the keys. Lucian, can your pack help carry her?"

Lucian nodded, his face a mix of relief and weariness. "Yes, we can manage that."

"Damien, are you taking on the role of King now?" I asked, my curiosity getting the better of me.

He shook his head slowly. "I'm not sure what this means yet. I need to talk to my Queen about her place at my side, but for now, let's focus on this victory. We should savor it."

"Let's get back home and celebrate," I said, feeling a surge of relief. "We've earned this moment. We'll deal with the witch's remains when we get back."

"Agreed," Damien said. "The journey home will be long, so let's get started."

As we prepared to leave, I glanced at the stone figure of Vivian, feeling a strange mix of triumph and unease. "I'll cast a cloaking spell to keep her hidden until we figure out what to do next. Do any of you know a spell for that?"

Lucian shook his head. "I don't know one off the top of my head."

"I've got it covered," I said, stepping forward with determination. "Let's do this."

I began the incantation for the cloaking spell, my hands weaving through the air as I chanted the ancient words. A veil of invisibility enveloped Vivian, hiding her from view.

"There," I said, satisfied. "She's hidden from sight, at least for now. We'll need to stay alert, but we can enjoy our victory for a while."

Damien smiled, a genuine smile for the first time since our arrival. "Thank you, Amy. We did it."

The coven gathered around, the tension easing as we began our journey back. The forest path was quiet, the only sounds were the rustling leaves and the occasional call of distant creatures.

"We'll face whatever comes next," Damien said, his tone filled with resolve. "But for now, let's enjoy the peace we've earned."

As we rode through the forest, the weight of our victory settled over us, a comforting blanket against the chill of the night. The battle was won, but the war was far from over.

We rode on in silence, each of us lost in our own thoughts, but united in our triumph. For now, we had the upper hand, and that was enough.

Chapter 12

Our victory was undeniable. We'd vanquished the evil witch, freed the captives from her dark clutches, and uncovered a handful of ordinary souls who had been dragged into this shadowy realm. Now, the real work began—ensuring that these people returned to their lives without the weight of their harrowing experiences. If the world knew what lurked in Tridion, our existence would be at risk.

I took a deep breath and gathered everyone around. "Okay, listen up," I said, my voice steady as I looked at the group of weary but relieved faces. "We need to make sure these people don't remember what happened here. I know a spell that will erase their memories and guide them back to their homes. Damien, I could use your help."

Damien nodded, his eyes focused on the task at hand. "Let's do this. We need to get it right."

"Everyone, join in," I instructed. "We're going to chant the incantation ten times. As we do, imagine a shimmering path leading them home."

I started the spell, my hands weaving through the air as I spoke the ancient words. The coven followed my lead, their voices merging with mine in a rhythmic chant.

As we repeated the chant, the mundane souls began to fade from sight, their bodies dissolving into shimmering threads of light that wove a path back to their homes. I watched as they disappeared, a mixture of relief and sadness settling over me.

"We did it," I said softly, glancing at the others. "They're on their way back."

Damien gave a small smile. "Thank you, Amy. That spell was crucial."

With the immediate danger behind us, we started our journey back to Lucian's place. The mood was lighter, our spirits buoyed by the victory.

As we walked, Lucian began to hum a familiar tune. "I don't even know where this song comes from, but it feels right to sing it now."

The melody was catchy, and soon we all joined in, our voices melding in a triumphant chorus.

(Chorus)
Lucian: singing
Marching on, with hearts so bold,
Through the fire, through the cold.
Victory's ours, the story's told,
In unity, we stand as one, behold!
(Verse 1)
Amy: joining in
Banners high, unfurling wide,
In the winds of triumph, we ride.
With each step, our spirits soar,
To the rhythm of victory's roar.
(Chorus)
All: singing together
Marching on, with hearts so bold,
Through the fire, through the cold.
Victory's ours, the story's told,
In unity, we stand as one, behold!
(Verse 2)

Damien: enthusiastically
Drums beating in thunderous sound,
Our triumph echoes all around.
In the face of every trial we've braved,
Our banner of victory unfurled and waved.
(Chorus)
All: singing in harmony
Marching on, with hearts so bold,
Through the fire, through the cold.
Victory's ours, the story's told,
In unity, we stand as one, behold!
(Bridge)
Mayson: with determination
Through every battle, every fight,
We've held our ground with all our might.
Now we march, with heads held high,
For victory's banner lights the sky.
(Chorus)
All: singing passionately
Marching on, with hearts so bold,
Through the fire, through the cold.
Victory's ours, the story's told,
In unity, we stand as one, behold!
(Outro)
Annie: with joy
So let our victory song resound,
Through valleys low and mountains crowned.
For in unity, we've claimed our right,
Marching forward into the light!

By the time we reached Lucian's home, the sun was just starting to rise. We were still high on victory, our voices tired but filled with the joy of our success.

Lucian and Damien set up champagne and glasses on the table. The bubbles in the champagne seemed to mirror the excitement we felt.

"To us," Lucian toasted, raising his glass. "To our unity as a team and a family."

We all clinked our glasses together, the sound of the glassware mingling with the laughter and the last strains of our victory song.

Damien reached for my hand, his touch warm and reassuring. "I'm grateful for this moment," he said. "It feels like we've lived through an entire saga today."

I squeezed his hand back, the connection between us comforting. "We really have," I said. "It's amazing what we can achieve together."

As the evening wore on, we shared stories of our journey, reminiscing about the battles we fought and the victories we claimed. Despite the exhaustion that tugged at us, we were buoyed by the success and the promise of what was to come.

Damien looked at me with a thoughtful expression. "There are still things we need to talk about, but for now, let's enjoy this moment."

I smiled, my eyes heavy with fatigue but also filled with hope. "Thank you, Damien. I'm ready for bed, though. It's been a long day."

With that, we said our goodnights and went to our rooms. As I climbed into bed, I felt a deep sense of satisfaction. Our bond had been tested and proven, and we had emerged victorious. I drifted off to sleep, grateful for the strength we had found in each other and the triumphs we had shared.

Chapter 13

Annie's voice cut through the fog of sleep like a siren. "Amy, wake up! I had the most amazing idea!" she said, her excitement so clear I could almost see it bouncing off the walls.

I groaned, dragging myself from the cozy cocoon of my blankets. The early morning light crept through the curtains, and I squinted at Annie's eager face. "Annie, it's barely dawn. What's this about?"

She bounced on her toes, practically vibrating with enthusiasm. "I had a dream about a fortune teller in New Orleans. We must go see her, Amy! Think of the answers we could find about our past lives!"

I rubbed my eyes, struggling to shake off the sleepiness. "You know Damien and Lucian are against messing with our past lives, right? It's risky business. Are you sure about this?"

Annie's eyes widened with determination. "We'll be back before they even notice. We can cast a time-slowing spell to make sure we don't get caught. Come on, Amy, this could be the chance of a lifetime!"

I sighed, considering her excitement against the nagging worry in the back of my mind. "Alright, but let's keep this on the downlow. We need a short spell, one that lasts just a few hours. Deal?"

Annie's face lit up like a sunrise. "Deal!"

We scrambled out of bed and grabbed the grimoire from the bookshelf. Annie found the time-slowing spell, and we chanted the incantation together, our voices blending into a focused hum.

"There, it's done," Annie said, her eyes sparkling with anticipation. "Let's get moving before we lose the best part of the day."

"Did you figure out how to reopen the portal?" I asked, my fingers drumming on the table. "And what about getting back? And making sure everything stays the same while we're gone?"

Annie waved her hand dismissively. "I've got it all covered. We'll slip in and out without a hitch. I've even got the return spell ready." She handed me a slip of parchment with the words written in careful script.

"Good," I said, taking the parchment. "Let's make sure everything's ready then."

With our preparations in order, we approached the portal. Annie started the chant, her voice steady and clear. The air around us shimmered as the portal opened, the familiar swirl of colors pulling us through.

Stepping out into the vibrant streets of New Orleans was like being wrapped in the city's electric pulse. Music from a nearby jazz bar floated through the air, mingling with the rich scent of beignets from a bakery on the corner.

Annie took a deep breath, her excitement almost tangible. "I love this city! Let's head to the Gypsy store. I can't wait to see what she must tell us."

We walked through the lively streets, dodging the occasional street performer and lost tourist. The city seemed to hum with a life of its own, its magic a faint but persistent undercurrent.

The Gypsy shop was tucked between two larger buildings, its entrance adorned with hanging crystals that tinkled softly as we stepped inside. The shop was filled with the rich aroma of incense and the warm glow of candlelight.

A woman stood behind a table covered in mystical trinkets. She looked up as we entered, her eyes sparkling with knowing anticipation. "Welcome, Amy and Annie," she said with a welcoming smile. "I knew you'd be coming today."

Annie and I exchanged glances of surprise. "Wow, you must be quite powerful," I said, trying to keep my voice steady. "How did you know we were coming?"

The Gypsy chuckled softly. "I'm a fortune teller, my dear. I see things before they happen. Now, let's get to your reading."

She gestured for us to sit at the table. "Focus on your deepest desires and hold them close to your heart. I will draw five cards for each of you and interpret their meanings. If I see something unfavorable, would you prefer to know, or should I keep it to myself?"

Annie looked at me, her eyes wide. "We want to know everything—the good and the bad. Especially about love."

The Gypsy nodded, her fingers moving deftly as she shuffled the deck. "Very well. Let's see what the cards reveal."

As she laid out the cards, the air seemed to thrum with an almost tangible tension.

"Amy, your cards are as follows," the Gypsy began, her fingers pointing to each card in turn. "The Death card signifies a profound transformation, not a physical end but a new beginning. The Ace of Wands heralds a surge of creative energy and new ventures. However, the reversed Empress and Queen cards suggest challenges in nurturing and emotional stability. You might need to focus on self-care and confidence. Finally, the Four of Pentacles advises you to find a balance between security and change. You have a bright future ahead, but it's important to remain open to growth."

I took in her words, the meaning of the cards settling in my mind. "Thank you. This is reassuring, though nothing from my past jumped out?"

The Gypsy shook her head gently. "No past-life details in this reading, Amy. It's more about the future."

She turned to Annie, and I watched with bated breath as the cards were laid out for her.

"Annie," the Gypsy began, "you have the upright Emperor, symbolizing leadership and structure. The reversed Queen echoes emotional instability, indicating a need for self-confidence and nurturing. The upright Death card suggests transformative change, while The Fool encourages you to embrace new beginnings with optimism. However, the reversed Six of Swords warns of resistance to change. Keep an open heart and mind as you face the future."

Annie absorbed the reading, her face thoughtful. "Thanks. But did you pick up anything from our past lives or anything extra?"

The Gypsy's eyes grew distant for a moment before she focused on us again. "Actually, yes. I see a premonition. Amy, in many past lives, you've faced death at the hands of a wicked witch. Despite your recent victory, her presence remains. Be vigilant; she will seek vengeance. The fate of both your world and the mundane one rests on your readiness for this battle."

A chill ran down my spine at her words. The thought that Damien's mother could still be a threat was terrifying. "We need to handle this carefully," I whispered to Annie, my mind racing with strategies. "We can't let Damien or the coven know about this yet."

Annie nodded, her face set in determination. "Agreed. We'll keep this to ourselves for now."

We left the shop, our minds heavy with the Gypsy's warning. I cast the return spell, and the portal opened once more, its familiar glow welcoming us back to Tridion.

Stepping through, I felt the weight of the Gypsy's prophecy pressing on my shoulders. Annie and I said nothing about what we had learned as we resumed our normal routines, the gravity of our new knowledge making us more cautious.

Our laughter from earlier in the day had faded, replaced by a quiet resolve. The peace we had fought for was fragile, and the battle ahead loomed large.

Chapter 14

I barely had time to drag myself to the room before Annie pounced on me. Her eyes were wide, almost manic, like she'd been brewing a big plan while I was asleep.

"Amy, we have to reverse the spell," she said, barely containing her excitement. "The sleeping spell we cast—if we don't lift it, they'll wake up and figure out we're gone!"

I rubbed my eyes and stifled a yawn. "Can't it wait until we've had a little more rest?"

"No way! The longer we wait, the more chance someone might notice we're missing," Annie insisted. "Let's get this over with."

We shuffled to the center of the room, and Annie grabbed the grimoire from the table. We kept our voices low, barely above a whisper as we recited the reversal spell. "By the stars above and the earth below, awaken those who slumber in peace," we chanted, the words slipping from our lips like a secret incantation.

A soft hum of magic filled the room as the spell took effect. I could almost hear the faint stirrings of life beyond our door. "Let's just hope they stay asleep for a bit longer," I murmured.

Annie nodded, her face glowing with satisfaction. "Let's move on. We need a new protective layer for the property before Damien and Lucian get up and start their routine."

I flipped through the grimoire, my fingers brushing over the worn pages until I found a suitable spell. "Here we go. I'll take Earth and Air. You do Fire and Sea. Let's make sure this barrier holds up."

Annie nodded and pulled out the candles and ingredients we'd need. "Ready?"

I set the candle in the center of the room, surrounded it with rose petals, and placed a bowl of water next to it. "Alright, let's do this."

We began the incantation, our voices merging into a chant that resonated with the ancient forces of nature. "By Earth's might, and Air's grace, by Fire's heat, and Sea's embrace, we build a shield, a sacred place."

The room seemed to hum with power as the spell wove itself into existence. "Done," I said, brushing the last bit of rose petal off the floor. "Now we just need to clean up and get some rest."

Annie looked up at me, a flicker of worry in her eyes. "Do you think we can keep this from Damien and Lucian? They're not exactly clueless."

"We have to try," I said, hoping my voice sounded more confident than I felt. "We'll just act like we're tired from a late night. We've pulled off crazier things before."

As if on cue, Christian and Grayson strolled into the hallway, their cheerful banter filling the space. "Morning, sleepyheads!" Christian grinned, leaning against the doorframe. "Burning the candle at both ends, huh? Everything okay?"

Annie and I exchanged a glance. We'd have to tread carefully here. I took a deep breath. "It's been a bit of a rollercoaster, honestly. We, um, went back to New Orleans earlier this morning to see a Gypsy."

Christian's eyebrows shot up. "You did what? Damien and Lucian are going to flip when they find out!"

"We know," I said, trying to keep my voice steady. "But we found out some serious stuff. Damien's mother—she's still a threat, even with her locked away in stone. And with Vivian and her followers out there, the danger isn't over."

Grayson's face grew serious. "What did you learn? What's our next move?"

"We've got it handled," I said, trying to sound assured. "We cast a new protection spell that covers our whole property, even the seaside. We're safe here."

Christian let out a sigh of relief. "Good to hear. At least we've got that going for us."

With the truth out and our defenses in place, there was a moment of calm between us. "Nice work, you two," Christian said. "But let's be real—sooner or later, Damien and Lucian are going to figure it out. We need a solid plan for when that happens."

Annie nodded. "Yeah, we get it. Let's just keep this between us four for now. Deal?"

"Deal," Christian and Grayson said in unison.

As we made our way downstairs, I kept up the façade of normalcy, my stomach growling at the scent of grilled meat wafting from the backyard. Damien and Lucian were busy preparing for a barbecue, the perfect distraction for us.

"Hey, you two are finally up!" Damien called, a wide smile on his face as he flipped the burgers. "Hope you got some good rest."

"Yeah, thanks," I said, trying to mask the exhaustion behind a bright smile. "We were just catching up on some sleep. All that magic can be draining, you know?"

Damien nodded, though his eyes lingered on me with a hint of concern. "You don't look too well, Amy. You sure you're not coming down with something?"

I waved him off, hoping to deflect his worry. "Just a little tired. We'll be fine. After lunch, we might head back to the room for a nap if that's okay."

"Of course," Damien said, his concern evident but not pressing. "Just let me know if you need anything."

Annie and I grabbed plates and served ourselves, trying to blend into the scene of cheerful camaraderie. The barbecue was in full swing, and we settled down with Alistair, Aeron, and Tina from the pack, their easy laughter and conversation a welcome distraction.

As we ate, I caught a glimpse of the television screen and blinked in surprise. "Is that a romantic comedy?"

"Yeah," Alistair said with a grin. "It's like their version of Netflix. They've got all kinds of shows and movies here."

Lucian's voice cut through the chatter. "You two seem to have settled in nicely. How was your morning?"

"We were just catching up on some sleep," Annie said, her tone light. "Nothing too exciting."

Lucian seemed to accept that. "Good to hear. We've been busy preparing for the day. I hope you didn't miss too much."

"Nope," I said, feeling a bit of tension ease. "We're just enjoying the downtime."

After the meal, we made our way back upstairs, keeping up appearances until we were safely behind the closed door of our room.

"Alright, let's get ready for the next phase of our plan," I said, checking our supplies. "We need to make sure we're prepared for whatever comes next."

Annie nodded, her eyes sharp with resolve. "Let's do it."

I set up the room for the next spell, arranging the candle, water, and rose petals just as we had before. "Ready?"

"Ready," Annie said.

We recited the incantation ten times, our voices echoing softly in the dim light. "With this spell, we seek the truth of our past lives," we chanted, hoping for answers.

Once the spell was complete, we cleaned up quickly and climbed into bed, the weight of our quest heavy on our minds.

"Here's to finding some answers," I whispered as I snuggled under the covers.

Annie's eyes were closed, her voice soft. "Same to you."

And then we let the darkness of sleep take us.

∞

The first memory hit me like a punch—shadows and fire, monstrous creatures pouring from the darkness, the witch's minions attacking us with ruthless intent. I saw myself fighting, every spell and strike desperate and fierce.

The scene shifted abruptly to a Christmas past, where Damien and I were a family, joyous and expecting a child, only for that peace to be shattered by betrayal. I could feel the icy sting of Christian's knife and the heartache of being left behind.

Another memory followed, one of darkness and despair, where the witch's malevolent presence tainted my vision, her black eyes looming over me as she delivered my doom once more.

I was thrust into a time when the coven had turned dark, a horrifying vision of us using our powers for harm, hunted down by witch hunters. The weight of betrayal from those I trusted was nearly unbearable.

Then there was a fleeting moment of joy—a ball, laughter, dancing—before it was consumed by flames and chaos. The witch hunters were back, their assault ruthless and unyielding.

The next memory was brutal, each coven member turning against me, the pain of betrayal searing through my dreams. I was stabbed one by one, the faces of my friends twisted with a cruel purpose.

The seventh vision was a fall from a cliff, the abyss below swallowing me as I plummeted into the unknown. I could feel the fear and confusion, but also the question of who had cast me down.

The eighth and final memory was a burning stake, the ultimate punishment for my supposed crimes. Faces of loved ones and enemies alike watched as I faced my fate, and I could only wonder why no one came to my aid.

"Why didn't anyone stop them?" I whispered in the dream, my heart aching with the weight of betrayal. "Why was I left to burn?"

Each memory seemed to swirl around a house, red and dark, ominous and unrelenting. Faces from the past, my coven, my family, and then a new face—familiar yet distant. My grandfather, I realized with a jolt, a figure from a forgotten past who might hold the key to breaking the curse.

I woke with a gasp, my heart racing. "

It's not just memories," I said to Annie, who was already stirring beside me. "They're connected. The house, the faces... there's something more we need to understand."

Annie looked at me, her eyes full of concern. "What do you mean?"

"I saw our grandfather," I said, the words spilling out. "He was there in the memories. He might be the key to breaking this curse."

Annie frowned. "But he's been gone for centuries. How could he still be alive?"

"I don't know," I said, frustration mingling with determination. "But we have to find out. We have to ask Mom when we get back."

Annie sighed. "I didn't see much—just happy moments, a future where the realms were at peace. I think we saw different things because the answers are meant for you alone."

I told her everything I had seen, and she listened, her face growing more troubled with every word.

"This is so messed up," Annie said finally. "We went into this hoping for answers, but all we've got are more questions. It's almost like the spell was meant to confuse us."

"We need another spell," I said. "Maybe we can find something that gives us more clarity."

Annie nodded. "Let's try it. We need to get to the bottom of this."

We recited a new spell, our voices quiet and resolute as we counted down from twenty. Before we hit ten, we were fast asleep again, the shadows of our past still lingering in our dreams.

In my next round of sleep, the same memories played out, and I felt the same pull of darkness. Annie and I were running, trying to escape an ever-encroaching evil. We cast spells, but they were futile against the darkness that pursued us into oblivion.

As we fled, the darkness seemed to close in around us, and the struggle to find light, to find hope, was as elusive as ever.

Chapter 15

Damien sat on the edge of my bed, his hand gently squeezing mine as if he could pull me from the abyss of my dreams.

"Amy, are you alright?" His voice was a blend of concern and confusion. "You were screaming so loud it cut through the music downstairs. It must have been quite the nightmare."

I tried to shake off the lingering fear from my dream. "I'm fine. I didn't mean to wake everyone," I said, glancing over at Annie, who was still curled up in her bed, blissfully unaware of the commotion. "Annie's still out cold, though. We have to wake her up."

Lucian appeared at the doorway, his eyes sharp as he took in the scene. "Annie, wake up, sweetheart. We've got a situation."

Annie stirred groggily, rubbing her eyes as she blinked up at us. "What's going on? Why is everyone shouting?"

"Thank goodness you're alright," I said, relief washing over me as I met her sleepy gaze. "I just had a really bad dream, and I'm afraid it might mean something."

Annie sat up slowly, still disoriented. "I had a weird dream too, but I'm not sure what it was about. Do you think it's connected?"

Lucian stepped forward, offering a reassuring smile. "How about we put the nightmare behind us and grab some dinner? It's ready downstairs."

"Sounds great," Annie said, her stomach growling in agreement.

"Count me in," I said, eager to shift focus away from the dark shadows of my dream.

We hurried downstairs, the excitement of a good meal enough to distract us from the uneasy feelings that lingered from the nightmares. The scent of grilled meat and roasted vegetables filled the air, and for a moment, the comfort of normalcy felt like a balm to my nerves.

As we settled around the table, I couldn't help but replay the images from my dream: the old house with its pristine white walls and green door. There was something about it that gnawed at me, a sense of familiarity mixed with dread.

I took a bite of the juicy steak on my plate and tried to focus on the here and now. "This is fantastic, Damien. You really outdid yourself."

Damien smiled, a bit of pride in his eyes. "Thanks. I figured you two could use a good meal after everything."

As the conversation flowed around the table, I glanced at Annie, who was lost in her own thoughts. Her eyes met mine, and I could see she was thinking about the same things I was.

After dinner, we retreated to our room to talk. The weight of the dream was heavy on my mind, and I knew it was time to dig deeper into the mystery of that house.

"Annie," I began as I sat down on the edge of the bed, "we need to figure out what that house is all about. I feel like there's something we're missing."

Annie nodded, her expression serious. "Yeah, I get it. We need to know more. What did you see?"

I told her everything from the visions—the dark magic, the past lives, the memories of the house. "There was this house, a three-story place with white walls and a green door. It had a picket fence and a yard full of creatures. It seemed so peaceful, but there was something off about it."

Annie listened intently. "You think it's in Tridion?"

"Yeah, it has to be. I've never seen it in New Orleans," I said. "We need to ask Damien and Lucian about it. Maybe they know where it is."

We made our way downstairs again, the house now quiet as everyone seemed to have settled into their own routines. Damien and Lucian were lounging in the living room, watching an old black-and-white film on the TV.

I took a deep breath and sat down next to Damien, catching his eye. "Damien, can I ask you something?"

He turned to me, his gaze gentle. "Of course, Amy. What's on your mind?"

I flashed him a soft, genuine smile. "Earlier, I had a dream—a vision, really. It was about this old house, a charming three-story place with white walls, a green door, and a picket fence. I was wondering if you knew anything about it. Was it part of our past?"

Damien's eyes widened slightly, a flicker of recognition crossing his face. "Ah, you must be talking about the house across the forest. Yes, I know it well. It was your family's home long ago."

"Why would I be remembering something so dark?" I asked, a shiver running down my spine. "Could it be that our ancestors were involved in something evil?"

Damien's expression grew serious. "It's possible. The house had a troubled history, with dark forces lurking beneath its charm, not unlike the Amityville Horror legend."

I looked at him, trying to grasp the full implications. "Then what does that mean for us? Does this mean we were part of something sinister?"

Damien nodded slowly. "Our ancestors dabbled in dark magic, but it's not a reflection of who you are now. Did you see anything else in your dream?"

I took a breath, my voice trembling slightly. "Yes, there were other visions. I saw our coven engaging in dark magic, and it seemed like I was at the center of it all. Was I the one responsible for leading them down that path?"

Damien's eyes softened with concern. "It's hard to say. The past is a tangled web, and you may have been part of it, but that doesn't define who you are now."

"And what about Annie?" I asked, glancing at my sister. "Did she see the same things?"

Annie met Damien's eyes. "Yes, I saw the darkness of our past, but I also saw the possibility of a different future. We've chosen to fight for good now, not evil."

Damien gave a thoughtful nod. "The past can haunt us, but it's what we do in the present that matters. But you seem determined to know more. What do you need from me?"

I looked at him, feeling the weight of my resolve. "I need you to help Annie and me see our past lives, just for a glimpse. I want to understand what we were and how we can avoid repeating those mistakes. Can you help us with that?"

Damien's eyes searched mine, weighing my request. "I can help, but I must warn you—delving into the past can be dangerous. It's easy to get lost in it."

"I understand," I said, my voice steady. "But we need to know if we're to have any hope of changing our fate."

Damien sighed, his hand reaching out to hold mine. "Alright, we'll do it. But we'll need to be careful."

"Thank you," I said, feeling a surge of hope. "We'll do it together."

Lucian looked over from where he was sitting, a thoughtful expression on his face. "Are you ready for this? Once we dive into the past, there's no going back."

Annie nodded firmly. "We're ready. We need to face our past to move forward."

With a determined look, Damien stood up. "Then let's prepare for this journey. We'll start first thing in the morning."

As we made our way back upstairs to our room, the weight of the task ahead settled over us. I glanced back at Damien and Lucian, who were already discussing the preparations.

The old house from my dream was more than just a memory—it was a key to our past, and understanding it might just be our only hope for the future.

∞

The night passed quickly, filled with restless anticipation. In the early hours of the morning, I found myself unable to sleep, my thoughts racing with the possibilities and dangers that lay ahead. I glanced at Annie, who was still sound asleep, and then at the window where the first light of dawn was just beginning to break.

The old house and the dark legacy it held were pulling at me, a mystery that I was determined to solve. I knew that the journey into our past was not just about-facing old ghosts but about finding the strength to confront our destiny.

I took a deep breath and turned to Annie, ready to face whatever awaited us.

Chapter 16

After Damien heard our terrifying tale, he agreed to help us. Sitting in the dimly lit living room, the weight of our mission hung heavy in the air.

Christian, looking more serious than I'd ever seen him, cleared his throat. "We need to perform a spell—something to dive into your memories, tracing back to the start. Damien, Lucian, we need your help. Dark magic can be unpredictable, and we might face dangers from the past."

Damien nodded, his eyes steady. "We're with you. Whatever it takes to fix this."

"Thank you," Christian said, relief evident in his voice. "We need to cleanse our old home and free the trapped spirits there."

I stepped forward, my hands trembling slightly. "Let's begin. We need to open ourselves to the past, to see the truth of what we did."

Lucian handed me an old grimoire. "Are you ready?"

"Yes," I said, taking the book from him. "Let's embrace the past and find the answers we need."

We gathered around the circle of candles on the floor, the faint glow casting shadows on the walls. I took a deep breath and began the incantation, my voice steady despite the fear in my heart. "We call upon the forces of time, to unveil the shadows of our past. Let the memories come forth and guide us."

A soft hum filled the room as the air around us shimmered. "May the past reveal itself to us," I added, focusing on the words of the spell.

In an instant, the room was engulfed in a blinding light, then plunged into darkness. I clutched Damien's hand, feeling his warmth as a beacon in the void.

The scene that unfolded was a strange mix of clarity and shadow. I saw myself dressed in a crimson cloak, standing around a flickering fire pit with Annie and the others. The atmosphere was thick with darkness, the edges of the memory obscured and foreboding.

A book lay open on a wooden altar in front of us, its pages blank and dark. We chanted in a language I didn't recognize, our voices merging into a haunting melody. Shadows writhed around us, and the fire blazed higher, consuming the air and our resolve.

Figures writhed in agony around the edges of the circle, their suffering a stark reminder of the cost of our actions. The flames roared, their heat oppressive, a visible symbol of the doom we had unleashed.

The memory shifted, and suddenly we were pulled back to the present. I looked around, my heart pounding. The weight of what we'd seen pressed down on me.

"That was... awful," I said, my voice trembling. "We have to learn from it, but we can't let it define us."

"Agreed," said Christian, his eyes dark with the gravity of our shared experience. "We must move forward and find a way to break this curse."

"What now?" Arielle asked, her face pale but resolute.

"We need to reach out to our grandfather," I said, though my voice wavered with the uncertainty of our task. "We have to see if he can help us break the curse."

Annie sighed, clearly not thrilled about the plan. "It's a long shot, and Mom's not going to be happy about this. Plus, we don't even know if he's alive."

"True," I said, nodding. "But it's the only lead we have."

With a determined resolve, we left Damien and Lucian downstairs and headed up to my room.

"This is something we have to do ourselves," I said firmly.

Damien and Lucian exchanged glances, but they didn't argue. They knew we were set on this course, no matter what.

We entered my room, and Arielle was already on the floor, the grimoire spread open beside her. "I found a spell," she said, excitement lacing her voice. "We need a few things to perform it."

"Like what?" I asked, my eyes scanning the list of ingredients she held.

"A photo of him would be best, but since we don't have one, we can work with just his name," Arielle explained. "We'll need his full name, a few drops of your blood in the cauldron, and then we recite the spell three times."

Annie and I exchanged a look. "Do you remember Mom's maiden name?" Annie asked.

"Wasn't it Brody Bloodmoon?" I suggested, though I wasn't entirely sure.

Arielle nodded. "Let's use that then. We'll need to write it down and perform the spell."

I took a deep breath and cut my palm just enough to let a few drops of blood fall into the cauldron. I scribbled *Brody Bloodmoon* on a piece of paper, placing it into the cauldron as well.

We began the incantation together, our voices merging in a rhythmic chant. "By the blood of the past, and the name of the lost, we summon the one we seek. Hear our call and appear before us."

The room was filled with a blinding flash of light. When it faded, there he was—our grandfather, his presence cold and commanding.

"What do you want?" he growled, his eyes sharp with disdain. "You dare summon me?"

Annie stepped forward, her voice shaking. "We need your help. We want to break the curse you placed on our mother and the coven."

He sneered, his anger palpable. "Help you? After what your mother did? Do you think I owe you anything?"

Tears sprang to my eyes. "Please, Grandfather. We can't live under this curse any longer."

He shook his head slowly, a sinister smile curling on his lips. "You think you deserve mercy? No, it's time you suffer a new curse, one far worse than before."

Fear tightened around us, but we had no choice. "Alright," I said, barely above a whisper. "We'll leave you be."

With another flash of light, he was gone, leaving us with a sinking dread and a sense of failure.

The room fell silent, the crackling of the fireplace the only sound as we stared at the empty space where he had been.

"I can't believe it," Annie whispered. "We thought maybe he'd help us."

Christian stepped forward, his face set in grim determination. "We can't let this defeat us. We need to find another way."

"But how?" Arielle asked, her voice tinged with desperation.

"We will figure it out," Mayson said firmly. "We can't give up now."

I took a deep breath, trying to push the despair away. "We won't give up. We'll find a way to break this curse. I promise.

We gathered closer together, drawing strength from one another.

"We will find a way," I said, my voice steady. "We will have normal lives."

The room was thick with unresolved tension, but there was a quiet agreement among us to keep this encounter with our grandfather buried deep. We had been threatened with a new curse, and we would have to find another path forward.

"I can't shake the feeling that there's something more we're missing," I said, breaking the silence.

Annie's eyes widened. "I feel it too. Like there's another piece to this puzzle we haven't seen."

I nodded, sensing that there was a greater force at play. It didn't make sense that our suffering could be the result of our own actions alone.

"We need to go back," Grayson said firmly. "We have to uncover the truth of what happened to us."

The decision was made. We would perform the spell again, to travel back to that dark moment in our past and seek the answers we needed.

"I'm with you," Arielle said, her voice resolute. "We need to know the truth."

One by one, the coven agreed. With the spell recited from memory, we prepared ourselves for another journey into the past, hoping this time to uncover the hidden truths.

As we prepared for the spell, a sense of grim determination filled the room. We knew the journey ahead was fraught with peril, but the hope of redemption drove us forward. We chanted the incantation, the air around us shimmering as we were pulled back into the shadows of our past.

The scene unfolded before us—our former selves surrounded by darkness, the ritual that summoned the ancient evil now a vivid, haunting memory. The weight of our past sins pressed down on us, but we knew we had to face it to seek forgiveness and redemption.

In the depths of that dark memory, we vowed to confront the evil we had unleashed and to fight for a future free from the shadows of our past.

As we returned to the present, the heaviness of our mission settled over us. We had seen the horrors of our past, and the path forward was uncertain. But we were united in our resolve to break the curse and reclaim our lives.

"We will find a way," I said quietly, more to myself than anyone else. "No matter what it takes."

The coven gathered close, our resolve hardening against the darkness that had haunted us for so long. Together, we would face the challenges ahead, driven by the hope of a brighter future.

The quest was far from over, but for now, we took solace in our unity and our determination to overcome the past and forge a new path.

Later that night, as we sat together, the air filled with tense silence, a question lingered at the edges of my mind:

Was it better to remain ignorant of the darkness that had shaped us, or should we pursue understanding, no matter the cost?

Chapter 17

As we rode up the gravel driveway to our old house, the air was thick with the scent of damp earth and decaying wood. Shadows cast by the evening sun stretched across the overgrown lawn, giving the place an almost spectral quality.

"It's even more eerie than I remember," Annie whispered, her voice barely cutting through the rustling of leaves and the distant call of a raven.

Christian, ever the leader, scanned the dilapidated facade of the house. "Let's stick together. We don't know what's waiting for us inside."

We dismounted from our horses and approached the house in silence, the crunch of gravel beneath our boots breaking the eerie stillness. The front door, half off its hinges, creaked open with a groan that seemed to echo from the depths of the house. We stepped inside, our footsteps echoing off the walls as if the house itself were whispering secrets.

"Let's split into pairs," Christian suggested. "We'll cover more ground that way."

The rest of us nodded and paired up—Arielle with Mayson, Annie with Gwen, and Grayson with me. We avoided the basement. None of us was eager to confront the shadows we knew lurked there.

Room by room, we searched. Dusty furniture and broken picture frames greeted us, relics of a past we barely remembered. The silence of the house was oppressive, broken only by the occasional creak of the floorboards beneath our feet.

After a couple of hours, we reconvened outside the weight of our unfruitful search evident in our tired eyes.

"We didn't find much," Arielle admitted, her voice edged with frustration as she brushed the dust off her coat.

"There has to be something we missed," Grayson said, eyes scanning the old house one last time.

"Yeah, we'll have to keep looking," I agreed, trying to push down the disappointment. "Let's head back and go through what we brought."

As we rode away, the shadows seemed to shift and whisper behind us, the secrets of the old house tantalizingly out of reach.

Back at the cabin, breakfast was a subdued affair. We set up in the main room, laying out everything we had found—two old books, some artifacts, and a handful of trinkets.

"The Book of Celestial Beings" and the "Evil Book of Shadows" lay on the table, stark contrasts to each other. The celestial artifacts—golden angel wings, ornate knives, old coins, tarot cards, and jewel-encrusted plates—sparkled faintly in the morning light.

"I've been dying to see what's inside that book," I said, picking up the "Book of Celestial Beings." I turned to the others. "Let's see if there's anything useful in here."

Mayson leaned over my shoulder, examining the items. "Do you think these artifacts can help us tell the difference between good and evil?"

Christian nodded. "Maybe they have some sort of power or knowledge we can use."

"It's possible," Mayson said. "But we'll need to study them carefully. Rushing in could lead to more trouble."

I flipped open the ancient book, its pages filled with intricate symbols and glowing scripts. "We need to be cautious," I agreed. "Especially with that 'Evil Book of Shadows.' We have to find a way to destroy it."

Damien and Lucian volunteered to help. "We'll get rid of that book if it's the last thing we do," Damien said firmly.

We gathered outside, Damien and Lucian starting a fire in the backyard. The flames roared to life, but the "Evil Book of Shadows" remained untouched.

"This book doesn't burn like it should," Damien said, frustration evident in his voice.

"Let's check the 'Grimoire,'" Arielle suggested. "There might be a spell for this."

Gwen nodded. "If there's a way to destroy it, the 'Grimoire' will have it."

I took a deep breath and flipped through the ancient tome, finally landing on a passage about banishing dark artifacts. "Alright, everyone," I said, rallying the coven. "We need to perform this spell carefully. Damien, I'll need you and the rest of the pack to stay close in case anything goes wrong."

Lucian nodded. "We're ready. Let's get this done."

We formed a circle around the fire, each of us holding a black candle in our left hand and placing our right hand over our hearts. "Our intentions must be pure," I reminded them. "Focus on banishing the darkness."

As the flames flickered and danced, we chanted together.

"As the flames illuminate, I release this tome's grasp," I began solemnly, holding the book aloft.

"Shadows of malevolence flee; their power shall lapse," Gwen continued, her voice steady.

"With fire's embrace, I cleanse and purify," Arielle added, her eyes fixed on the blaze.

"May this transformative act herald peace anew," I finished, lifting my hands towards the fire. *"Into the inferno's embrace, where darkness may sway."

We chanted the spell ten times, our voices rising and falling with the crackling of the flames. Yet, the book remained unscathed.

"We need more power," Annie said, her brow furrowed. "Damien, channel your strength with ours."

Damien stepped forward, focusing all his energy on the spell. We chanted again, our combined force finally igniting the book. The flames roared higher, consuming the pages until all that was left were ashes.

"We should bury the ashes," I suggested. "Let's make sure it's buried deep so it can't be resurrected."

"Good idea," Gwen agreed. "We have the right spell for that."

Annie's eyes gleamed with anticipation. "Can we do it?"

Gwen nodded. "Yes, let's get to it."

We gathered around the pit where we'd burned the book. "Gratitude to Earth, Air, Fire, and Water," Meghan began, her voice calm and reverent. "For their watchful shield in this critical hour."

"May their blessings guide us steadfast and true," I added, focusing on the spell to seal the burial site.

As we completed the ritual, the site was protected, and sealed from any future disturbance.

∞

Later that day, we huddled around the grimoire once more, our faces lit by the soft glow of the candles.

"There has to be a spell in here to decipher the celestial texts," Arielle said, her eyes scanning the pages for anything that might help.

I flipped through the book until I found a passage about understanding ancient languages. "Alright, everyone," I said, gathering their attention. "We need to perform this spell to read the celestial texts. Follow my lead and focus on the book."

We recited the incantation together, and a soft glow surrounded the pages, making the ancient writing legible.

As the text revealed itself, we learned about the celestial beings' rebellion against God and their subsequent fall to Earth. Their influence had turned the once-peaceful realm of Tridion into a place of chaos and darkness.

"We have to find them," Meghan said, her eyes blazing with resolve. "They need to answer for what they've done."

"It won't be easy," I said, scanning the texts for any leads. "But we have to try."

"Maybe a summoning spell could work," Meghan suggested cautiously. "Though it's risky."

"It's a last resort," I agreed, feeling the weight of the decision. "But if we can't find another way, we'll need to use it."

As I continued to read, a plan began to form. "Alright, listen up," I said, calling everyone's attention. "The full moon is tomorrow. Lucian and the pack will be out in their wolf forms. We'll stay inside for safety. After the full moon, we'll perform the summoning spell and make them pay for their crimes."

"Agreed," the coven said in unison, their voices filled with determination.

With our plan set, we prepared for the coming night, knowing that the full moon would bring us one step closer to justice.

As we settled into our usual routine, the anticipation of tomorrow's ritual hung in the air, a tangible reminder of the task that lay ahead.

Chapter 18

The Full Moon hung low and heavy in the sky, its light casting eerie shadows on the world below. The tension in our meeting room was palpable, a stark contrast to the usual warmth of our coven gatherings.

"Why do we have to stay locked up, Amy? It would be incredible to see them transform," Meghan asked, her gaze fixed on the moon outside the window.

I shook my head, though I understood her curiosity. "Lucian warned us that their wolf forms are dangerous. They lose their human control and act on primal instincts. It's not safe for us to be around them during the Full Moon."

Arielle frowned, clearly not convinced. "But we're all allies here. Why would they harm us?"

I sighed, recalling Lucian's grave explanation. "Their animal instincts take over, and they can't control their actions. Even Lucian can't fully manage his pack during the Full Moon. He told me that trying to use any magic to counteract it would be dangerous."

Annie's eyes were troubled. "Even though Lucian's my love, the thought of him being a danger to us is terrifying."

"I did suggest a protection spell," I admitted, remembering the heated argument we'd had. "But Lucian was adamant that we stay out of their way. He was ready to fight if we pushed it."

Annie looked at me with a mix of relief and worry. "What happened when you threatened to leave?"

"He gave in," I said. "'Alright, Amy, you got your way,' he said. It wasn't just about him; he was worried about us." I smiled at the memory of his resignation. "I told him it was for everyone's safety. He said, 'You better get moving then. The full moon is closing in fast.' I assured him we'd be fine."

So here we were, huddled together in my room, surrounded by ancient books and arcane symbols. Each of us was clutching a tome or a charm, ready for what the night might bring.

"Alright, everyone," I said, excitement buzzing in my voice. "Let's combine these spells into one powerful incantation. We'll use items from each pack member to create a protective circle."

We gathered mementos from Lucian's pack—fur, a broken collar, a worn leather glove—and arranged them in a circle on the floor.

"Hold hands," I instructed, "and focus on the spell."

Damien stepped forward, his eyes glowing faintly as he began channeling his energy into the ritual. "Ready when you are, Amy."

"Let's do this," I said. We began chanting, the words blending in a harmonious flow of magic.

"Did it work!?" Richard's eyes were wide, his excitement barely contained.

"We'll see," I said. "We need to test it. If the wolves come near, we'll observe their reaction. If not, we might need another layer of protection."

Annie glanced nervously at the door. "Maybe we should consider casting another protection spell just to be safe?"

I shook my head. "I have a spell that might help. It's like a jolt of energy that can startle them if things go wrong. I discovered it during our fight with Damien's mother. I should have mentioned it sooner, but that night was a blur."

"You can shoot energy from your fingers?" Grayson's eyebrows arched in surprise.

"Yeah, it's a bit strange," Christian said with a grin.

"Well, let's remember that I'm probably the most powerful witch you've ever met, so it makes sense that I have a few tricks up my sleeve," I said confidently.

"Very well said, my love," Damien said, his eyes flashing red for a moment as he gave a pointed look around the room. "You have our respect."

"Let's not get into a debate," I said quickly, sensing the rising tension. "I'll go outside and check things out. I'll let you know when it's safe."

"I'm coming with you," Damien said firmly, stepping up beside me.

I raised an eyebrow. "You're really going to follow me?"

"Of course. I have other powers, like flying," he said casually, a hint of mischief in his eyes.

"You can fly? Since when?" I asked, taken aback.

"It's a vampire thing," Damien said with a smile. "Part of the package deal."

As I stepped outside, the cool night air greeted me, and the Full Moon's light was almost blinding. I approached the edge of the woods, where the wolves were gathered, their eyes reflecting the moonlight.

They were tense, their bodies shifting as they began to transform. I watched in awe as the familiar faces of Lucian's pack turned into powerful wolves. Their eyes met mine, and I felt a sense of recognition.

The wolves moved closer, sniffing at the air around me. Their howls filled the night, a chorus of raw, primal energy. I reached out a hand, and one of the wolves nudged it gently. They seemed to sense that I was not a threat.

Back inside, the coven was on edge. "It worked!" Arielle whispered, her voice a mix of excitement and relief.

Damien stayed by my side, his eyes scanning the wolves for any signs of aggression. "They're behaving well. Let's just hope they stay this way."

The wolves began to roam, their instincts taking over as they vanished into the shadows of the forest. I looked over at Damien. "They're not attacking. I think the spell worked."

Hours later, when the wolves returned, Lucian was waiting for us at the door, his face a mask of fury.

"What were you thinking, Amy?" he growled. "You could have been killed. I would never forgive myself or the pack if something happened to you."

I took a deep breath, standing my ground. "Relax, Lucian. I was in control of the situation. We're all safe, and the spell worked."

"You didn't have to take such risks," Lucian continued, his anger not quite fading. "Annie would never forgive me if I harmed you."

"She knows you wouldn't harm me, Lucian. Besides, Damien was with me," I said.

Lucian seemed surprised. "Damien was there? Why didn't we sense him?"

"Yes, he was by my side the whole time," I confirmed.

"That's very peculiar," Lucian said, looking thoughtful. "If he's a half-vampire and half-witch, we should have sensed him."

The room fell silent as we mulled over this new information. There was clearly more to Damien than we had realized.

"Well, let's not dwell on it now," I said, trying to focus on the immediate task. "We have more pressing matters to attend to."

The coven nodded in agreement. We had a lot to do, and the challenges ahead were daunting. But tonight, had been a success, and that was a step in the right direction.

With that, we gathered around the books and scrolls, ready to dive back into our research, our eyes set on the next phase of our quest for justice.

Chapter 19

After the chaos of the full moon, our coven was back in the attic, buried under a mountain of old tomes and scrolls. The scent of candle wax and the crackle of parchment filled the room as we dug into our research. I flipped through a dusty old grimoire, the pages yellowed and delicate under my fingers.

"I realized something fascinating," I began, my voice breaking the silence. "Our mystical abilities are tied to celestial events. The alignment of stars and planets can affect our magic."

Gwen looked up from her own book, her eyes sparkling with interest. "Really? How does that work?"

I leaned back in my chair, staring at the patterns on the ceiling. "The stars and planets influence the ebb and flow of magical energy. It's like a cosmic rhythm that we're all part of."

Arielle looked up from her notes, her brow furrowed. "So you're saying the angels weren't just doing random acts of evil? There was a reason behind their actions?"

"Exactly," I said, nodding. "Their actions seemed designed to push us towards destruction instead of peace."

Meghan's lips pressed into a thin line. "But why would celestial beings—who are supposed to be protectors—want to harm us?"

"It's confusing," I admitted. "Angels are supposed to be the guardians of the divine order, not instigators of chaos."

Nancy, usually quiet, spoke up. "What could have driven them to such malevolence? We must have done something to provoke their wrath."

"Have we really done anything to deserve this?" Grayson asked, his voice heavy with doubt. "It feels like we're just pawns in some larger game."

We were all silent for a moment, the weight of unanswered questions pressing on us.

"Amy, maybe we should take a break," Nancy suggested gently. "We could all use some rest."

"Yeah, I think we need it," I said, rubbing my eyes. "Let's call it a night. We can regroup tomorrow."

As we packed up the books and closed the grimoire, Gabriella's voice broke through the gloom. "We'll make them regret the day they messed with us."

We agreed, and for once, we allowed ourselves to relax. We climbed into our beds, hoping for a few hours of peace before facing the harsh realities of our quest again.

The next morning, sunlight streamed through the attic windows, warming the cold room. Eleven hours of sleep had left us refreshed; the exhaustion of our previous work replaced by a tentative hopefulness.

Outside, the world was blanketed in snow, the air crisp and cold. But Lucian had set up a warm-water pool, a little oasis amidst the winter chill. We were drawn to it like moths to a flame.

"Ready for a break?" I called, my voice echoing with relief.

"Yes!" Nancy said, her eyes lighting up. "Let's enjoy it while we can."

We changed into swimsuits, braving the chill to reach the pool. The warmth of the water was a balm for our weary spirits. Damien and Lucian started a spirited game of water volleyball, the splash and laughter filling the space between us. Seth and Winston manned the grill, the smell of sizzling meat mixing with the crisp winter air.

Annie watched the game with a grin, her laughter ringing out. "Look at you two! I thought vampires didn't play games."

"Just because I'm a vampire doesn't mean I can't enjoy a good challenge," Damien said with a smirk, splashing water in her direction.

As the day wore on, the fun and games were a welcome distraction. We played, ate, and laughed until the sky turned a dusky gray.

"Dinner's ready," Lucian called from the kitchen. "And I've got movies lined up for us."

"Sounds perfect," Annie said, already heading inside.

We followed her, slipping into the cozy warmth of the kitchen. The smell of food and the hum of the TV were comforting after our long night of research.

Later, when we gathered around the table, I felt a rare moment of peace.

"This is nice," Gabriella said, her voice filled with contentment. "We've earned this break."

As we ate, the conversation turned to plans for the future.

"We have our work cut out for us," I said, my mind already shifting back to our mission. "It's time to start preparing for the confrontation with the dark forces."

Christian's voice trembled slightly. "Is there really no other way?"

"I wish there was," I said gently. "But we've explored every option. This is the only way forward."

Christian nodded, though doubt still lingered in his eyes. "What about the spell to uncover who cast it on us?"

"I have a suspicion," I said, feeling the weight of the moment. "But there's something else I need to tell you."

Damien looked up from his plate, concern in his eyes. "What is it, Amy?"

I took a deep breath, the words feeling heavy on my tongue. "Damien, your mother is still alive. And she's likely already plotting against us."

Damien's eyes widened. "How do you know this?"

"She's powerful," I said. "As you said, she can't be killed. We need to be ready for her."

Damien's face grew dark. "I see."

I offered a strained smile. "We've cast a protective spell around ourselves and the house, but we need to stay vigilant."

The room was silent as we absorbed the news. Damien gave a tight nod before retreating into his thoughts.

As the day turned to evening, we prepared ourselves for the next phase of our battle. With the weight of our mission before us, we knew that rest would be fleeting.

The time had come to put our plans into action.

"Let's get to it," I said, steeling myself. "We need to summon our enemies and find out what really happened that night."

With a firm resolve, I prepared the spell, gathering the herbs and oils we would need.

"Are you ready?" Nancy asked, her voice steady despite the tension.

"Yes," I said. "It's time."

I began chanting, drawing on the power we had gathered. The air grew heavy, the darkness pressing in as black smoke swirled and the celestial beings began to manifest.

Zachariah appeared first, his gaze cold and unyielding.

"How dare you summon us," he growled, his voice dripping with contempt.

"We dare," I said, my voice unwavering. "You owe us answers for the wrongs you've committed."

His eyes glinted with something like amusement. "You think you can challenge us?"

"Yes," I said, stepping forward. "We're the Crescent Coven. We're not afraid of you."

Zachariah sneered. "You have no idea what you're dealing with."

"We know enough," I said. "And we're ready for whatever comes next."

As the confrontation unfolded, the tension in the room was almost palpable. Lucian and the pack stood behind us, their presence a formidable force.

"Are those scars from the fire?" I asked, my gaze fixed on Zachariah's face.

He flinched, though he quickly masked it. "It was not our doing."

"Then who?" I demanded. "Which demons did you manipulate us into summoning?"

Zachariah's smirk faltered. "You were used as pawns. The demons were summoned to ensure your eventual vengeance."

"Give us their names," I said firmly. "Or face the consequences."

With a reluctant sigh, Zachariah began to write. "I will cooperate, but remember, this is not the end."

"Consider it a beginning," I said, watching as he penned the names of the demons.

When he was done, I dismissed him with a wave of my hand. "Leave now. And know this: I will track you down if you cross us again."

Zachariah and his fellow beings vanished into the shadows, leaving us alone with our new knowledge and a renewed sense of purpose.

"We have work to do," I said, rallying the coven. "Let's start planning for the battle ahead."

Christian's eyes were wide. "Is there really no other way?"

"I wish there was," I said, my voice steady. "But we've come this far. We can't turn back now."

Damien's face was a mix of resignation and determination. "We'll face whatever comes."

With that, we set to work, ready to confront the challenges that lay ahead.

The night was quiet, but it was the calm before the storm. We knew that the real battle was just beginning.

Chapter 20

We'd been expecting it. Zachariah had promised that the celestial beings would behave differently, but I wasn't about to take a chance on his word. I knew how angels were: deceptive and ruthless. Now that he'd seen what we could do, I was sure he'd find ways to counteract us. It left me feeling uneasy and exposed, like we'd given away our best move in a game of chess.

"Hey guys," I said, hoping to break through the tension, "anyone here have connections to dragons? You know, someone who might have them or know where to find them? We could use their help."

Damien and Lucian exchanged glances, then burst out laughing.

"What's so funny?" I asked, bewildered.

Lucian wiped a tear from his eye. "Seriously, Amy? Dragons? Are you planning to start an epic quest or something?"

"Yeah," I said. "We're gearing up for a showdown. With Damien's mother and the celestial beings coming back, we need every advantage we can get."

Damien looked at me skeptically. "But we have the protection spell up. That should keep them at bay, right?"

"It's not enough," I said. "Zachariah saw what we're capable of. He'll be working on a way to get around our defenses. We need to surprise them."

Damien sighed. "You're jumping ahead. We still need to focus on the demons and the trapped spirits from the old house."

"I know, but I have a plan," I said. "Dragons are the first thing that came to mind. Is it that crazy?"

"It's not that," Lucian said. "It's just unusual for you. You've been on edge ever since we summoned those celestial beings."

"I'm trying to think outside the box here. So, do you know anyone with dragons or not?" I pressed.

Lucian raised his hand, almost like he was back in school. "Actually, I do. I can get in touch with Gregory Ravenswood. He's my cousin and the alpha of his pack. He's also known for his dragons."

"Great!" I spoke. "Can you contact him?"

Lucian chuckled. "It's not like I can just send him a text. I'll have to go to Silverhaven to see him."

"Alright, take Damien with you. What about Seth? Isn't he friends with Gregory too?" I asked.

"Yeah, Seth knows him as well. I'll bring both. Last I heard, Gregory had about ten dragons," Lucian said. "Maybe he has more now."

"Sounds like a solid plan," I said, feeling a bit of relief. "How long will it take?"

"It's a tough trip. Two days there and two back, if everything goes well. If not, it could take longer," Damien said. "But we'll manage."

"Alright, then I'll get to work on some protective amulets for you guys. I'll need until morning to finish them," I said, already thinking about the enchantments.

Lucian nodded. "That works. We'll set out first thing in the morning."

With that, I left them to their preparations and started working on the amulets. The hours slipped by as I crafted spells and charms, the weight of our upcoming battle pressing on me. By the time morning came, I was both anxious and hopeful.

After a quick breakfast, I saw Damien and Lucian off, watching as they disappeared into the snowy distance, heading towards Silverhaven and Gregory Ravenswood.

The next few days dragged on, filled with a flurry of activity. We reinforced the barriers around the house, brewed potions, and made sure every spell was ready for when they returned. The hours felt like days, and the days like weeks.

Then, one night, as I was finalizing a particularly tricky protection charm, a noise shattered the quiet.

"Annie, wake up!" I whispered urgently, shaking her shoulder.

"What's wrong?" she mumbled groggily.

"I heard something outside. What if Zachariah has found us?" I said, my heart racing.

Annie's eyes widened. "Oh no. We're not ready yet. What should we do?"

I grabbed her hand and we slipped out of the room, our footsteps silent as we headed down the hallway to Christian and Grayson's room.

"Christian! Wake up!" I said, shaking him gently. "There's something going on outside."

Christian blinked awake as we heard a loud crash. "They've found us! What do we do?"

I looked around, panic rising. "We need to hide. Fast. I've got an idea.

We raced through the house, waking up Milo, Mason, Arielle, Gwen, Andy, Meghan, Gabriella, and Nancy. We huddled together in the safest room we could find, and I began the incantation for the cloaking spell.

"Whispers soft as a gentle breeze, shadows deep like secrets wrapped in dreams," I chanted, the words flowing from me as we became invisible.

We huddled in silence, trying to keep our breathing steady as we heard the angels moving around downstairs, searching for us with determined precision.

"They must have had a tip-off," I whispered. "How could they know we're here?"

Annie trembled beside me. "Maybe they've been watching us. I thought our protection spell would be enough."

"They're cleverer than that," I said. "They won't leave until they find us."

We waited in tense silence, the sounds of the angels' search echoing through the house. Each footstep and whisper from them seemed to stretch out the minutes.

"Amy, why won't they leave?" Annie asked, her voice barely more than a whisper.

"I think they believe we're still here," I said. "They're not going to stop until they're sure we're gone."

We followed the angels' movements as they made their way through the house, sticking to the shadows. I made sure the cloak covered everyone, even Tina and Pamela, who were still asleep on the sofa.

Hours passed like this until we finally heard a commotion from the front of the house.

"They're gone!" I whispered, barely believing it.

The door creaked open, and Damien and Lucian stumbled in, exhausted but triumphant.

"Are you guys okay?" Damien asked, his eyes darting around. "Did they hurt you?"

"No, we were hiding," I said, my voice breaking. "We managed to stay out of their sight, but I thought it was over for us."

Damien pulled me into a hug. "You're safe now. We brought reinforcements. Gregory and his dragons are on their way."

I almost cried with relief. "Thank you, Damien. I didn't know if we'd make it."

He smiled at me, his expression both reassuring and tired. "Gregory's dragons are impressive. We'll be ready for the next fight."

The dragons were a sight to behold. When Gregory arrived, his pack and their majestic creatures filled the room with a powerful presence.

"Meet Gregory Ravenswood," Lucian said. "He's the alpha of his pack and the dragon master we needed."

Gregory gave a nod, his eyes assessing the room. "You must be Amy. Lucian's told me a lot about you."

"Yes, thank you for coming," I said, feeling a bit shy. "I'm glad you're here."

Gregory looked around at the group. "Let's get ready. We have a battle ahead of us."

With that, the room was filled with a renewed sense of purpose. We had our dragons, and we had a plan. We would be ready for the celestial beings when they returned.

As the night went on, I went back to my grimoire, studying hard to make sure we were as prepared as we could be. I wouldn't let the angels underestimate us again.

For now, we had a moment of peace, and it was enough to fuel our preparations for the coming storm.

Chapter 21

The crisp night air hit me as we stepped outside, and I had to blink a few times to take it all in. Dragons. Real dragons. The sight of them was almost more than I could handle. They soared and circled in the dark sky, their scales glistening like the stars, their fiery breath painting the night with bursts of brilliant flame.

"Wow," I breathed out, my eyes following a dragon as it unfurled its wings, sending ripples through the cool night air. "This is incredible."

Gregory, standing tall beside us, seemed to notice my awe. "Glad you think so. We don't get to show off the dragons too often. They're quite the sight, aren't they?"

Damien, standing next to me, was practically vibrating with excitement. "These dragons are legendary. I've heard stories but seeing them up close is something else."

Annie's eyes were wide as she looked up at the dragons. "I've read about Draconis the Flameheart. I never thought I'd see him in person."

I glanced around at the group, noticing the way Gregory's pack and our coven were forming a circle, their faces illuminated by the dragon's fiery breath. Each of the dragons had a presence that made the wolves and us seem almost insignificant in comparison.

"Draconis the Flameheart blazes with the intensity of a thousand suns," Damien began, his voice low and reverent.

Aetheria the Skyborn glided overhead, her wings creating a serene pattern against the dark sky. "And Aetheria the Skyborn, soaring with the grace of dawn and dusk," Annie added, her voice almost a whisper.

Christian pointed towards the shadows where a dark form loomed. "Nidhoggr the Shadowcaster, a creature of the night, blending into the darkness."

Nancy caught the light of the fire from the nearby barbecue, her gaze following a particularly radiant dragon. "Aurelia the Sunwing spreads warmth and life wherever she goes."

Gwen's eyes tracked a dragon weaving through the air with majestic movements. "Tiamat the Stormbringer commands the fury of storms and the thunderous roar of the skies."

Mason pointed out the shimmering scales of a serpent-like dragon. "And Leviathan the Sea Serpent glides through the depths, his scales a mysterious sapphire."

"And lastly," I said, trying to sound as reverent as Damien, "Azurea the Frostwing, her icy blue scales reflecting the ancient glaciers of the north."

Gregory's eyes widened, clearly impressed. "You know your dragons. I like that."

"We try," I said with a smile. "The last dragon we encountered wasn't exactly friendly. But that's a story for another time. Right now, we should focus on preparing for the battles ahead."

Gregory chuckled, his eyes twinkling. "Sounds like you've been through a lot. I guess we're all here to make sure we come out the other side in one piece."

Lucian slapped Gregory on the back. "Yeah, we've been quite the magnet for trouble lately. But we've got a plan."

"That's the spirit," Gregory said, nodding. "So what's the plan?"

I glanced at Lucian and Damien. "Let's bring Gregory and his pack up to speed. We need to catch them up on everything we've been through."

Damien stepped forward. "Alright, Gregory. Time to dive into the details. We've had our share of battles, and there's more to come."

As the night deepened, we moved to a quieter spot where the dragons continued to patrol the skies. Lucian, Damien, and Gregory huddled together, discussing the finer points of our situation while the rest of us set up our temporary base.

"Alright, let's get these spells up and running," I said, breaking off from the group. I laid out candles and arcane symbols on the ground in a careful arrangement. "We need to fortify our defenses and make sure we're not overheard."

Annie and Christian joined me, their hands deftly moving through the motions of the spellcasting. "Let's start with the protection spells," Annie suggested, holding up a glowing candle. "We want to make sure that our wards are strong and effective."

Christian took a deep breath. "We'll need to recite the incantations ten times to ensure maximum potency."

We gathered around the symbols and began the ritual. "By the powers of the earth and sky, we shield this place from every eye," we chanted, our voices blending together in a rhythmic cadence.

The candles flickered, their light casting long shadows that danced along the ground. As we worked, the air grew thick with the scent of burning wax and the hum of magic.

∞

After hours of weaving enchantments and protective wards, I took a step back, surveying our work. "We did it. We've set up an impenetrable barrier."

Annie looked relieved. "Let's hope it holds. I'd rather not have to deal with another surprise visit."

Christian nodded; his face flushed with the effort of the spellcasting. "We've got a solid defense now."

Grayson was practically buzzing with excitement. "We even have a way to identify friend from foe. This is going to be a game-changer."

I smiled at my coven, pride swelling in my chest. "Excellent work, everyone. Let's celebrate our success with a feast."

We moved to the makeshift dining area where a barbecue had been set up. The smell of fish, prawns, and mussels filled the air, a comforting reminder of home.

"Crawfish! I've been craving this since we got here," I said, grabbing a plate.

Lucian grinned as he looked at the spread. "Looks like you're in for a treat."

"Everything's perfect," I said, savoring the flavors of the seafood. "This is just what we needed."

The celebration was full of laughter and stories, a rare moment of peace in our tumultuous lives. But the joy was short-lived.

Just as we were beginning to relax, the blaring sound of the alarm cut through the night, shattering the calm.

"That's our cue," I said, my voice steely with determination. "Summon the dragons. We've got company."

Lucian and Gregory wasted no time. "Dragons, to arms!" Gregory shouted, and the dragons roared to life, their presence a formidable force against the encroaching threat.

The intruders who had dared breach our defenses were met with a fury they hadn't anticipated. Flames roared through the night, and the clash of dragon claws and demon flesh filled the air.

"We're ready for them," I said as the battle raged on. "Let's show them what happens when you challenge us."

The fight was intense but swift. The dragons' might proved to be more than enough for the demons who had dared to invade our sanctuary. As the last of the enemies fell, the night quieted once more.

"Now we turn our attention to the next challenge," I said, catching my breath. "Zachariah and the fallen angels, and Damien's mother. We've beaten back this threat, but there's more to come."

Damien placed a reassuring hand on my shoulder. "We're ready. We'll face whatever comes next."

With that, we prepared for the battles ahead, knowing that our unity and strength would be our greatest assets.

Chapter 22

The sun was just starting to creep over the horizon, painting the sky in shades of gold and pink. We gathered in the warm morning light, ready for the day's mission. Damien and Lucian stood beside me, their presence a steady anchor in the sea of our anticipation.

"We've prepared for this moment," Damien said, his voice calm but resolute. "Together, we will rid our realm of these demons and bring peace to the souls trapped here."

Lucian's gaze was sharp and focused. "We stand united against the darkness. Our strength, combined with the dragons, will see us through."

We gathered around a table for breakfast, the smell of sizzling bacon and fresh bread filling the air. Gregory, now part of our group, was enthusiastically digging into a plate of eggs and toast. "So, what's the plan for today?" he asked between bites.

Lucian took a sip of his coffee and looked around at us. "We need to be prepared for anything. Our first stop is the haunted house where we'll face the demons. We have our spells, our potions, and our allies. Let's make sure we use them wisely."

Gregory grinned, his eyes glinting with excitement. "Count me in for the fight. I'm ready to take on some demons."

I nodded at him. "We're glad to have you, Gregory. Your help will make a big difference."

Annie, sitting across from me, was busy checking her spell book. "I've tailored the spells specifically for each type of demon we might encounter," she said, her voice filled with the kind of careful concentration that only comes from meticulous preparation.

"We can't underestimate these creatures," I said. "They're powerful, and we need to be ready for whatever they throw at us."

Once we finished our meal, the last of the preparations were made. Gregory suggested we bring along a dragon companion for additional support. The idea was met with unanimous agreement. I couldn't help but smile as Gregory summoned Fire, his dragon companion, a magnificent creature with scales like molten lava.

Damien approached me with a worried look. "Are you sure you're okay with flying? It's not too late to stay on the ground."

I gave him a reassuring grin. "I'm excited, Damien. I'll be fine. Fire and Gregory are the best companions we could ask for."

With a nod, Damien stepped back, though his eyes lingered on me with concern. Gregory and I climbed onto Fire's back, and with a powerful leap, we soared into the sky.

As we flew, I marveled at the sprawling landscape below us—the rolling hills, the winding rivers, and the distant mountains. The beauty of the world below was a stark contrast to the darkness we were about to confront.

When we arrived at the haunted house, its decrepit facade seemed to welcome us with a cold, menacing air. I took a deep breath, feeling the weight of the task ahead. Gregory and I quickly unloaded the supplies, setting up our gear as the rest of the coven arrived.

Lucian, taking charge, led us into the house. The interior was cloaked in shadows, and the air was thick with the remnants of past malevolence. We descended into the basement, where the presence of evil was almost tangible.

I glanced at Annie, who was preparing the potions and spells. "Are we ready?" I asked, my voice steady despite the chill in the air.

She met my gaze with a determined nod. “Let’s do this.”

As we reached the center of the basement, where the demons had once been strongest, we paused for a moment. The oppressive darkness seemed to pulse around us, but our collective resolve was a beacon of light against it.

“Ready?” I asked, my heart pounding with anticipation.

Lucian raised his hand, his voice steady as he began the incantation. “By the power of the coven, we cast away the darkness.”

We threw the potions, and the air erupted in a swirl of smoke and energy. The demons appeared, and as the vanishing spells took hold, they began to dissipate into nothingness.

The fight was swift, our combined magic overwhelming the demons before they could mount any real resistance. Smoke billowed around us, and as it cleared, the basement was once again silent.

“We did it,” Annie said, her voice a mix of relief and exhaustion.

“Now for the final task,” I said. “We need to guide the trapped souls to the celestial realm.”

∞

We began the ritual, channeling our combined energy into a powerful beacon of light. The glow illuminated the dark corners of the basement, and as the spell took effect, the souls were gently lifted from the shadows, moving towards their eternal rest.

When the light finally faded, the weight of our burden seemed to lift. The house, once a place of despair, now stood as a symbol of hope.

As we emerged from the house, the sunset was beginning to paint the sky in brilliant hues of orange and pink. The beauty of the evening was a welcome contrast to the grim task we had just completed.

“Looks like we made it through,” Gregory said, his eyes shining with admiration. “Amy, your coven is something else. I thought we’d be battling with swords and fists, but you all just handled it like it was nothing."

I laughed, the sound ringing out in the cool evening air. "Thank you, Gregory. We like to be prepared for anything. It's not just about power—it's about knowing how to use it."

Gregory grinned. "Well, if I were our enemies, I'd be pretty scared of you all. Maybe we should let everyone know just how strong you are."

I chuckled. "What's the fun in that? We'd miss out on all the dramatic moments if everyone was too afraid to fight us."

The coven laughed together, the camaraderie lifting our spirits as we made our way home.

Back at our place, the atmosphere was alive with celebration. The scent of food wafted through the air, and the sound of lively music filled the room.

"Looks like we've got a feast waiting for us," Lucian said, his tone filled with satisfaction.

The meal was delicious, a spread of seafood and other treats that made my mouth water. I took a moment to savor the flavors, enjoying the rare chance to relax.

Gregory looked around at the happy faces. "You all really know how to celebrate a victory. This is awesome."

"Yeah," I said, raising my glass in a toast. "Here's to our success and the battles still to come."

We cheered, and the room filled with laughter and song. It was a well-earned break, a chance to enjoy the fruits of our hard work and prepare for whatever was next.

As the night wore on and we finally headed to our rooms, exhaustion took over, but so did the warmth of our success.

"Good night, everyone," I said, my voice tired but happy. "Tomorrow we'll face whatever comes next. But tonight, we celebrate."

The laughter and music continued, a promise of the adventures yet to come.

Chapter 23

With the darkness vanquished and our realm finally at peace, the excitement in the air was almost tangible. We were standing on the brink of new adventures, eager to see what the future held for us.

"Alright, everyone," Damien said, his eyes gleaming with purpose, "we've got a lot ahead of us. Training starts today, and I know we're all ready for the challenge."

Lucian gave a nod, his expression serious but encouraging. "Yes. We'll begin with one-on-one combat training and dragon riding. It's crucial we're prepared for whatever comes our way."

I stepped forward, feeling the weight of our mission on my shoulders. "And in exchange for their guidance, we'll help the dragons master various spells and set up some solid defenses. We need all the supernatural protection we can get."

The first day of training was buzzing with energy. Lucian stood in front of us, his stance commanding attention as he began the session. "Combat is about more than just fighting," he said, demonstrating a series of moves. "It's about strategy, agility, and control. Your opponent will be relentless, so you must be relentless in return."

Annie looked a bit hesitant, her eyes shifting nervously. "But what if we're scared of getting hurt, Lucian? I'm not really up for bruises."

Lucian approached her, his voice gentle but firm. “Fear is a part of this. The key is to face it, not to let it hold you back. You’re stronger than you know, Annie. Trust yourself, and you’ll get through this.”

He placed a reassuring hand on her shoulder. “You’ve got this. Embrace the challenge, and you’ll become even stronger.”

The coven members paired off, the sounds of grunts and the clash of bodies filling the training yard as they practiced their strikes and defenses. Lucian moved among them, offering tips and pushing us to reach our potential.

Meanwhile, Gregory was at the edge of the clearing, standing beside a massive, majestic dragon. His voice carried across the field, full of authority. “To ride a dragon is to command the skies,” he said, his eyes shining. “It takes trust, unity, and unyielding courage.”

The members of the Wolf Packs listened intently as Gregory explained dragon riding techniques. One by one, they mounted their dragons and took to the skies, their movements becoming more fluid as they practiced aerial maneuvers.

I joined the training just in time. As I approached, I felt a shiver of excitement. Gregory noticed me and smiled. “Ready for your turn, Amy?”

I nodded, trying to keep my excitement in check. “Absolutely. I can’t wait to meet my dragon.”

Gregory’s eyes twinkled. “Then let’s get started. But remember, Shadowfire is a legendary creature. Respect her power, and she will show you what she’s capable of.”

Just then, a majestic black dragon descended from the sky, her scales glistening in the sunlight. She landed gracefully in front of me, her eyes meeting mine with an intense, knowing gaze.

“You have been chosen,” her presence seemed to say, a voice echoing in my mind.

With trembling fingers, I reached out to touch her sleek scales. A rush of warmth and power flowed through me. "I will call you Shadowfire," I whispered, awe and reverence in my voice.

Gregory's voice cut through my reverie. "In time, you'll learn to harness more of her power. For now, let's see what you can do together."

I glanced at Shadowfire, feeling the weight of the moment. "Just a moment to connect with her," I said, my heart racing.

"Take your time," Gregory replied, his tone encouraging.

I took a deep breath and placed my hands gently on Shadowfire's head. "Let's show them what we're made of," I said softly, my thoughts reaching out to her. "I'm ready if you are."

Shadowfire's eyes gleamed with a fierce determination. "Yes, Amy. Let's show them our strength. I will protect you as we soar."

"Thank you, Shadowfire," I whispered, feeling a deep sense of connection

With a powerful leap, Shadowfire took to the skies. The sensation of flying was exhilarating, the world below a blur of colors. Flames danced from her jaws, lighting up the sky as we practiced aerial maneuvers together.

From the ground, the coven and the Wolf Packs watched in awe as Shadowfire and I soared gracefully through the air, a perfect display of our newfound bond.

When we finally landed, the clearing erupted into cheers. I dismounted, feeling a mix of pride and relief. Shadowfire gave me a gentle nudge before taking off again, her wings spreading wide as she flew back to her den.

"That was incredible, Amy," Gregory said, his eyes filled with admiration. "You're a quick learner, and the bond you share with Shadowfire is already remarkable."

"Thank you, Gregory," I said, my voice filled with gratitude. "Shadowfire is amazing. I feel so fortunate to have her as my dragon. I believe we can face anything together."

Annie looked at me with wide eyes. "How did you connect with her so quickly, Amy?"

I shrugged, still awed by the experience. "I'm not entirely sure. It just happened. Has anyone else here had a chance to bond with a dragon?"

Annie shook her head. "Not yet. Dragons are very selective about their riders. It's a special thing when it happens."

Gregory nodded. "The bond between a dragon and rider is a rare and sacred connection. We'll keep trying, and hopefully, everyone will find their match in time."

"Thank you, Gregory," the coven echoed, their voices a harmonious blend of appreciation.

"It's been an amazing day," I said, feeling both exhausted and exhilarated. "What's for lunch, Lucian? I'm starving!"

Lucian grinned, a playful glint in his eyes. "Well, considering you've found your dragon, I'd say you can have anything you want."

A smile spread across my face. "In that case, can we have a seafood barbecue?"

"Absolutely," Lucian said with a nod. "Damien, Gregory, help me get things ready? Amy and the rest of the coven deserve a good meal after all this."

Damien and Gregory jumped to the task, leaving us to unwind and recover from the day's activities. The promise of a delicious meal and a chance to relax was a welcome change.

As we settled in for lunch, the mood was light and joyful. We talked about our adventures and what was to come, a sense of anticipation hanging in the air.

After the meal, as we sat together, I looked around at my friends and family, feeling a deep sense of gratitude. "It's been an incredible journey," I said. "But now it's time to think about our next steps."

"What do you have in mind, Amy?" Damien asked, curious.

I took a deep breath, feeling the weight of the moment. "I think it's time to go back to New Orleans. We can show our parents what we've built here and tell them we're planning to stay."

Annie's eyes lit up with excitement. "That's a great idea! We've made a life for ourselves here, and we should share that with them."

Arielle nodded enthusiastically. "Yes! We should go together and show them how far we've come."

The coven buzzed with excitement as we discussed the details of our plan.

"I think it'll make a difference if they see what we've accomplished," I said, feeling hopeful. "And I can keep writing my novels from our new home. Tridion feels like the right place for us."

With the decision made, we spent the rest of the day celebrating, savoring our victory and our newfound purpose. As the night wore on, we laughed and talked, the bonds between us stronger than ever.

We had a bright future ahead, and together, we were ready to face it.

The festivities continued late into the evening, a perfect end to a day full of triumph and new beginnings.

Chapter 24

I looked around the cozy kitchen of our Tridion home, taking in the sight of the breakfast dishes and the warm sunlight filtering through the windows. This would be the last time I'd see this place for a while. I hefted my bag onto my shoulder, trying to ignore the twinge of sadness at leaving Shadowfire behind. The dragon had been my companion through countless battles, and now I had to trust Gregory to take good care of her.

"Goodbye, Shadowfire," I said softly, stroking her smooth, black scales. "I promise I'll come back for you."

Shadowfire's eyes gleamed with a knowing light. "I'll be here when you return, Amy. Take care of what you must and know that our bond is unbreakable."

I stepped back, my heart aching. "I will. I'm going to miss you, but I know you're in good hands here."

With a final look at my majestic friend, I turned to the rest of the group. Damien, Annie, Lucian, and the others were ready for the journey. We had decided to leave early to catch our parents before they might start worrying too much.

"It's time for us to begin our return journey back to New Orleans," I said, my voice wavering slightly. "I'm excited but also a bit nervous about how this conversation is going to go."

Damien gave me a reassuring smile. "We've faced worse challenges than this. We can handle a conversation with our parents."

Annie squeezed my hand. "We're in this together. Let's just be honest and hope they understand."

We stepped through the portal, the familiar swirl of colors and sensations enveloping us. I glanced at Annie as the world around us shifted. "Remember when we first went through this portal? We barely knew what we were doing."

Annie chuckled. "Yeah, and now we're old pros at it. Let's hope we're just as good at convincing our parents of our new path."

As we emerged in the Crescent City, the hustle and bustle of New Orleans greeted us like an old friend. The energy of the city was the same, but it felt different now, as if we had grown beyond its streets. We made our way to our old house, and there, waiting on the porch, was a surprising sight—our parents had gathered, clearly concerned.

"Looks like they've been waiting for us," Lucian observed.

"Guess we arrived just in time," I said, trying to steady my nerves.

We walked up the steps and into the house, where the familiar scent of old wood and faint lavender greeted us. Our parents sat around the living room, a mix of relief and suspicion on their faces.

"Mom, Dad," I began, stepping forward. "Sorry we've been away for so long. We need to talk."

Mom's eyes widened as she took in Damien and Lucian. "Damien? Lucian? What are you two doing here? And why haven't you been around? What's going on?"

"Relax, Mom," I said, trying to calm her down. "They're part of our family now. We have a lot to explain."

I gestured for everyone to sit, and we took our places in the living room. I took a deep breath, readying myself for the explanation.

"A few months ago," I started, "we cast a spell to make it seem like we were still here while we were actually in Tridion. We've been there, exploring our past, fighting battles, and, well, we've made some big decisions. We've decided to stay in Tridion. Our future is there, and we want you to understand why."

Mom's eyes grew wide. "You were in Tridion? Fighting battles? What are you talking about?"

I nodded, feeling the weight of our actions. "Yes, we were. We fought against demons, saved souls, and discovered truths about ourselves. And today, we've come back to tell you that we won't be returning to New Orleans. We're staying in Tridion to pursue our futures. We've grown a lot, and we have a new life there. I've even bonded with a dragon named Shadowfire."

"Wait," Mom interrupted, "you released what?"

I took a deep breath. "We freed some trapped spirits from the house there. We thought they were innocent souls, but it turns out they were the Maleficent Ones, and we might have just let out a great evil."

Mom's face turned pale. "Do you have any idea what you've done? Those spirits were sealed away for a reason. They were the source of great suffering in Tridion. By releasing them, you've put Tridion in grave danger."

Annie's eyes widened. "But we thought we were doing the right thing. We didn't know—"

"Of course you didn't know!" Mom said, her voice rising. "We should have told you the truth long ago. But now, you must help us fix this."

I nodded. "We need to find the spirits and put them back where they belong. How do we do that?"

Mom took a deep breath and looked at me with a mixture of regret and resolve. "We'll need to locate a spell from one of our most powerful books. You'll have to summon the Maleficent Ones and re-seal them. It won't be easy, but we'll help you."

"Wait," I said, trying to wrap my head around this. "You're the Head of the Elders? You never told us?"

Mom nodded. "Yes, I am. And yes, we should have been more open with you. We wanted to protect you from the truth until you were ready."

"Well," I said, feeling the weight of our mistakes, "we need to fix this now. What's the next step?"

Mom looked at me with a stern yet hopeful expression. "We need to search for the spell and prepare for a ritual. We'll start upstairs. It'll take time, so you should wait here."

As they disappeared up the stairs, I turned to my friends. "Looks like we have some time to kill. Any thoughts on how we're going to fix this mess?"

Lucian rubbed his chin thoughtfully. "We'll have to rely on the strength of our coven and the knowledge of the Elders. It's a heavy burden, but we've overcome greater challenges before."

Damien nodded. "And we will overcome this one, too. We need to focus on the task at hand."

Annie squeezed my hand. "We've come this far together. We can handle whatever comes next."

We settled into the waiting, our thoughts filled with the enormity of the task before us. The quiet hum of anticipation filled the room as we prepared ourselves for the ritual that would determine the fate of Tridion.

Hours passed as we waited, the tension growing with each minute. When Mom and Dad finally came back downstairs, they carried an ancient tome between them, its cover worn but exuding an aura of power.

"We have the spell," Mom said, her voice steady. "Are you ready to begin?"

I took a deep breath, steeling myself for what lay ahead. "We're ready."

With the book in hand and our resolve firm, we moved towards the next chapter of our journey, ready to face the darkness we had inadvertently released and prove that we were more than just a coven—we were a family bound by strength and love.

Chapter 25

When Mom finally came downstairs, she carried a massive book with golden embellishments that glittered even in the dim light of the dining room. The book seemed almost to hum with a hidden power, and I couldn't help but think of the old volumes we'd found in the attic and the mysterious artifacts that had always fascinated us.

"Everyone, gather around," Mom said, her voice steady but with an edge of urgency. She carefully placed the tome on the polished dining room table, her fingers clad in white gloves as though she were handling a relic of great importance.

Damien had disappeared the moment Mom started handling the book. I glanced around, catching a glimpse of him slipping into the shadows, but there was no time to wonder about his sudden departure. I turned my full attention to the book, curiosity and unease mingling within me.

Mom cleared her throat, her eyes serious as she addressed us. "This book contains the spells we need to confront the Maleficent Ones. It's known as the *Codex of Chronomancy*, a repository of ancient and powerful magic."

I leaned in, my eyes wide. "I've heard of this book. We saw it in the library but didn't know its significance."

Mom nodded. "Yes, it's been in our family for generations, but it was kept hidden for good reason. Its spells are dangerous, and its knowledge is meant to be wielded with extreme caution."

Annie shifted nervously. "What exactly do we need to do?"

Mom opened the book, and the pages seemed to glow with a faint, otherworldly light. "We are going to perform a spell from the section on Time Manipulation. This spell will allow us to rewrite certain events from the past."

"Rewrite events?" I echoed, trying to wrap my head around it. "That sounds like something out of a story."

Mom's eyes met mine. "It's a reality that's more dangerous than any story. Messing with time isn't something to be taken lightly. There are ten potential consequences listed here, and they are all severe."

She turned the book around so we could see the text. "Changing events in the past can create unforeseen ripples in the present or future, leading to major disruptions."

"Like what kind of disruptions?" Lucian asked, leaning forward

"Things like paradoxes where you might erase your own existence," Mom explained. "Or getting trapped in a time loop where you repeat the same events over and over."

"Can it really cause that much damage?" I asked, feeling a shiver run down my spine.

"Yes," Mom said grimly. "It can destabilize reality itself. There could be entities that guard time and might come after us for tampering with it. We might even incur karmic debts or lose control over the spell. And there's a risk we could become isolated from reality, existing in a separate time plane."

Annie gulped. "And what do we do if we face one of these consequences?"

Mom took a deep breath. "For now, we need to focus on the spell. We must proceed carefully and hope we can navigate the risks."

I looked around at my friends and family, feeling the weight of the moment. "Are we ready for this?"

Mom nodded, her eyes filled with a mix of hope and worry. "We don't have much choice. If we don't act, Tridion will face the full wrath of the Maleficent Ones."

She turned back to the book and began reciting the spell. Her voice was steady, filled with a gravity that drew us all in.

"By the whisper of the wind and the dance of the stars above, I invoke the powers of time, the essence of eternal love," she chanted, her hands moving in graceful patterns as though conducting an invisible orchestra of magic

We followed her lead, our voices blending in the ancient incantation. The air around us seemed to thrum with power as we chanted the spell in unison.

"From the dawn of creation to the twilight's fading hue, I command the tides of time, reshaping what once was true," Mom continued, her voice like a beacon guiding us through the darkness.

"With the flicker of a candle and the flicker of my mind, I traverse the ages, leaving ripples far behind," she said, her gaze intense and unwavering.

"As the sands of time slip through my fingers, I hold them firm and tight," she intoned, her hands weaving through the air as if she were pulling threads of time into place.

"Through the corridors of history, I walk with measured stride," she declared, her words echoing with the weight of centuries.

"With each incantation spoken and each gesture of my hand," she chanted, her eyes reflecting the ancient wisdom of the tome.

"I unlock the mysteries of time, where the boundaries expand," she said, her voice rising with a sense of command.

"For time is but a tapestry woven with threads of fate," Mom proclaimed, her voice resonating with the force of the spell.

"And I, the chronomancer, hold the key to unlock its gate," she continued, her hands moving in a final, decisive gesture.

"In the labyrinth of time's embrace, I wander without fear," she recited, her expression serene and determined.

"For time is mine to command, a force that knows no bounds," she finished, her eyes glowing with the magic of the spell.

"So let the sands of time be still as I weave my intricate spell," she concluded, her voice ringing with authority.

I felt the spell's power envelop us, a palpable force that seemed to stretch out into the very fabric of time. The room grew still as we chanted the final words, our combined energy focusing on the task before us.

Mom looked at us, her face set in a serious expression. "This spell was never meant to be used lightly. It holds the power to alter time itself, a forbidden magic we have now embraced out of necessity. We hope for the best, but we must be prepared for the worst."

I took a deep breath, feeling the gravity of our situation. "Let's hope we don't face any of those consequences."

Mom nodded. "Let's begin the next phase of our plan. We need to find where the Maleficent Ones were released and start the process of putting them back."

As we prepared to move out, I glanced at my friends and family, a mix of fear and determination in my heart. "We can do this," I said, trying to reassure everyone. "We've faced impossible odds before. We can face this one."

We set out, our minds focused on the task ahead, ready to confront the darkness we had unleashed and to protect the future of Tridion.

Chapter 26

The spell had just finished echoing through the room when the future's dark visions unfurled before us like a grim tapestry. Shadows of demons and the clash of humanity against an insidious force played out in fleeting glimpses. Control, temptation, and deceit danced across the scenes like dark flames.

I tried to steady my voice. "We need to act fast. But what's our next step?"

Mom's eyes were sharp, her determination unwavering. "We have to put our heads together and think. This is our moment to be resourceful. Let's meditate on it. Sometimes the answers come when you're quiet."

We nodded and shuffled into the lounge. The room was dim, lit only by the flickering flames of the candles we had set up earlier. We sat in a circle on the floor, our hands joined, each of us closing our eyes and trying to clear our minds.

"Focus on the visions we saw," Mom instructed softly. "Let them guide your thoughts."

We sat in silence, each of us lost in our own contemplation. The weight of the spell's revelations hung in the air like a dense fog.

A few minutes later, I broke the silence. "Mom, we've come up with some ideas. I think we should talk about them."

Mom looked up, her gaze expectant. "Let's hear them, Amy."

I took a deep breath. "We thought about a few things. First, there's banishment and exorcism—rituals to expel the demons and cleanse the corrupted. Second, we discussed setting up protection measures like barriers or sigils to keep the demons out. And third, we thought about spiritual cleansing—meditation, prayer, and rituals to purify ourselves and our surroundings."

Mom nodded, her eyes narrowing as she considered each idea. "Anything else?"

I hesitated for a moment, then continued. "We also thought about seeking divine intervention but realized you're the highest authority we have. We discussed researching ancient texts for hidden knowledge and forming alliances with other magical beings or groups. Annie even mentioned empowering individuals as champions or guardians. And there was also the idea of offering redemption to the demons, though that seems like a long shot."

"Those are all good ideas," Mom said, clearly impressed. "And there was also the notion of cleansing specific locations or objects tainted by demons. We also need to stay vigilant and ready for any threats."

Annie added, "We might need to be on constant alert and prepared for any surprises. It's not a perfect plan, but we have to start somewhere."

Christian leaned forward, adding his own thoughts. "We should also remember that this ceremony will be complex. Every detail must be handled with care."

Mom's face showed approval. "Well done, everyone. You've come up with some remarkable strategies. We have a solid foundation to build on."

A surge of pride filled me. We had brainstormed effectively, and it was empowering to see our collective creativity take shape.

Just then, Damien reappeared, standing beside Lucian. Their serious expressions spoke of urgent conversations and hidden concerns. I wondered what they were discussing, but the weight of our own task was enough to keep me focused.

"Alright, everyone," I called out, drawing the group's attention. "It's time to put our plans into action. We need to perform a powerful group ritual to protect our village and the mundane world from the demonic threats."

Annie nodded firmly. "We've got a lot to do. This ceremony will be intricate, and we need to gather the right resources and perform every step correctly."

Lucian stepped forward; his expression intense. "Every step must be perfect. There's no room for errors."

We set to work with a newfound determination. We gathered the items we needed: protective amulets, enchanted herbs, and sacred artifacts. Each object was selected with care, imbued with our intentions to shield Tridion from harm.

As we prepared for the ritual, I couldn't ignore the way Damien kept glancing at me. His silence was unsettling, and the questions I had for him were pushed to the back of my mind as I focused on the task at hand.

Mom and Dad made their final preparations for their absence. Their commitment was clear, even though their professional lives would be on hold for this mission. They were ready to face the coming darkness with us.

With everything in place, we set out for Tridion. The weight of the responsibility we carried was almost palpable. I glanced at Damien again, but he still avoided my gaze. The suspicion gnawed at me, but I knew I had to keep my focus on the battle ahead.

As we walked towards the village, the familiar streets of Tridion seemed both comforting and foreboding. I took a deep breath, the cool night air filling my lungs, and tried to push my concerns about Damien out of my mind.

"Let's stay sharp," I said to the group, trying to sound more confident than I felt. "We've prepared for this. We can handle whatever comes our way."

Annie gave me a reassuring smile. "We've got this. Together."

We pressed on, ready for the fight that lay ahead and the challenges that would test every bit of our resolve.

Chapter 27

We stepped through the portal and into Tridion, and the change was immediate. The magical realm's serene atmosphere enveloped us, a stark contrast to the chaos of our last adventure. I could feel the difference in time here—a day might stretch into years, and every moment was thick with potential. Despite the calm around us, a gnawing worry had settled in my chest. Damien had been distant, slipping away for secretive meetings with Lucian, and it had left me feeling unsettled. I knew I couldn't ignore it any longer.

Damien stood outside with Gregory, who was busy polishing his silvered sword. The sight of Damien's brooding figure made my heart ache. I walked over, my resolve as strong as my unease.

"Damien, we need to talk," I said, trying to keep my voice steady.

He looked up, surprise flickering in his eyes. "What's wrong, Amy?"

I took a deep breath, feeling the weight of unsaid words pressing against me. "We can't keep going on like this. There are too many secrets between us, and it's tearing us apart. I need to know what's going on."

Damien's gaze dropped, and he rubbed the back of his neck as if trying to pull out the right words. "I didn't know how to tell you, but it's time you knew the truth."

"Whatever it is, we'll face it together," I insisted. "Just tell me what's going on."

His eyes met mine, full of regret and fear. "Alright," he said quietly. "But we need to get everyone together. This isn't just about us."

I nodded, and we headed into the lounge where the coven had gathered. The atmosphere was tense, everyone sensing that something important was about to be revealed. I could see Lucian in the corner, his face a mask of controlled worry.

"Damien," I said, trying to keep my tone even, "what's happening?"

Damien took a deep breath, then started, "I went to see the vampire elders for advice. What I learned is... it's bad. Really bad. We're facing a serious threat, and if we don't act carefully, it could be fatal."

I glanced around at the group's anxious faces. "What kind of threat?" I pressed.

Damien hesitated, then said, "My mother is back in power."

A murmur of shock swept through the room. I felt a chill, but Damien wasn't finished. "There's more," he continued, his voice heavy. "Kaitlin... our daughter... she's alive."

The words hit me like a cold wave. "That can't be right," I stammered. "She died with me. How can she be alive?"

Damien's eyes were full of sorrow. "I don't know how. But I saw her. She's out there, and we need to find her."

My head spun as I tried to grasp the enormity of what Damien had just revealed. The grief of losing Kaitlin, the hope that she might still be alive—it all crashed over me like a storm. I felt the world tilt beneath me, and then everything went dark.

When I came to, the room was still and quiet. Damien sat beside me, holding my hand as if it were the only thing keeping him anchored. His eyes were distant, reflecting a struggle that I couldn't quite understand.

"Are you alright?" he asked, his voice strained.

I squeezed his hand, trying to pull myself together. "Damien... I don't even know where to start. Kaitlin—our daughter—how is this possible?"

Damien's grip tightened on mine. "I wish I had answers. All I know is that she's alive, and she's somewhere in this world."

Memories of Kaitlin—the way her laugh would fill a room, her tiny hands reaching out for us—flooded back to me. The grief of losing her had been a void in my life, and now that void was being filled with a whirlwind of questions.

"Where has she been all these years?" I asked, my voice trembling. "Who's taken care of her?"

Damien shook his head. "I don't know. But we need to find her and bring her back. We owe her that much."

A steely resolve began to form within me. I had to find Kaitlin, to uncover the truth of her fate, and to confront whoever had kept her from us.

"I will find her," I said, my voice hardening with determination. "We will find her. We'll get to the bottom of this and make things right."

Damien's eyes met mine, and for a moment, the weight of the past and the hope for the future mingled in his gaze. "We will," he agreed. "But first, we have to deal with the threat my mother poses. That has to be our priority."

The reality of our situation set in. We had a looming battle ahead, but now there was also a personal quest: to find Kaitlin and reclaim the family we had lost.

Lucian stepped forward, breaking the silence. "We have much to prepare for. But first, we need to strategize and make sure we're ready for what's coming."

Annie and Christian moved closer, their faces set with resolve. "We'll need to strengthen our defenses and figure out how to confront the demons threatening Tridion," Annie said.

Christian nodded. "Let's focus on the immediate danger first. We can plan our search for Kaitlin once we've secured our position here."

We gathered around the table, the weight of our new mission pressing on us. Damien laid out the details of the threat, and we began to organize our approach. Every step we took was a step towards both protecting our world and finding our daughter.

As the planning began, I took a moment to look around at my friends and family. Their faces were a mixture of fear, determination, and hope. We were united by a common cause, ready to face the darkness that loomed over us.

But even as we made our plans, my thoughts kept drifting back to Kaitlin. She was out there, and I would not rest until I found her.

The battle for Tridion was just beginning, and the search for Kaitlin was now a part of our fight. Together, we would face whatever came next, and we would do it for her.

Chapter 28

The revelation of Kaitlin's existence felt like a tidal wave crashing over me. The joy of knowing she was alive was tempered by the sorrow of all the lost years. The idea that she might be older than me seemed almost impossible, like something out of a fantastical tale. I was desperate to see her, to finally meet the child I had never known.

But Damien's reluctance to share what he knew was like a thorn in my side. Despite his promises of a reunion, his silence only added to my anxiety. My emotions welled up, and I struggled to keep them in check as tears threatened to spill.

"Damien, why are you holding back?" I asked, trying to keep my voice steady despite the lump in my throat.

He looked at me with a mix of sadness and resolve. "I wanted to wait until you were ready. It's a lot to take in, and I didn't want to overwhelm you."

I wiped at my eyes, taking a deep breath. "Well, I'm ready now. I need to know everything."

Damien nodded, though he still seemed weighed down by the gravity of the situation. "Alright. I've been keeping a close eye on you while you were asleep. I've also been busy finding out more about Kaitlin."

I glanced around the room. "How long was I out, anyway?"

He looked a bit sheepish. "You've been asleep for almost a month."

I blinked. "A month? I thought maybe a few days."

Damien's eyes softened. "You needed the rest. Your mother insisted on letting you heal properly. I've been here, just waiting for you to wake up."

"Did anything happen while I was out?" I asked, a bit of worry seeping into my voice.

He shook his head. "Nothing of consequence. Most of us have been in a magical sleep. Your mother foresaw that we'd need to be well-rested for what's coming."

I couldn't help but be impressed. "Mom really does think of everything."

Damien smiled faintly. "She does. And Annie's been staying with Lucian."

I grinned. "I'm not surprised. And you've been in her bed this whole time?"

He chuckled softly. "Well, yes. But mostly I've been here keeping watch. The sleep spell affects you more than it affects me."

"Fair enough," I said, giving him a teasing wink. "I guess you've been a good caretaker then."

He leaned in and pressed a gentle kiss to my forehead. "Let's get you up. I have a little surprise for you."

I raised an eyebrow. "A surprise? What is it?"

He just smiled and headed out of the room. I got up, stretching and feeling the stiffness from the long sleep. I quickly dressed and went downstairs, my curiosity piqued by Damien's hint.

As I descended the stairs, my eyes fell on a little girl sitting by the fireplace, surrounded by my parents. My heart skipped a beat as I recognized her. It was Kaitlin. She looked so small, so delicate, and yet there was something undeniably familiar about her.

I moved closer, my steps unsteady as I tried to process the sight before me. "Damien... is that Kaitlin?"

He nodded, his eyes glistening with emotion. "Yes. I found her at an orphanage in New Orleans. She's been with the nuns there for as long as I can remember."

I turned to him, my eyes wide. "She lived with nuns? How did they find her, and how did they know she was special?"

Damien took a deep breath. "The nuns knew she was different from birth. They had records predicting her arrival, saying she would be a protector. They showed me documents and a picture from as far back as 1403 AD."

I was overwhelmed. "This is so much to take in. Did you learn anything else?"

Dad stepped forward. "We suspected she might have survived, but we had no way of knowing for sure until now. We didn't even know you had a child until we found out you'd carried her to term."

"Wow," I said, trying to steady my emotions as I looked at Kaitlin. She seemed shy but also curious, reaching out a little as she gazed at me.

Damien gently guided her over. "Say hi to your mommy, Kaitlin."

She looked up at me with wide eyes, her little voice barely a whisper. "Hi, Mommy."

My heart swelled with a mix of joy and sadness. "Hi, my sweet girl," I said, pulling her into a gentle hug. I could feel her trembling slightly in my arms.

"She's tired," Damien said softly. "Let's get her to bed."

"Goodnight, Kaitlin," I murmured, feeling a lump in my throat as she waved sleepily.

As Damien led her away, I suddenly felt a rush of images and sensations flood my mind. I was back in the delivery room, surrounded by nuns in the same attire as the ones from the orphanage. Pain and exhaustion overwhelmed me as I saw another baby being born—a second daughter. It was like reliving a forgotten memory.

Tears began to fall as I pulled away from the vision. "Damien... we have two daughters," I said, my voice trembling.

He looked at me, confusion etched on his face. "Two? What do you mean?"

I took a shaky breath, trying to explain. "I had a vision of the birth. I saw the nuns holding one baby while another was being born."

"That can't be right," Damien said, furrowing his brow. "The nuns never mentioned another child. How could they have kept that from us?"

Mom joined us, her face serious. "Maybe they kept it a secret for some reason. We need to find this second child."

I nodded. "Yes, we need to find her. She's a half-witch, half-vampire, and she could be in danger."

Mom's eyes shone with determination. "I'll find a spell to locate her. We have all the ingredients we need."

"Thank you, Mom," I said, squeezing her hand. "When can we start?"

"Right away, but we'll need Damien and Kaitlin for the spell to work," Mom said. "Let's go get them."

We moved swiftly back to Kaitlin's room, where Damien was tucking her into bed. "Damien, we need you and Kaitlin for a spell," I said, my urgency clear.

Kaitlin looked up at me with a hint of fear. "No, Momma. I don't want to find Paige. She scares me."

"Why does she scare you, sweetheart?" I asked gently.

Kaitlin's voice was barely above a whisper. "The nuns said she was possessed. They said she was bad."

My heart ached at her words. "We need to help her, Kaitlin. It's important. Please, come with us."

With a fearful nod, Kaitlin took my hand as we headed to the main room. The Coven and the elders were ready, their faces set with resolve as they prepared the ritual space.

Mom stood at the center of the room, her voice steady as she addressed us all. "We will perform the spell to find Paige. Damien, Kaitlin, and Amy will focus on their intentions while the rest of us complete the ritual."

I nodded. "Let's bring Paige back to us."

Mom began to recite the spell, her words weaving a tapestry of magic and hope. We chanted together, our combined will channeling the power of the spell.

The room grew heavy with magic as the spell took effect, and we were transported back to a dark and foreboding scene.

Damien's voice cut through the tension. "We can't let this stand. Paige needs our help."

"We need a plan," I said, trying to stay focused. "We can't just rush in."

Mom's face was resolute. "We will call on our allies. The dragons, the werewolves—anyone who will stand against the darkness."

Dad added, "And we must be cautious. We can't risk Paige's safety with a reckless approach."

"Right," I agreed, my mind racing. "We need to act fast. Every moment under the demon's influence puts her at greater risk."

"We'll gather our forces and make a plan," Damien said, determination in his voice. "We will save Paige, no matter what it takes."

With our resolve set, we began to reach out to our allies, preparing for the battle to come. We knew the path ahead was fraught with danger, but we were united in our mission to bring Paige home and ensure she knew the love and safety she had been denied.

Chapter 29

The ancient forest of Starfall seemed alive under the moon's silver light. Each leaf and shadow whispered secrets of the old world, and we moved through it like a tide of purpose and resolve. The air was thick with magic, the kind that made your skin tingle and your heart race. We were all here for one reason: to rescue my daughter and confront the dark forces that had taken her.

"Are we all ready?" I asked, trying to keep my voice steady, though it wavered under the weight of my fear and hope.

Elara, the Coven's leader, stepped forward. Her eyes glowed with a gentle light, the kind that comes from deep, ancient power. "We are with you, Amy. We'll see this through."

I turned to Lucian, the alpha of the werewolf pack, who was crouched low, his muscles coiled like a spring. "What about you and your pack?"

Lucian bared his fangs in a fierce grin. "We're ready to shred through whatever stands in our way."

The rumble above drew my gaze skyward. The dragons soared gracefully, their scales reflecting the moonlight in a dazzling array of colors. "And the dragons?" I asked.

The eldest dragon, a massive creature with scales like burnished gold, roared. "We will burn away the darkness."

I nodded, my heart swelling with a fierce, fierce pride. This was our army. This was our stand against the night.

We moved as one through the forest, our path lit by the light of the dragons and the flickering torches carried by the Coven. The forest itself seemed to part for us, the ancient trees shifting to reveal the crumbling chapel in the distance. The chapel was a shadow of what it once was, dark and ominous against the glowing backdrop of the forest.

"We're here," I whispered, though the enormity of the moment left me almost speechless.

The witches formed a circle around us, their voices rising in a chant that wove together the threads of power and protection. The werewolves spread out, their senses sharpened and alert for any hint of danger. The dragons circled above, their wings casting shadows like moving specters.

With a nod from the Elders, the battle began.

Elara's voice cut through the night. "Now!"

The witches' magic surged like a storm, tendrils of energy crackling in the air as they wove barriers of protection. The werewolves leaped into action, their howls mixing with the clash of steel as they met the corrupted priest's minions head-on.

Above us, the dragons unleashed torrents of flame, the fire roaring down to consume the chapel and the dark forces within.

In the chaos, I caught sight of the priest—a gaunt figure whose eyes burned with an unnatural light. Beside him, the demon writhed and twisted, a nightmare of claws and shadow.

"Come on!" I shouted over the cacophony of battle. "We have to finish this!"

The dragons, roaring with primal fury, unleashed a final, massive blaze that enveloped the chapel. Flames roared and cracked, a cleansing fire that seared away the darkness.

As the last of the smoke cleared, we stood in the midst of ruin and ashes. And there, amidst the rubble, I saw her—my daughter, Paige, held gently in the arms of a nun.

A wave of relief washed over me, and I rushed forward, tears streaming as I took Paige into my arms. "You're safe now," I whispered, my voice breaking with emotion. "I'm so sorry."

The head nun, Sister Marianne, stepped forward. Her eyes were kind, though tired. "We did what we could. She's safe now."

"Thank you," I said, choking on my gratitude. "You saved her. You have our protection and our thanks. We won't forget what you've done for us."

Sister Marianne smiled; her relief evident in her eyes. "We will remember your kindness as well."

With Paige in my arms, I looked around at the devastation, my heart aching. But amidst the wreckage, there was hope. The Coven began to set to work, and the werewolves were already moving to help clear the debris.

"We'll rebuild," Gregory said, his voice carrying the steady resolve of his pack. "Together, we'll make this place stronger than before."

Annie, her hands still glowing with the residual energy of the battle, stepped forward. "And I'll enchant it with protective wards. This chapel will be safe again, for you and for the nuns."

I hugged Paige close, feeling the warmth of her small body against mine. "Thank you," I said to everyone, feeling the strength of our shared resolve. "Let's rebuild, and let's do it as a testament to our strength."

As the Elders and the Coven began to clear the wreckage and start the restoration, a profound sense of peace settled over me. The chapel would be rebuilt, stronger and more resilient than before, a symbol of our victory and our unity.

The morning sun began to peek through the trees, casting golden light over our work. We had faced the darkness and emerged victorious. And with that victory came the promise of new beginnings.

I looked at my family and allies—our bonds forged in battle and strengthened in the face of adversity.

"We did it," I said softly, almost to myself.

Damien put a comforting hand on my shoulder. "And we'll face whatever comes next together."

As we worked side by side, our hearts were light with the knowledge that no matter what challenges lay ahead, we would face them as one, a united force against the darkness.

Our journey was far from over, but today, we had won a great victory. We would rebuild, and we would stand strong. Together.

∞

With the chapel's restoration underway, I knew that this was just the beginning of a new chapter. We had reclaimed my daughter, defeated our enemies, and forged bonds that would see us through whatever came next.

In the heart of Starfall's ancient forest, under the watchful gaze of the dragons and the protective spells of the Coven, we began to look forward to the future, knowing that as long as we stood together, there was nothing we could not face.

Chapter 30

We trudged home through the dim light of dawn, the weight of our victory settling on our shoulders. The air was cool, tinged with the scent of charred wood and smoke from the battle we'd just fought. The moon still hung low, a silent witness to the night's struggle.

Damien walked beside me, his eyes scanning the surroundings with practiced vigilance. "You ready for this?" he asked, his voice steady despite the exhaustion in his eyes.

"As ready as we'll ever be," I said, gripping my sword tighter. The blade had been our guardian through countless battles, and now it felt heavier than ever. I glanced back at our allies—Lucian and the Coven, the werewolves and dragons, all prepared for the next fight.

Lucian's eyes gleamed with determination. "The fate of the world is on our shoulders now."

"I know," I said, trying to ignore the shiver that ran down my spine. "But we've got a solid team here."

Gregory's pack of werewolves stood close, their fur bristling with the anticipation of what was to come. "We've fought demons and dark forces before," Gregory said, his voice a low growl. "We'll handle this just as well."

Stormfire and the other dragons circled high above us, their powerful wings stirring the air as they waited for my command.

"We'll be ready to burn a path through whatever comes our way," Stormfire's voice echoed in my mind, a deep rumble of power.

"Good," I replied mentally, feeling the weight of responsibility settle in. "We'll need every bit of that strength."

We moved forward, the forest giving way to the remnants of ancient structures—crumbling stone walls and broken archways that hinted at forgotten times. The darkness we faced now was ancient, its origins lost to history but its effects felt in every shadow.

The ground shook beneath our feet, a tremor that seemed to echo the heartbeat of the world itself. "They're coming," Damien said, his hand on the hilt of his sword.

A roar split the air as Lucian and Gregory led their packs into battle, the werewolves leaping forward with primal ferocity. "Let's show them what we're made of!" Gregory's voice carried over the din, rallying his pack into the fray.

Above, the dragons descended with a deafening roar, their fiery breath searing the air as they engaged the ancient beings that had risen from their slumber. Stormfire's flames crackled, lighting up the night with fierce brilliance.

The Coven was in the thick of it too, their chants weaving protective spells that shimmered around us. Elders stood at the heart of their magic, their faces lined with the wisdom of ages as they called forth elemental forces to shield us from harm.

Amidst the chaos, my thoughts kept drifting to the source of this malevolence. Who had summoned these ancient evils? Was there a greater threat lurking in the shadows? My mind raced as I fought, trying to keep focus.

Tina, holding Paige close behind the safety of a protective barrier, kept watch over her. I could see the worry on her face, but she kept Paige safe, her own strength a silent shield.

"We'll handle this," Tina said softly, her eyes meeting mine as I fought. "She's safe here."

"I know," I said, nodding gratefully. "Thank you."

The battle waged on, a grueling clash of power and will. I fought alongside Damien, our swords flashing in the moonlight as we took on the ancient beings. Exhaustion set in, our movements slower, but we pressed on with a fierce resolve.

With a final, powerful chant from the Coven, a blinding wave of magic swept over the battlefield. The ancient beings fell, their dark forms dissipating into the ether. But the cost was evident—two of Gregory's pack lay injured, and three of the ancients had escaped into the night.

"We still have a lot of work ahead," Damien said as we caught our breath, the battle's toll evident on his face. "But we made it through."

"It was a close fight," I agreed, though the sense of triumph was undeniable. "But we prevailed. We'll face whatever comes next, together."

"Absolutely," Damien said, his smile a rare but welcome sight. "We fought well. Now we rest."

We gathered around a small fire that Damien and Lucian had started, the flames crackling and providing a much-needed warmth. The hunger from our battle gnawed at me, a reminder of our physical strain.

"We should eat while we can," Lucian said, handing out the food he'd prepared. "We've earned it."

Paige sat beside Tina, her eyes wide as she looked at the food spread out before us. "Did you see the dragons? They were awesome!" she exclaimed, her excitement a bright spot during our weariness.

"They were," I said, a smile tugging at my lips. "And you were very brave too, staying safe while we fought."

Stormfire's voice brushed against my mind. "You used the power I gave you. I'm glad it worked."

"I didn't expect it to," I admitted. "But it was a relief to have you backing us up."

The thought of Paige's role in the battle was a constant hum in my mind. Tina's explanation—that her powers might have been at play—left me with a mix of pride and concern. She was so young, but already her potential was immense.

"We'll figure it out," Damien said, sensing my thoughts. "We face things as a family."

I nodded, feeling a deep sense of connection. "She's already showing great strength."

"She is something special," Damien said, glancing at Paige as she played with Tina. "She's definitely more than we expected."

With our bodies and spirits refreshed by the meal, we settled in for the night. The moonlight cast a gentle glow over our camp, the peacefulness a stark contrast to the battle we had fought. The pack took turns keeping watch, their presence a comforting assurance.

As we lay down to sleep, I whispered a prayer of gratitude for our victory and the strength of our unity. "We'll protect her," I said softly, knowing the weight of the promise. "No matter what."

Damien's hand found mine in the darkness. "Together, we can face anything."

As we drifted off, the soft rhythm of our breathing and the warmth of our bond were a soothing balm to the weariness of the day. We had faced the darkness and won, but there were more battles to come. For now, though, we rested, readying ourselves for the future.

And as the night enveloped us, I knew that whatever challenges awaited, we would meet them as one. Our strength, our resolve, and our unity would guide us through the shadows.

∞

As the moonlight bathed our camp in a serene glow, I felt a quiet hope. We had won a battle, but the war was far from over. The true test of our strength lay ahead, and we would face it together, with courage and determination.

"We'll meet whatever comes next," I murmured into the night.

Damien squeezed my hand, his voice a calm promise. "Yes, we will. Together."

With those words, we fell into a peaceful sleep, the promise of a new day and the strength of our bonds carrying us forward into the unknown.

Chapter 31

The first light of dawn filtered through the curtains, painting the room in soft hues of gold. I stretched, feeling the gentle pull of the muscles in my arms and the comforting warmth of the blankets around me. The battle was behind us, and for now, my daughters were safe, sleeping peacefully in their beds.

I turned to Damien, who was just beginning to stir beside me. The morning light softened the lines of exhaustion on his face, and when our eyes met, there was a shared sense of relief. "Good morning," I whispered, a smile tugging at my lips.

"Morning," Damien replied, his hand finding mine under the covers. "I guess we made it through another night."

"We did," I said, giving his hand a gentle squeeze. "But there's still so much to do."

After a quick breakfast—bread, fruit, and the last of the battle rations—we gathered everyone in the living room. The Coven members, the Elders, Lucian, Gregory, and his pack of werewolves stood together. Stormfire, now nicknamed Fire, perched proudly by the window. I'd been practicing tricks with her in the days since our return, and she seemed to enjoy her new name. Her blue eyes sparkled with excitement as she let out a happy trill.

"Morning, Fire," I said, reaching out to give her a quick scratch. "How's my dragon today?"

Fire's scales glinted in the sunlight as she nuzzled my hand. *"Ready for action, as always!"* Her mental voice was bright and eager.

"Good to hear," I said, giving her a final pat before turning to the group. "Let's get moving. We have unfinished business at the old house."

The atmosphere grew tense as we approached the house. The once-familiar place now held a dark weight, a reminder of the battles we had fought and the shadows that still lurked.

As we crossed the threshold, a shiver ran down my spine. The darkness in the house was palpable, almost like a physical force pressing against us. But we weren't here to be intimidated—we were here to confront it.

We gathered in the center of the room, forming a protective circle. The Coven began to chant, their voices rising in a harmonic melody that wove around us, creating a shimmering barrier. The Elders stood at the heart of the circle; their eyes closed in concentration as they channeled the ancient powers we needed.

Damien stepped forward; his expression serious as he recited the resurrection spell. The air around us crackled with energy, the ancient words resonating with a power that filled the room. Each syllable seemed to pull at the very fabric of reality.

The ground trembled as the spell took effect. Shadows danced along the walls, and the chilling presence of the demons and lost souls began to stir from their slumber. It was an oppressive force, a dark tide threatening to sweep over us.

With a collective effort, we channeled our strength to bind the resurrected beings. The room was alive with the energy of our combined magic, the ancient entities trapped once again within the house's confines. As the final echoes of the spell faded, we took a deep breath, the weight of our success settling over us.

"We did it," Damien said, his voice carrying a mix of exhaustion and relief.

"Yeah, we did," I replied, wiping the sweat from my brow. "This was one of the toughest things the Coven's ever faced, but we had the Elders' guidance, and we pulled through."

Damien nodded, though his brow was furrowed. "I hope there aren't any side effects from that spell. We should stay alert."

"We will," I said, placing a reassuring hand on his shoulder. "For now, let's go home and enjoy some time with the girls."

We returned to our new home, where Kaitlin and Paige greeted us with bright smiles and open arms. The relief of seeing them safe and happy was a balm to my soul.

"We missed you, Mommy and Daddy," Kaitlin said, her voice full of warmth as she threw her arms around us.

"We missed you too, sweetheart," I said, hugging her tightly. "We've got a lot of time to make up for."

Paige looked up at Damien with big, hopeful eyes. "Can we play outside, Daddy? Please?"

"Of course," Damien said, ruffling her hair. "Let's go have some fun."

The afternoon sun was warm on our faces as we played games with the kids in the yard. The laughter of my daughters, the playful banter with our allies—it was a welcome distraction from the shadows of our recent battles.

As the sun began to set, we made our way to the swimming pool. The dragons joined us, and Fire hovered nearby, her eyes glinting with mischief. Every so often, she'd splash us with water, her joyful roars filling the air.

"It's almost full moon again," Damien said as we relaxed by the pool, his arm around me.

"The werewolves will be out soon," I said, leaning into him. "But for now, let's enjoy this moment."

We watched as Kaitlin and Paige splashed around in the pool, their laughter ringing out under the twilight sky. The dragons swirled above us, their scales catching the fading light as they played.

As the evening deepened, we gathered around the fire pit, roasting marshmallows and sharing stories. The warmth of the flames was a stark contrast to the cold darkness we'd faced.

"The stars are so bright tonight," Kaitlin said, pointing up at the sky.

"They are," I agreed, smiling at her wonder. "Just like the twinkle in your eyes."

Damien took my hand, his gaze soft as the firelight danced in his eyes. "Can you believe how far we've come?" he asked, a hint of awe in his voice.

"I can't," I said, resting my head on his shoulder. "From battling demons to sharing this peaceful moment—it's been a wild ride."

"I wouldn't trade it for anything," Damien said, squeezing my hand gently. "Not for anything."

As we sat there, surrounded by the warmth of the fire and the laughter of our children, I felt a deep sense of peace. The battles we'd fought and the darkness we'd faced seemed far away, overshadowed by the love and joy that filled this moment.

"I'm so grateful for you, Damien," I said, looking into his eyes. "For our family, for everything we have."

His gaze was tender, his voice thick with emotion. "Me too, Amy. You and the girls mean everything to me."

In that quiet, starry moment, I knew that despite the darkness that lay beyond our peaceful existence, we had found a little piece of forever. Our journey had been filled with challenges, but it had led us here—to a place where love and hope flourished.

As the stars began to fade and the night deepened, we huddled together, our hearts full of gratitude and love. We were ready to face whatever came next, confident in the strength of our bond and the promise of a brighter future.

"Together," I whispered to Damien as we prepared to sleep under the stars.

"Together," he echoed back, his voice a soft promise in the night.

And with those words, we drifted into a peaceful sleep, the love we shared a shield against whatever the future might hold.

∞

As the first rays of dawn peeked through the curtains, I woke to the sounds of the world beginning anew. I stretched, feeling the comforting weight of the battles we had fought and the hope of what lay ahead. I glanced over at Damien, his eyes still closed in peaceful slumber, and I felt a surge of gratitude for the life we had built together.

With the day stretching out before us, I was ready for whatever came next. We had faced great darkness, but we had emerged victorious and together. Our love and our family would see us through any future trials.

"Together," I murmured to the empty room, the promise of a new day warming my heart.

And with that promise, I knew that no matter what the future held, we would face it side by side, our love a beacon in the darkness.

Chapter 32

The soft light of dawn filtered through the canopy of trees, casting dappled patterns across the forest floor. I woke to the gentle warmth of the sun on my face and the comforting sounds of the forest coming to life. Birds chirped their morning songs, and the breeze rustled the leaves above us.

I stretched lazily, glancing around at our makeshift camp. Damien lay beside me, his dark hair tousled and his breathing deep and steady. Our daughters, Kaitlin and Paige, were still curled up in their blankets, their faces peaceful and serene in sleep.

A contented sigh escaped my lips as I sat up, feeling the weight of recent battles lift just a little. This was a rare moment of peace, and I was determined to savor it.

"Morning, love," Damien mumbled, his eyes blinking open. He yawned, stretching his arms above his head. "I don't think I've ever slept this well outside."

"Good morning," I said, my voice gentle. "I guess the fresh air did us some good."

Damien gave me a lazy smile, his eyes still heavy with sleep. "Yeah, it feels nice to wake up surrounded by nature instead of chaos for a change."

I reached over and gave his hand a squeeze before leaning in for a quick kiss. "Today's going to be special," I said. "We're going to make the most of it."

With that, I gently shook Kaitlin's and Paige's shoulders. "Wake up, sleepyheads! It's a new day, and we have adventures planned!"

Kaitlin stirred first, rubbing her eyes and yawning. "What are we doing today, Mommy?"

"We're going to have a fun day together," I said. "Riding horses, flying with the dragons, and then a picnic for lunch."

Paige sat up, her eyes brightening. "And we can play games?"

"Absolutely," Damien said, sitting up beside me and ruffling Paige's hair. "How about we start with a ride through the forest?"

The girls' faces lit up with excitement as they scrambled out of their blankets. "Yes, let's go!" Kaitlin said, hopping out of bed.

The morning was filled with laughter as we saddled up the horses. The cool breeze blew through the trees, and the dragons soared high above, their wings catching the sunlight.

"Look at Fire go!" Paige squealed, pointing up at the blue dragon as she looped and swooped through the sky.

Lucian and Annie joined us, each leading a horse and guiding their dragons as well. "Ready for a day of fun?" Lucian asked, a grin on his face.

"Definitely," I said. "We've earned this break."

The forest was alive with colors and sounds as we rode through the trees. The horses' hooves thudded softly on the forest floor, and the dragons' shadows danced on the ground. The sense of freedom and joy was almost intoxicating.

When the sun reached its zenith, we set up for lunch by a small clearing near a babbling brook. Lucian and Annie took charge of the barbecue, the scent of sizzling meat mixing with the fresh smell of the forest.

"Looks like we're in for a feast," Damien said, pulling up a seat next to me.

"Can't wait," I replied, grinning as I watched the children run around, their laughter echoing through the trees. "Today's been perfect so far."

We ate and talked, sharing stories from our past adventures and making plans for the future. Lucian was regaling us with a tale of a prank he'd pulled on the Elders, and we all laughed as he described their horrified reactions.

As we finished eating, the dragons gathered around, nosing at the scraps. "They're just as eager for leftovers as the kids," Damien said, scratching Fire behind the ears.

"Yeah, they've been great companions through all of this," I said. "I'm glad we have them with us."

The afternoon was all about soaring through the skies. We climbed onto the dragons' backs, and with a powerful leap, we were airborne. The world below looked like a patchwork quilt of green and gold, and the rush of the wind against my face was exhilarating.

"Hold on tight!" Damien shouted over the roar of the wind as we looped through the clouds.

Paige's laughter rang out as Fire did a playful roll. "This is the best day ever!"

Kaitlin was beside her, grinning as she held on to her dragon's reins. "I'm never coming down!"

Eventually, we descended and landed softly on a hill overlooking the sunset. The sky was ablaze with colors, a magnificent canvas of orange, pink, and purple.

∞

As evening drew closer, we gathered around a crackling fire. The flames cast a warm glow over our faces, and the stars began to twinkle overhead, their light shimmering through the darkness.

"Isn't this just perfect?" Damien said, draping an arm over my shoulders.

"It is," I agreed, leaning into him. "It's everything we've dreamed of."

Kaitlin and Paige were toasting marshmallows, their faces illuminated by the firelight. "Mommy, tell us a story," Kaitlin asked, her eyes wide with anticipation.

I smiled, brushing a stray lock of hair from Paige's face. "Alright, how about a story of brave heroes and magical creatures?"

The kids snuggled closer as I began to spin a tale of daring quests and enchanted lands. As I wove the story, the fire crackled and the night creatures sang their songs. I watched as their eyes widened with each twist in the tale, their laughter and gasps mingling with the sounds of the forest.

When the story ended, Kaitlin clapped her hands, her face alight with excitement. "That was amazing, Mommy!"

"Thank you for the story," Damien said, pressing a kiss to my forehead. "You always know how to take us on an adventure."

With the fire burning low and the stars glittering above us, we settled in for the night. The cool night air brushed against our faces, but the warmth of our love kept the chill at bay.

"I've been thinking," I said quietly, breaking the comfortable silence.

"What's on your mind?" Damien asked, turning to me with a curious look.

"I want to start writing again," I said, my voice steady with determination. "I've missed it, and I think it's time to follow that dream."

Damien's eyes sparkled with excitement. "That's wonderful, Amy! I always knew you had a talent for storytelling. I can't wait to read your novels."

"Thank you," I said, feeling a rush of gratitude. "I couldn't do it without your support."

We sat together, the fire's last embers glowing softly. I felt a profound sense of peace, surrounded by the people I loved and the dreams I hoped to fulfill.

As the night deepened, we wrapped ourselves in blankets, enjoying the serene beauty of the forest and the promise of a bright future. The gentle rustling of leaves and the occasional hoot of an owl became a soothing lullaby.

"Tell us more stories, Mommy," Paige murmured sleepily.

I brushed a strand of hair from her face and began another tale, my voice soft and warm. "Once upon a time, in a land of magic and wonder..."

The fire's glow faded to embers, and the stars moved slowly across the sky. I could see the joy in my family's faces as they listened, their eyes reflecting the flickering firelight.

When the story ended, I saw in their eyes the same wonder and love that had always been there.

"That was the best story ever, Mommy!" Kaitlin said, her eyes sparkling.

"Thank you, Amy," Damien said, holding me close. "You've brought us so much joy."

As the fire died down and the night grew quiet, we held each other close, our hearts full of hope and happiness. We had found a little piece of paradise, and I knew we would face the future together, whatever it might hold.

The next morning, the sun rose bright and clear, painting the sky in shades of gold and pink. I woke with a renewed sense of purpose, ready to embrace the day with my family.

"Good morning, everyone," I said, stretching my arms and greeting the new day.

"Good morning, Mommy!" Kaitlin and Paige chimed in, their voices filled with excitement.

We prepared breakfast together, the aroma of sizzling bacon and fresh coffee mixing with the forest's early-morning freshness. As we ate, the forest around us came alive, birds singing and the breeze rustling through the trees.

"Today we could go for a hike or have a picnic by the river," Damien suggested, packing up the last of the picnic supplies.

"That sounds perfect," I said, feeling a sense of wonder at the life we had built together. "Let's make it another great day."

As we set off, the laughter of our children and the chatter of the pack and Coven in the distance reminded me of the simple joys that filled our lives. I was grateful for these moments of peace and the love that surrounded us.

We walked to our favorite spot by the river, the same place where Damien and I had shared our first picnic. As we settled in, I took out my notebook, eager to start outlining my novel.

"Mommy's writing a story?" Paige asked, peering over my shoulder.

"Yes," I said, smiling as I wrote. "It's going to be a story about love and magic."

Damien sat beside me, his eyes glancing at the notebook. "What's it about?"

"It's a tale of forbidden love," I explained, "a story where there are no battles, just peace and happiness."

"That sounds wonderful," Damien said, squeezing my hand. "I can't wait to read it."

As we enjoyed our picnic, the children played, and I sketched out ideas for my novel. I was filled with excitement at the prospect of bringing my story to life.

The day passed in a blur of laughter, joy, and love, a perfect continuation of the beautiful day before. We played games, explored the forest, and basked in the simple pleasure of being together.

As the sun began to set, painting the sky with vibrant hues, I felt a deep sense of fulfillment. We had found our little slice of paradise, and I knew that whatever challenges lay ahead, we would face them as a family.

"Let's make the most of tonight," Damien said, his arm around me as we watched the sunset.

"Absolutely," I agreed. "Here's to our family, our love, and the future we're building together."

As we headed back to the camp, the forest was bathed in the warm glow of the setting sun. The promise of tomorrow was bright, and with my family by my side, I felt ready for whatever came next.

The night was filled with laughter, dreams, and the peaceful hum of the forest. Wrapped in blankets and each other's arms, we fell asleep under the stars, our hearts full of hope and joy for the future.

Chapter 33

Morning sunlight filtered through the canopy, casting golden beams on the forest floor. The gentle rustling of leaves and the occasional chime of bells were the only sounds in the serene clearing. I was lying on the grass, enjoying the calm with Damien and the kids, when two figures emerged from the trees. Their presence was almost otherworldly, as if they had stepped out of a legend.

"Good morning," said the taller of the two, her voice like a soft melody carried on the breeze. "I am Trinity, Queen of the Fae, and this is my husband, Jasper, King of the Fae."

I sat up, blinking at the sight of the Fae monarchs. Their appearance was both beautiful and imposing, their eyes filled with an urgent light. Lucian had warned us that the Fae might come uninvited, and here they were, just as he'd predicted. I quickly recalled that Lucian had said they would come empty-handed, but these two seemed to carry a heavy burden.

"Good morning," I said, trying to steady my voice. "I'm Amy. What brings you to us?"

Trinity's gaze met mine, her eyes reflecting a deep sadness. "We come seeking your help. Our kingdom has been overrun by ogres—monstrous creatures who have driven us from our lands. We have no other recourse."

Jasper stepped forward, his face lined with concern. "We've heard of your strength and your allies. We hoped you might help us reclaim our home."

The plight of the Fae resonated with me. We had faced our own battles and struggles, and I knew the fight against the ogres would be formidable. My thoughts flickered back to the ogres we had fought before—the ones that had taken Vivian and fled after Damien's mother was turned to stone.

"We will do everything we can to help," I said, determination in my voice. "But we can't make any promises. Our resources are stretched thin, and the ogres are fierce."

Trinity's hand touched mine, her touch light and reassuring. "We understand, Amy. But please, will you at least hear us out? We have warriors, but they are no match for the ogres. And yes, a witch with long red hair leads them—my sister, Vivian."

My heart sank. I knew that Vivian was Damien's sister and that she had fled with the ogres. This was a fight we couldn't ignore. "We know what we need to do. Gather your people and meet us at the edge of the forest before sundown. We will come up with a plan.

Trinity's eyes brightened with hope. "Thank you, Amy. We'll be there."

With a final nod, Trinity and Jasper turned and disappeared into the forest. I watched them go, feeling a mix of apprehension and resolve. This mission would not only challenge our strength but also test our unity.

I found Damien sitting by the picnic blanket, looking concerned. "What's on your mind?" he asked.

I took a deep breath, knowing that this would be a difficult conversation. "Trinity and Jasper asked for our help. The ogres and Vivian have taken over the Fae's kingdom."

Damien's eyes darkened. "Ogres are brutal enemies, and Vivian... you know she's powerful. We need to prepare for a tough fight. But if anyone can do this, it's us. We need to think through our strategy carefully. Expect the unexpected."

I nodded, grateful for his support. "We will make it through this. We have to."

We gathered the coven and the wolf packs around the fire, preparing for a long discussion. Lucian's sharp eyes met mine as he noticed the gravity of the situation.

"Something on your mind, Amy?" he asked.

I explained, "Trinity and Jasper have asked us to help them fight the ogres and reclaim their kingdom. We need to plan our approach carefully."

Gregory's eyes widened. "Ogres are no small challenge."

"We will help them," I said firmly. "Trinity and Jasper are waiting for us at the forest's edge to discuss a plan before sundown."

Lucian, Gregory, and the others nodded, their faces set with resolve. We left the dragons behind for now; we needed to build trust with the Fae before revealing our full strength.

As we approached the meeting spot, Trinity and Jasper were waiting, their faces marked by a mix of hope and anxiety.

"Thank you for coming," Trinity said, her voice filled with relief. "We weren't sure if you would."

Damien offered a reassuring smile. "We may not know your world well, but we know how to fight monsters."

Trinity's eyes softened with gratitude. "You have no idea how much this means to us."

We sat in a circle, and Trinity and Jasper shared stories of their homeland—a place of magic and beauty. They spoke of emerald forests, crystal-clear streams, and enchanted castles reaching towards the sky.

"Now, let's talk strategy," I said, feeling the weight of our responsibility. "We need to assign roles for the battle."

Trinity and Jasper listened intently as we outlined our plan. "We will use swords as our primary weapons," I said. "They need to be sharp and ready."

"Our swords will be our strength," Trinity agreed.

"And our dragons," I continued, "their flames can be our greatest asset."

Jasper's eyes lit up. "We've heard about your dragons. How did you bond with them?"

I smiled. "Shadowfire chose me. It was a deep connection, and I believe the other dragons will find their riders in time. For now, we work with what we have."

Lucian and Gregory set about preparing supplies for the coming battle, while the rest of us finalized our strategy. We planned to use illusions to confuse the ogres and to set up scouting parties for reconnaissance.

As night fell, we made camp and prepared for the battle ahead. Trinity and Jasper were offered a room for the night, and the rest of us gathered around the fire.

"It's been a long time since we had guests," I said, watching as the firelight danced on everyone's faces.

Trinity smiled wistfully. "We miss our home, but this kindness helps ease the pain."

"We'll do everything we can to help you reclaim it," I promised.

We shared stories and laughter, bonding over our shared experiences. As the night deepened, I felt a strong sense of unity and purpose among us.

Before long, the fire burned low, and we decided it was time for rest. "We leave at first light," I said, trying to sound confident despite my own exhaustion. "We have to be ready for whatever comes next."

Tina agreed to watch the twins, and we all prepared for sleep, knowing the next day would bring the battle we had been preparing for.

Dawn broke over the horizon, painting the sky with hues of gold and pink. Damien and I stood at the edge of the forest, our allies gathered around us. Lucian, Annie, Gregory, the dragons, the Coven, and the Fae stood ready, weapons in hand.

"Are you both ready for this?" I asked Trinity and Jasper.

Trinity took a deep breath. "We're ready."

"Let's go then," Damien said with determination. "It's time to save a kingdom."

The dragons descended from the sky, their scales shimmering. We moved out, our hearts set on the task ahead. Lucian led the charge with the werewolf packs, Gregory and his dragons provided aerial support, and I flew beside Fire, gripping my sword tightly.

As we neared the Fae's homeland, the sight before us was grim. The once-beautiful landscape lay in ruins, smoke rising from the shattered remains.

"We need to move quickly," Damien urged. "Every minute we delay causes more damage."

We sprang into action. The wolves shifted into their wolf forms, and the Coven engaged the ogres on the ground. Fire and I swooped down, cutting through the ogre ranks with swift precision.

The battle raged on. The ground shook under the clash of weapons and the roar of dragons. I fought with all my strength, Fire's flames lighting up the battlefield as we struck down the ogres. Damien fought with grace and fury, his movements fluid and powerful.

Just as victory seemed within reach, a dark figure appeared—a cloaked figure wielding shadowy magic. It was Vivian.

"We can't let them win," I shouted, rallying our forces. "We must keep fighting!"

With renewed determination, we pressed on. The clash of magic and steel filled the air as we faced our greatest challenge yet. We fought as one, driven by our desire to save the Fae and restore their home.

In the end, our unity and strength prevailed. We captured Vivian and the ogres, imprisoning them in the Fae's dungeons where they would remain for eternity.

Trinity and Jasper approached us, their faces reflecting deep gratitude. "Thank you," Trinity said, her voice trembling. "You've saved our home."

I smiled, feeling a swell of pride. "We couldn't have done it without you. We're all in this together."

As we tended to our wounds and prepared to rest, Trinity and Jasper invited us to stay with them and recuperate. "It's the least we can do for all you've done," Trinity said sincerely.

"We accept your offer," I said, touched by their generosity. "And we're grateful for the chance to rest."

We set up camp amidst the ruins, finding comfort in the warmth of the fire and the company of our new friends. Lucian and Annie tended to the wounded, while Gregory and the dragons kept watch.

As the stars emerged in the sky, we shared stories and memories, forging new bonds in the aftermath of battle. We had fought for a noble cause, and the victory we had won was a testament to our courage and unity.

The battle for the Fae was over, but our journey was far from complete. We knew that there would be more challenges ahead, but for now, we could take solace in the knowledge that we had made a difference.

The road ahead was uncertain, but we faced it together, with hope in our hearts and determination in our souls. And as we looked towards the future, we knew that whatever came our way, we would face it as one.

Chapter 34

As we trudged along the familiar forest path back to our homeland, a dense fog of unease clung to my thoughts. We had just fought and won a battle, but the victory felt hollow. There was an ominous chill in the air, a sense of danger that lurked just out of sight.

"Damien," I murmured, my voice almost lost in the rustling leaves, "do you feel it? Like there's something wrong?"

Fire landed beside me, her fiery eyes scanning the horizon. I knew she could sense it too. Damien glanced over at me, his expression a mask of concern.

"I feel it," he said, his voice low. "It's like a storm is brewing on the edge of the world. We need to stay alert."

I nodded, glancing back at the trail of the pack and the dragons. Our allies walked in somber silence, their usual banter replaced by a tense quiet. The dragons flew overhead, their wings beating in steady rhythms as they kept watch.

"What do you think it could be?" I asked, trying to ignore the sinking feeling in my stomach.

Damien's brow furrowed as he stared into the distance. "It's hard to say. But after everything we've been through, I wouldn't be surprised if it's my mother."

The mention of Damien's mother sent a shiver down my spine. "Do you think Vivian freed her? Is she behind this?"

Damien's jaw tightened, his eyes darkening. "It's a real possibility. We have to be prepared for anything."

We walked on in uneasy silence, the landscape of our homeland coming into view but offering little comfort. The familiar sights felt tainted by the unease that had settled over us.

Suddenly, a dark figure appeared on the horizon, barely visible against the dimming light. A chill ran down my spine as the figure drew closer, moving with a deliberate, menacing pace.

"Is that—" Damien began, his voice trembling slightly.

"It's her," I said, my heart pounding as the figure stepped into the open. The cloak's hood fell back, revealing the cold eyes of Damien's mother.

"I've come for what's rightfully mine," she said, her voice like the crackle of ice.

Before we could react, a distant roar echoed from our homeland, followed by the unmistakable sounds of battle—clashing steel, shouts, and cries.

"My daughters!" I gasped, my heart leaping into my throat.

Damien and I exchanged a desperate glance, our fear for the safety of Kaitlin and Paige propelling us forward. The rest of our group moved with us, urgency spurring us on.

As we crested the final hill, the scene before us was chaos. Tina stood at the forefront, her wolf form a fierce silhouette against the flames and smoke. Beyond her, Damien's mother commanded a horde of dark creatures, her laughter echoing through the night like a sinister melody.

"We can't let her win," Damien said, his voice firm despite the chaos surrounding us.

"We face this together," I said, trying to steady my own nerves. With Fire by my side and my sword drawn, I prepared for the battle ahead.

Annie stepped forward, her eyes glinting with resolve. "We've faced dangers before. We can overcome this one too."

With that, we charged into the fray. Lucian moved with deadly precision, cutting through enemies with swift strikes. Annie wove magical barriers, shielding us from the relentless assault. The dragons unleashed torrents of fire from above, their roars reverberating through the battlefield.

Damien and I fought side by side, our movements synchronized as we pushed against the tide of darkness. His blade flashed in the light, a beacon of hope amidst the chaos. I focused my magic, channeling it to fortify our defenses and strike down our foes.

The battle raged on. We fought with everything we had, but Damien's mother was a formidable opponent. Her dark magic was overwhelming, pushing us to our limits. I could hear Fire's voice in my mind, calm and reassuring.

"Trust in your strength, Amy," she urged. "Draw upon the power we share."

Drawing deep from Fire's power, I unleashed a surge of energy. The sky crackled with lightning, and the earth trembled beneath us. Damien's mother faltered, a hint of surprise in her eyes.

"Let's finish this," Damien said, his voice filled with renewed determination.

The Coven gathered around me, their collective energy amplifying my magic. We aimed a powerful bolt at Damien's mother, but she anticipated the attack and unleashed her own beams in retaliation. Annie's barrier held for a moment but was soon overwhelmed.

Wolves and other creatures joined the fray, trying to distract Damien's mother. Fire and the dragons hurled fireballs, but they seemed ineffective against her dark powers.

During the chaos, I heard Fire's voice again. "You need more power, Amy. Take what you need from me."

"Thanks, Fire," I said, my voice steady despite the gravity of the situation.

Drawing on Fire's energy, I focused on protecting my daughters. I knew that to save them, I had to defeat Damien's mother. I could feel the power surging through me as lightning streaked across the sky and rain began to fall.

With a final, fierce concentration, I directed a lightning bolt at Damien's mother. The strike was true, and the force of it scattered her and her dark army into the void.

Exhausted but triumphant, I sank to my knees. Fire descended beside me, her warm presence a comforting embrace.

"You did it, Amy!" the Coven cheered, their voices a mix of relief and admiration.

"You defeated the wicked witch!" they exclaimed, their faces shining with the thrill of victory.

Fire gathered me up, placing me gently on her back. "Home isn't far. I'll help you recover," she said softly.

I woke a few hours later, feeling revitalized and stronger than ever. Fire's power had renewed my strength, and I realized that together we had achieved something incredible. The battle was over, and Damien's mother was defeated.

With a newfound energy, I knew that no matter what challenges lay ahead, Fire and I were ready to face them together.

Chapter 35

The winter winds swept through Tridion, casting a blanket of snow over our new home. It was that magical time of year again—my favorite season, blending the warmth of Thanksgiving with the joy of Christmas. I couldn't help but smile as I watched the flakes fall gently against the window, transforming the world into a winter wonderland.

Inside, the house buzzed with activity. The crackle of the fireplace was a constant companion to the laughter and chatter filling the room. The Elders, the packs, and the coven were all gathered, creating a tapestry of warmth and camaraderie.

"Remember when Lucian tried to cook a turkey without thawing it first?" Gregory's eyes sparkled as he shared the memory.

Lucian gave him a good-natured glare. "Oh, yeah. The turkey was more of a rock than a meal."

"And Liam," Gregory continued, "wasn't happy about it. Your mom had to step in and save the day."

I frowned, trying to recall the name. "Liam? That sounds familiar."

"Oh, Liam's another cousin," Gregory explained, waving a hand dismissively. "He's an alpha too, but you only met him once ages ago. Nothing major, but you might see him again someday."

Annie and I were busy preparing for the feast. “We can’t forget Amy’s famous pumpkin pie,” Annie said, her eyes dancing with excitement.

“Oh, of course!” I said, my heart warmed by her enthusiasm. “I’m on it.” I mentally checked off the list of ingredients I’d need to make the pie.

Outside, Gregory, Damien, and the girls busied themselves with decorating the house. Twinkling lights draped over the eaves, and festive ornaments hung from the tree they’d just cut down. The smell of fresh pine filled the air.

I caught a glimpse of them through the window—Damien helping the girls untangle a string of lights. “Let’s make sure we get a picture of this,” I said to Annie, snapping a few shots with my phone. “It’s not every day you see Damien in holiday mode.”

Annie chuckled. “I can’t wait to see the finished tree. I’m sure it’ll be beautiful.”

The buzz of activity made it easy to forget that we were also planning a trip back to New Orleans. It was a chance to reconnect with the city where our journey had begun.

“Any news on the agents for your book?” Annie asked as we whisked flour and sugar together.

“Not yet, but I’m hopeful,” I said, my fingers working the dough. “It’ll be nice to have a change of scenery. I’m excited to see what’s next.”

Thanksgiving Day arrived, and the house was a sanctuary of laughter and warmth. We gathered around the table, hands clasped and shared our gratitude for the blessings we had and the ones we hoped to find.

“Here’s to family, to dreams, and to the journey ahead,” I said, raising my glass.

“To a wonderful holiday and the promise of a bright future,” Damien added.

The girls looked at us with wide eyes, their excitement barely contained. "Can we open presents now?" Kaitlin and Paige asked in unison.

"Yes, girls," I said, smiling at their eagerness. "Let's wait for your dad, though. He's coming down any minute now."

As if on cue, Damien appeared at the top of the stairs, his usual cool demeanor softened by the festive mood. "Did I hear my name?" he asked with a grin.

"You did," I said, laughing. "We're just waiting for you."

He joined us by the tree, and I handed him the first gift. "For you, my love," he said, presenting me with a beautifully wrapped box.

I opened it to find a delicate necklace, the kind that made my heart flutter. "Thank you, Damien. It's gorgeous," I said, hugging him tightly.

He gave me another, larger box. "And this is for your writing," he said. "I know how much it means to you."

I tore off the wrapping paper to reveal a new laptop, complete with notebooks and pens. "Wow! Thank you, Damien. " I said, my eyes brimming with tears of gratitude.

Next, I gave Kaitlin and Paige their presents—a personalized book filled with family memories and photos, along with matching necklaces and lockets.

"Thank you, Mommy! We love it!" they said, their faces alight with joy as they hugged me.

Damien's surprise for the girls was a beautifully crafted Barbie house and new dolls. "Thank you, Daddy!" they squealed, their excitement evident.

∞

As we exchanged gifts, I was touched by how well everyone knew us. My parents had gifted Annie and me Louis Vuitton luggage and a selection of clothes and makeup. "They know us so well," I said to Annie, marveling at the thoughtful presents.

After the gift exchange, we sat down for a Christmas breakfast prepared by Lucian. The table was laden with crumpets, croissants, toast, eggs, bacon, and sausages.

"Wow, Lucian! You've outdone yourself," I said, savoring the delicious spread.

Lucian grinned, a hint of pride in his eyes. "It's the least I could do. I hear you and Annie have big plans for New Orleans."

"Yes, we do," Annie said. "We were thinking Lucian could explore a career as a chef once we're back."

Lucian's eyes lit up at the suggestion. "That's an idea worth considering. I'd love to try my hand at something new."

After breakfast, we settled in for some Christmas movies. The living room was cozy, the fire crackling in the hearth, and the mood was perfect.

"We're going to miss this," I said, my voice tinged with sadness as I thought about leaving.

"Yeah," Annie said, "but it's only for a little while. We'll be back before you know it."

Gregory raised his glass. "We'll be here, waiting for you. Follow your dreams and come back with great stories."

"Safe travels," Tina said, her eyes shining with unshed tears. "We'll be thinking of you every day."

Seth stepped forward; his face serious but kind. "I'll help Gregory and Tina take care of Fire while you're gone. We'll keep everything in order."

"Thanks, Seth," I said, feeling a wave of relief. "It means a lot to know we can leave things in good hands."

Seth shook Lucian's hand. "No parties, I promise."

Lucian chuckled. "I'm counting on you. Just keep the house in one piece."

"We'll do our best," Seth said with a wink. "And we'll keep the dragons happy."

With that, we raised our glasses for one last toast.

"To family," Damien said, "and to the adventures that await us."

"To dreams and the promise of reunion," I added.

As we clinked our glasses together, I knew this Christmas had been everything I could have hoped for. The love and joy shared with family made the thought of leaving bittersweet.

"Thank you, everyone," I said, my voice full of emotion. "We will be back before you know it."

"And we'll be waiting for you," Gregory said, his smile warm.

The day drifted by in a haze of joy and love, ending with a promise to return and share our new adventures. As I looked around at the faces of those I loved, I knew that no matter where our journeys took us, the bonds we shared would always bring us back together.

Outside, I met with Fire one last time before we left. She was already waiting for me, her scales glinting in the winter light.

"Merry Christmas, Fire," I said, reaching out to pat her gently.

"Merry Christmas, Amy," she replied in my mind, her thoughts tinged with sadness. "I'm going to miss you."

"I'll be back before you know it," I promised, stroking her warm scales. "Gregory will take good care of you, and we'll have our adventures when I return."

"True," Fire said with a hint of playfulness. "I'll be waiting for those flights."

"It's a deal," I said, smiling as I felt the warmth of our bond.

I turned back towards the house, ready to join the others for supper.

What a Christmas it had been—full of love, laughter, and the promise of a new chapter to come.

At the table, we enjoyed our last meal together before the trip.

"Thank you, everyone," I said, raising my glass one final time. "We'll be back before you know it with stories to tell."

"To family and new beginnings," Damien said, his eyes shining with pride.

"To the future," Annie added.

"To great adventures," Gregory said, smiling.

"To returning home," Tina said, her eyes glistening.

As we clinked our glasses and enjoyed our meal, I felt a deep sense of contentment. This Christmas had been perfect, a moment of peace before the next journey began. And with that thought, I looked forward to what lay ahead, knowing that no matter how far we traveled, our hearts would always bring us back home.

Chapter 36

As the end of the year draws near, a palpable excitement hums through Tridion. The air feels charged with anticipation for our trip back to New Orleans, a city that's as much a part of us as our own home. I can't help but smile at the sight of Kaitlin and Paige, their faces bright with the thrill of the journey ahead.

"We're going to see the city where you and Daddy started your adventure!" Paige bounces up and down beside me, her curls bobbing with each jump.

"That's right," I say, brushing a stray lock of hair from her face. "We're going to celebrate the New Year where it all began for us."

Damien joins us, his usual calm demeanor showing a hint of excitement. "And we have a lot to look forward to. The dragons are in good hands with Seth and Gregory, and we've got so many plans for New Orleans."

Gregory's voice echoes from the back of the room as he hands us a bag of emergency supplies. "Don't worry about a thing. We've got the packs and the dragons covered. Just focus on enjoying yourselves."

"Thanks, Gregory," I say, giving him a grateful hug. "We'll miss you guys, but I know everything's in good hands."

We say our goodbyes and head out, the winter chill biting at our cheeks as we load the last of our bags into the car. I catch Damien's hand and give it a squeeze. "Ready for the road trip?"

"Absolutely," Damien replies with a smile. "Let's get this adventure started."

The drive to New Orleans is filled with chatter and laughter. The city's outline starts to emerge on the horizon, and Kaitlin and Paige's excitement only grows as we get closer.

Once we pull up to my parents' house in the Garden District, the familiar sight of the old oak trees and the sprawling garden fills me with a deep sense of nostalgia. The house stands as it always has, a beacon of cherished memories.

"Mommy, look at the flowers!" Kaitlin exclaims, running towards the magnolia trees that are just beginning to bloom.

"The magnolias are gorgeous," I agree, watching as the girls twirl around in the garden. "Remember how we used to climb those trees?"

Paige's eyes widen. "Did you really climb them?"

"Yep," I say, laughing as I picture those carefree days. "And sometimes we'd sit up there and make up stories."

Annie catches up with us, her eyes sparkling with the same excitement. "How about we take the girls on a little tour of the city? Show them the places we used to hang out?"

"That sounds perfect," Damien agrees. "Let's start with the schools. I'm sure they'd love to see where you and I spent so much time."

As we walk through the streets of New Orleans, the past and present blend seamlessly. We visit my old high school, where the hallways still seem to whisper echoes of teenage dreams and friendships.

"Mommy, did you really have to study in the same hallway?" Kaitlin asks, her eyes wide as she takes in the old lockers and classroom doors.

"Yes, and it was just as chaotic as it looks," I say with a chuckle. "But it was a lot of fun, too."

We wander through the French Quarter, the lively streets filled with the sounds of jazz and the rich aroma of Cajun cuisine.

"This place hasn't changed a bit," Damien observes, glancing around at the familiar storefronts and street performers. "It's like stepping into a time machine."

"It does have that effect," I agree, taking in the vibrant colors and the lively energy of the street performers. "New Orleans has a way of feeling timeless."

The Mississippi River is as majestic as ever. We take a moment to stand by the water's edge, the gentle current reflecting the sunlight in a mesmerizing dance.

"It's peaceful here," I say, watching the river flow by. "I used to come here to think and dream."

"That sounds wonderful," Damien says, his arm wrapping around me. "You've come so far since those days."

Before long, it's New Year's Eve. We're back at my parents' house, the decorations gleaming with the promise of a new beginning.

"Look at the fireworks!" Paige squeals as the first bursts of color light up the sky.

I pull Damien into a warm embrace, my heart swelling with joy. "This is incredible."

"Congratulations on the book deal, Amy," Damien says, his voice filled with pride. "You did it."

"Thank you," I say, tears of happiness slipping down my cheeks as I hold up the contract. "It feels like a dream come true."

"Mommy, Daddy, can we have our presents now?" Kaitlin asks, her eyes sparkling with excitement.

"Soon, sweetie," I say, smiling. "But first, let's enjoy the fireworks and the celebration."

As the clock ticks closer to midnight, the air fills with the sound of laughter, music, and the crackle of fireworks. We raise our glasses, toasting to the new year and the future that awaits us.

"To new beginnings," Damien says, his eyes meeting mine.

"To adventures yet to come," I add, feeling the weight of the past year lifting off my shoulders.

The jazz music swells around us, and we dance under the stars, our spirits lifted by the city's magic and the promise of what's to come.

∞

Days after the New Year, we immerse ourselves in New Orleans. We stroll through the Garden District, the scent of magnolias and the sound of jazz creating a perfect backdrop for our explorations.

One afternoon, we discover a charming bookstore tucked away among the historic homes. The scent of old paper and the soft strains of jazz draw us inside.

"Look at this!" Kaitlin says, pointing to a display. "It's Mommy's book!"

I gaze at the cover, my heart pounding. "It's really here."

Damien chuckles beside me. "I guess there's some magic after all. I checked the contract, and it was only signed two months ago. I thought it would take longer."

I reach out and touch the cover of my book, a rush of excitement and disbelief flooding over me. "I can't believe it's real."

We flip to the dedication page, and I read the heartfelt note from the publisher. My eyes well up with tears, the weight of the journey we've been on crashing over me.

"Thank you for sharing this moment with me," I whisper to Damien as we leave the bookstore.

"Your book is a testament to your hard work," Damien says, his arm around me. "And this city is the perfect place for it to begin its journey."

As we continue to explore New Orleans, a sense of purpose fills me. The city's vibrant spirit and rich history inspire me, reminding me of why we embarked on this path in the first place.

Under the canopy of live oak trees and the soft glow of gas lamps, Damien and I walk hand in hand, our hearts full of hope and gratitude.

"New Orleans has a way of making everything feel new," Damien says, glancing around at the elegant mansions and lively streets.

"It does," I agree, feeling a deep connection to the past and excitement for the future. "It's like we're rediscovering a piece of ourselves."

Damien's fingers gently brush mine. "Some things, like our love, remain constant no matter where we are."

We pause under an ancient oak tree, the branches forming a natural arch over us. "Remember when we used to come here?" Damien's voice is soft, tinged with nostalgia.

"I do," I say, my heart aching with fond memories. "We dreamed of so many things back then. It's nice to see some of those dreams coming true."

"And there are still more dreams to chase," Damien says, his eyes shining with a mixture of hope and love.

I lean into him, feeling his warmth envelop me. "I'm excited for all that's ahead."

As the sun sets, casting a golden glow over the city, we walk back to the house, our hearts light and our spirits high. The past and future intertwine, and we are ready for whatever comes next.

In that moment, I know that no matter where life takes us, we have each other, and that's the greatest adventure of all.

Chapter 37

The anticipation for the New Year's ball at my parents' opulent house in the Garden District was almost tangible, hanging in the crisp New Orleans air like the sweet scent of magnolias.

Annie and I decided to turn dress shopping into a special event, bringing along my mom, my daughters Kaitlin and Paige, and the girls from the coven—Nancy, Arielle, Gabriella, and Meghan. We were on a mission to find the perfect dresses for the ball, and the idea of doing it together made the day even more exciting. We set out early, laughter bubbling up as we navigated the lively streets of the French Quarter, our hearts racing with the thrill of the hunt.

Our first stop was a quaint boutique known for its vintage-inspired gowns. The shop's interior was a feast for the eyes: racks of shimmering dresses, delicate fabrics in every hue, and the gentle hum of jazz from the speakers overhead. Kaitlin and Paige's eyes grew wide as they took in the spectacle.

"Look at this one, Mom!" Kaitlin held up a flowing emerald dress, its fabric catching the light like a thousand tiny stars.

"It's beautiful, sweetheart," I said, touching the soft fabric. "But let's see what else we can find."

Mom was already deep into the racks, her eyes scanning for something that would make my heart skip a beat. "Amy, try this one on," she said, handing me a deep blue gown adorned with intricate beadwork.

Annie, caught up in the excitement, picked out a delicate lavender dress and held it up to herself, twirling in front of Kaitlin and Paige. "What do you think, girls?"

"You look like a fairy princess, Aunt Annie!" Paige said, her eyes sparkling.

Nancy, Arielle, Gabriella, and Meghan were busy exploring the racks, their chatter a blend of excitement and fashion talk.

"Nancy, you have to try this one!" Arielle held up a bold red dress with a daring neckline.

Nancy laughed, her eyes shining. "Alright, let's see if I can pull off this bold look."

Gabriella picked up a sleek black gown, her eyes twinkling as she showed it to Meghan. "What do you think of this one?"

Meghan grinned. "It's perfect for you. You'll be the star of the night."

We spent hours trying on dresses, each of us finding our own version of magic in the garments. The shop attendants were patient, bringing us more options and offering suggestions as we laughed and admired each other's choices. It was more than just dress shopping—it was a chance to bond and create memories.

After we finally made our selections, we headed to a nearby café for a break. As we sipped hot chocolate and nibbled on pastries, the conversation turned to the ball and the excitement of the night to come.

"I can't wait to see everyone dressed up," Kaitlin said, her eyes dancing with anticipation.

"Me too," Paige agreed. "It's like a fairy tale."

Nancy looked around at the group with a warm smile. "These are the moments that make life special, aren't they?"

Gabriella nodded. "Absolutely. It's all about celebrating with the people we care about."

Arielle added with a grin, "And finding the perfect dress, of course!"

Mom reached over and squeezed my hand. "I'm so glad we're having this day together," she said softly.

Annie smiled and raised her cup. "To great memories and a fabulous evening!"

We finished up and headed back to my parents' house, the excitement building as we prepared for the ball. The house was buzzing with activity as friends and family began to arrive, their faces lighting up at the sight of the elegant décor and the promise of a wonderful night.

Upstairs, the air was filled with the sounds of hurried preparations. Mom helped Kaitlin and Paige into their dresses, while Annie and I worked on our makeup and hair. Nancy, Arielle, Gabriella, and Meghan were in the guest rooms, sharing beauty tips and last-minute adjustments.

"Annie, can you help me with this zipper?" I asked, struggling with the back of my gown.

"Of course," Annie said, stepping over to assist. "You look amazing, by the way."

"Thank you!" I replied, glancing at her lavender gown. "So do you."

From down the hall, I heard Kaitlin giggling as Mom adjusted her dress. "Hold still, Kaitlin," Mom laughed. "Or this bow will end up on your ear."

Paige twirled in front of the mirror, her dress flaring out like a princess's gown. "I feel like I'm in a fairy tale!" she said, her excitement bubbling over.

"You are a princess," I told her, giving her a kiss on the forehead.

Finally, we were all dressed and ready. As we descended the grand staircase, Damien and Lucian waited at the bottom, their eyes widening as they took in our ensemble.

"Wow," Damien said, his eyes locked on me. "You look breathtaking."

Lucian looked at Annie with admiration. "You look incredible, Annie."

Damien turned to Kaitlin and Paige. "And you two are the most adorable princesses I've ever seen."

"Thank you, Daddy!" Kaitlin and Paige said in unison, their faces glowing with joy.

Damien offered me his hand as I reached the bottom of the stairs. "I'm the luckiest man here," he whispered, kissing my hand gently.

Lucian extended his arm to Annie. "Tonight is going to be magical," he said, his eyes shining with excitement.

As we joined the crowd in the transformed living room, now a grand ballroom filled with twinkling lights and lush greenery, the atmosphere was electric. Friends and family greeted us with cheers and applause.

"Look at you all!" Nancy said, raising her glass. "You look like you stepped out of a fairy tale."

Arielle agreed, her eyes twinkling. "Absolutely. You all look amazing."

Gabriella and Meghan came over to admire our dresses. "You all outdid yourselves," Gabriella said, giving us a thumbs up.

"Let's make tonight unforgettable!" Meghan added, her excitement palpable.

As the evening unfolded, the doorbell rang with the arrival of more guests. I opened the door to find Mayson, Milo, Christian, Grayson, Richard, and Dylan standing there, looking sharp in their suits. Gwen and Andy were with them, dressed to impress.

"Welcome!" I said, pulling them into a warm hug. "It's so good to see you all."

"You all look fantastic," Mayson said, stepping inside and giving me a hug.

"Thanks, Mayson. You're looking pretty dashing yourself," I replied with a smile.

Gwen and Andy came in next, their eyes widening as they took in the transformed room. "This place looks incredible!" Gwen said. "You've outdone yourself."

"Thanks, Gwen. It was a lot of work, but it's worth it," I said, smiling at her enthusiasm.

Damien joined us at the door, greeting the newcomers. "Glad you could make it. The night's just beginning!"

Christian and Grayson eyed the dance floor with eager grins. "Who's up for some dancing?" Christian asked.

"Count me in!" Grayson said, pulling Andy along.

The band struck up a lively tune, and soon everyone was on the dance floor, moving to the rhythm of the music. The room buzzed with energy as friends and family twirled under the sparkling chandeliers.

Milo and Gwen led Kaitlin and Paige in a dance, showing them some moves. "Like this, see?" Milo demonstrated, making the girls giggle as they tried to follow along.

"You're a great dancer, Milo," Paige said, laughing.

Richard and Dylan were deep in conversation with Lucian and Annie, sharing stories and laughter. "It's great to be here with everyone," Richard said, raising his glass.

"It is," Annie agreed, her eyes sparkling. "Even without using any magic, tonight feels special."

Nancy, Arielle, Gabriella, and Meghan mingled with the other guests, their laughter ringing out. "This is exactly what we needed," Arielle said, toasting with Meghan.

The doorbell rang once more, and Lucian's pack walked in: Lee-Anne, Alistair, Anna, Alison, David, and Mark, all ready to join the celebration.

"Welcome! So glad you could make it!" I said, ushering them inside.

"Thanks for having us," Lee-Anne said, giving me a warm hug. "This place looks amazing."

David and Mark headed straight for the dance floor, while Alistair and Anna greeted Lucian with smiles and hugs. "Lucian, you know how to throw a party," Alistair said.

"We aim to please," Lucian said with a grin.

As the night went on, the room was filled with joy and celebration. Despite our magical lives, we reveled in the simple pleasures of the evening: the music, the laughter, and the company of those we loved.

At one point, Damien pulled me into a slow dance, his gaze fixed on mine. "This is perfect," he whispered, holding me close.

"It is," I said, resting my head on his shoulder. "I'm so glad we're all here together."

Around us, Lucian and Annie danced gracefully, while Kaitlin and Paige twirled with their friends. The pack mingled with the coven, blending our two worlds in a beautiful harmony.

Lee-Anne caught my eye and smiled. "This is a night to remember," she said.

"Absolutely," I agreed, feeling a deep sense of gratitude for the love and friendship surrounding us.

As the evening wore on, the excitement built toward midnight. The room was alive with the buzz of anticipation.

"Alright, everyone!" Lucian called out over the music. "It's almost time. Let's get ready for the countdown to 2025!"

Damien and I stood together in the center of the room, feeling the collective excitement of our friends and family.

"Ten minutes to go!" Christian announced, glancing at his watch.

Milo and Gwen ushered Kaitlin and Paige over to us. "Come on, girls," Milo said with a grin. "Let's get ready to ring in the new year!"

As the final moments approached, the band shifted to a softer melody, and glasses of champagne and sparkling cider were handed out.

"Five minutes left!" Arielle called out.

Lucian and Annie moved to stand beside us, their faces glowing with happiness. "This year is going to be amazing," Lucian said.

"It sure is," Annie agreed.

The room grew quieter as everyone turned their attention to the clock on the wall. Damien squeezed my hand gently. "Ready for a new year, love?"

"Ready as ever," I replied, feeling a swell of emotion.

"One minute to go!" Richard called out.

The room's energy was electric as the countdown began.

"Ten!" everyone shouted.

"Nine! Eight! Seven!"

Damien's hand was warm in mine, and Kaitlin and Paige were bouncing with excitement, their voices joining the countdown.

"Six! Five! Four!"

Nancy, Arielle, Gabriella, Meghan, and the rest of our friends and family were all smiling, their eyes full of hope and joy.

"Three! Two! One!"

"Happy New Year!" we shouted as the clock struck midnight. The room erupted in cheers, clinking glasses, and joyous exclamations.

Damien pulled me into a kiss, his lips soft against mine. "Happy New Year, my love," he whispered.

"Happy New Year, Damien," I said, feeling my heart swell with love.

Lucian and Annie shared a kiss, their happiness evident. "Here's to twenty-twenty-five," Lucian said, raising his glass.

"To twenty-twenty-five!" We all echoed, glasses raised high.

Kaitlin and Paige hugged us tightly. "Happy New Year, Mommy! Happy New Year, Daddy!" they shouted.

"Happy New Year, my sweet girls," I said, pulling them into a warm embrace.

The band struck up a lively tune, and soon everyone was back on the dance floor, the joy of the new year propelling us into a fresh wave of celebration. Lee-Anne, Alistair, Anna, Alison, David, and Mark joined in, their laughter blending with the rest of the party.

Nancy clinked her glass against mine. "Here's to making more wonderful memories," she said with a smile.

"Absolutely," I agreed, feeling a deep sense of gratitude.

As the first moments of twenty-twenty-five unfolded, we danced, laughed, and celebrated, surrounded by the people we loved most. It was a perfect start to the new year, filled with hope, joy, and the promise of all the beautiful things to come. For a few hours, we forgot about the magical challenges of our lives and embraced the joy of simply being together.

∞

The morning after, the sunlight filtered through the curtains, casting a gentle glow over everything. We awoke to the comforting aroma of freshly brewed coffee, courtesy of Lucian's expert touch.

"Good morning!" Lucian greeted us cheerfully from the kitchen.

"Morning, Lucian," I said, stretching and yawning.

Annie was setting out a delicious breakfast, her face beaming with warmth. "I hope you're all hungry," she said with a smile.

"Starving," Damien said, pulling out a chair for me.

We gathered around the table, savoring the food and reminiscing about the previous night's festivities.

"Last night was unforgettable," Kaitlin said, her eyes still sparkling with excitement.

"It really was," Paige added, her face aglow. "I'm so glad we could all be together."

In the cozy atmosphere of the kitchen, surrounded by loved ones and the simple pleasure of a good meal, I felt a deep sense of contentment. After breakfast, we decided to take a leisurely stroll through the Garden District, enjoying the crisp morning air.

As we walked beneath the ancient oaks, their branches reaching skyward, the morning sunlight danced on the cobblestones. The fragrance of blooming flowers filled the air, mingling with the distant strains of jazz from a nearby café.

"This place feels like a painting come to life," Damien said, his voice filled with awe.

"It always felt that way growing up here," I said with a fond smile. "It's like New Orleans has its own kind of magic."

Kaitlin and Paige skipped along the sidewalk, their laughter a sweet melody in the crisp morning air. "Mommy, look at that house!" Kaitlin pointed to a grand mansion with intricate ironwork gates.

"It's beautiful, isn't it?" I said, my heart swelling as I watched them marvel at the elegance around them.

Lucian and Annie walked beside us, their hands intertwined. "I hardly recognize some parts of the city," Lucian said, glancing at the bustling streets. "But there's something timeless about it."

Annie nodded. "That's the charm of New Orleans. It evolves but never loses its essence."

We turned a corner and discovered a charming café under a canopy of jasmine vines. The sound of live music floated out, inviting us in. "Shall we stop for coffee?" I suggested.

Damien's eyes lit up. "Only if they have beignets," he said, his grin infectious.

We laughed as we stepped inside, ready to savor the simple pleasures of a New Orleans morning. We settled into our seats, the vibrant ambiance of the café wrapping around us like a warm embrace. I knew this was a moment I would cherish.

After our coffee, we walked home, taking our time to admire the historic homes and lush gardens. Annie and I exchanged glances, sharing a silent understanding of how these moments connected us to our past.

Back at my parents' house, a feeling of tranquility washed over us. The morning had given us a renewed appreciation for the love and unity we shared. As we gathered on the veranda, basking in the sun's golden glow and each other's company, I knew these moments would be etched in our hearts forever, a testament to the beauty of simple joys and the enduring power of love.

Chapter 38

The next morning, New Orleans was alive with possibility. The sun peeked through the curtains of my parents' grand house, casting golden light over the breakfast table where everyone was gathering.

"Today's the perfect day for more exploring," I said, taking a sip of my coffee and looking around at the eager faces.

Damien, holding a cup of strong black coffee, nodded enthusiastically. "There's so much more to see, and I'm ready to dive in."

Kaitlin and Paige, sitting cross-legged on the floor, were deep into a board game. They looked up, their eyes wide with curiosity. "Can we go see the river?" Kaitlin asked, her voice brimming with excitement.

Damien grinned, ruffling Kaitlin's hair. "Only if you promise not to push me in," he teased.

Paige giggled, her eyes sparkling. "I promise, Daddy!"

I laughed, feeling a surge of joy at their enthusiasm. "It's a deal. Let's get ready and hit the streets of the French Quarter."

As we gathered our things, I glanced at the ornate chandelier overhead, its crystals casting rainbows on the walls. "What do you think? Should we head out now?" I asked, glancing at Damien.

He raised his glass. "To new adventures in New Orleans and the memories we'll make!"

Lucian walked into the room, carrying a platter of barbecue ribs and sausages. "Who's ready for breakfast?" he announced, setting the platter down with a flourish. "We need fuel for our adventures."

Annie followed close behind, her eyes twinkling. "Let's feast like kings and queens," she said, arranging the sides on the table.

We gathered around, plates filling with delicious food as laughter and stories flowed freely.

"Remember when we first arrived?" Annie asked, her eyes gleaming as she looked around the room.

"How could I forget?" I said, thinking back to the whirlwind of our arrival. "It was overwhelming, but also exhilarating."

"Yeah, it was like being thrown into the deep end," Damien said, taking a big bite of ribs. "But look at us now. We've settled in and found our rhythm."

Annie raised her glass. "To new beginnings and the adventures yet to come!"

We clinked glasses and dug into the feast, savoring every bite and moment. The room was filled with warmth, both from the food and the company.

As we finished up, Damien leaned back in his chair. "Alright, everyone ready for the river?"

Paige and Kaitlin bounced up and down in their seats. "Yes!" they shouted in unison.

"Let's do this," I said, feeling a thrill of excitement.

We made our way to the docks, the streets bustling with the usual French Quarter charm. The smell of beignets and coffee from a nearby café mixed with the salty tang of the Mississippi River.

"Look at that," Damien said, pointing to the Crescent City Connection bridge. "That bridge is like a gateway to all the possibilities New Orleans has to offer."

I leaned against the railing, taking in the view. "It's beautiful," I said, the bridge's arches framed by the bright blue sky.

Kaitlin and Paige peered over the edge of the boat, eyes wide. "Did you know the river used to be a major trade route?" Paige asked, her voice filled with wonder.

"Yes," I said, smiling at her insight. "The Mississippi River was crucial for trade and culture, shaping New Orleans into what it is today."

Annie joined us, her eyes lighting up. "And the steamboats! They were the lifeblood of the city, carrying goods and people up and down the river."

We watched as majestic cargo ships sailed past, their immense size dwarfing our boat.

"Wow," Kaitlin said, staring up at one of the ships. "It's like a floating city."

Paige nodded. "I read that steamboats helped build New Orleans' economy."

"That's right," Annie said, "and they played a huge role in the city's history. They connected the North and South, bringing together people and cultures."

As the boat glided along the river, the sunset painted the sky in hues of pink and orange. The city's skyline shimmered in the distance, and I felt a deep sense of connection to this place.

"This city has a way of getting under your skin, doesn't it?" Damien said, his eyes reflecting the colors of the sunset.

"It really does," I agreed, feeling the same pull in my heart.

The boat docked, and we stepped back onto solid ground. The streets of the French Quarter were alive with the sound of jazz. Street musicians played melodies that seemed to capture the very essence of the city.

"Shall we wander?" I asked, holding out my hand.

Everyone nodded, and we strolled down the lively streets, the music and laughter blending into a soundtrack for our exploration.

After a while, we found ourselves in a quieter part of the Quarter, where the lively facade of the city gave way to a more reflective atmosphere.

"Do you remember the last time we were here?" I asked quietly, glancing at Annie.

Annie's smile faded as memories of that night came rushing back. "How could I forget?" she said, her voice low. "It was a night we thought would never end."

Lucian's hand tightened around Annie's arm, a silent promise of protection. "You all got out of there just in time," he said, his voice steady.

I looked down at the scar on my arm, a dark reminder of that dark night. "And the mark," I said, my voice faltering. "It's always there, a reminder of everything we've been through."

Annie's eyes were filled with understanding. "But we made it through," she said softly. "We're stronger for it."

I nodded, trying to focus on the present instead of the shadows of the past. "We have to move forward," I said, more to myself than anyone else. "We can't let the past hold us back."

We wandered back to the bustling streets, the vibrant energy of the French Quarter lifting our spirits.

In the days that followed, we dove into the heart of New Orleans. We explored hidden jazz clubs with names like "The Spotted Cat" and "Preservation Hall," where the music felt like a heartbeat beneath the city's surface.

We dined at charming little restaurants, where the food was as rich as the history of the city. "This étouffée is amazing," Damien said, savoring the spicy, flavorful dish.

Lucian and Annie found their own ways to get involved in the city's life. Lucian took up a part-time job at a local bookstore, while Annie began writing articles for the local paper, capturing the city's essence with her keen eye for detail.

Kaitlin and Paige enjoyed the simpler pleasures of the city, like feeding the ducks at City Park and discovering the best spots for beignets.

In quiet moments, I took to writing in a corner of our rented apartment. The city's magic seeped into my stories, infusing them with a new life.

"It's like the city's alive," I told Annie one evening. "It's inspiring my writing."

Annie smiled, her own notebook open as she jotted down notes for her next article. "I feel the same way. There's something about this place that fuels creativity."

Damien and Lucian were adjusting to their new roles. Damien threw himself into his work, embracing the challenge of building something new from the ground up. Lucian, with his bookish demeanor, enjoyed the peaceful environment of the bookstore, finding solace in the pages of forgotten tales.

Together, we faced the highs and lows of life in New Orleans. We discovered new corners of the city and learned to navigate its complex, magical tapestry.

Our bond grew stronger, shaped by shared experiences and new adventures. The city tested us, but we met every challenge together, with unwavering resolve and optimism for the future.

As we continued to explore and settle into our new lives, the promise of new beginnings and the strength of our family's love guided us. We were ready to face whatever came next, confident that as long as we had each other, we could conquer any obstacle.

And as we looked ahead to the future, the mysteries of New Orleans beckoned us, promising that our story was far from over.

Chapter 39

January whipped past like a carousel of excitement and nervous anticipation. I was juggling the release of not just one but two novels—each a labor of love that had taken months to bring to life. The thrill of seeing my words on the page, of knowing they had touched readers far and wide, was almost more than I could handle.

One evening, Damien caught me staring at the glossy cover of my latest book, a smile stretching across my face. "Dreams do come true," he said, his eyes bright with pride as he held the novel up to the light.

I took his hand, feeling the warmth of his support. "I couldn't have done it without you," I said, pressing a kiss to his fingers. "You were there for every draft, every late night."

With the thrill of my book releases still buzzing, a new excitement arrived: an invitation to New York City for a prestigious writing award. I burst into the living room, where Lucian, Annie, and the kids were gathered around the table, crafting Mardi Gras decorations.

"We're going to New York!" I announced, my voice tinged with the thrill of the news.

"New York? That's amazing!" Kaitlin squealed, her eyes wide with excitement.

Paige jumped up, nearly knocking over a stack of beads. "Are we going to see the Statue of Liberty? Or maybe Central Park?"

I laughed, the excitement of the future blending seamlessly with the joy of the present. "Yes to all of it, but first we have Mardi Gras to prepare for!"

Our costumes for Mardi Gras were going to be something special. The kitchen table was cluttered with fabric swatches, paintbrushes, and glitter.

"We're going all out this year," I declared, holding up a piece of vibrant purple fabric. "We're going to be the best-dressed witches in the parade!"

Annie picked up a paintbrush, her face determined. "I'm not sure if we can top last year, but we'll give it our all."

Lucian grinned as he sketched out the float design. "We'll figure it out as we go. We always do."

With laughter and creativity, we dove into making our costumes and float. Glitter flew through the air like magical confetti, and our chatter was a mix of excitement for Mardi Gras and the upcoming trip to New York.

"I can't believe we're actually going to New York," Paige said, her hands covered in gold glitter. "It's like we're in a movie!"

"It's going to be an adventure," Damien agreed, his eyes twinkling. "But let's make sure we enjoy every minute of Mardi Gras first!"

The day of the parade arrived, and we decked ourselves out in our elaborate costumes. The streets of the French Quarter were alive with the buzz of the festival. We climbed aboard our float, which was a colorful masterpiece of magic and creativity, and began our march through the French Quarter.

"Here we go!" Lucian shouted, his voice nearly drowned out by the cheers of the crowd.

I looked around, soaking in the vibrant energy of the parade, the laughter, the music, the dancing. We threw beads and trinkets to the delighted onlookers, the weight of our months of hard work lifting off our shoulders.

"Look at them cheer!" Annie shouted over the music, her eyes sparkling with pride.

"We did it," I said to Lucian, squeezing his hand. "We really did it."

But amidst the joy and celebration, a shadow loomed at the edge of my vision. I caught a glimpse of the dark figure that had haunted us before, lurking in the shadows.

"There," Annie said, her voice low and urgent as she pointed to the corner where the figure had vanished.

I squinted into the darkness but couldn't make out any details. "We need to find out what it wants," I said, trying to mask the unease in my voice.

Christian, Grayson, Mayson, Nancy, Gabriella, Ariella, and Gwen gathered around us, their faces a mix of concern and resolve.

"We can't ignore it," Christian said, his brow furrowed. "It's been following us for too long."

"But how do we even start?" Mayson asked, his uncertainty evident.

Gwen stepped forward, her expression thoughtful. "We need to gather information. There must be others who have dealt with similar entities. Let's seek out their knowledge."

"Yes," I agreed. "And we must stay alert. We need to be ready for anything."

Grayson's eyes were serious. "We might need experts on this. There are people in New Orleans with the knowledge we need."

Annie nodded, her resolve steely. "We'll face this together, whatever it takes."

As the night wore on and the parade drew to a close, we returned to my parents' house, our minds racing with thoughts of the shadowy figure. If we didn't deal with this now, it could become a threat to New Orleans and to us.

In the attic, which had become our strategy room, we laid out our plan. I recounted our encounters with the figure, from the depths of the French Quarter to its appearance during the parade.

"My mom suggested we consult the elders' grimoire," I said, my voice steady despite the gravity of the situation.

My mom nodded, her expression solemn. "The grimoire might hold the answers we need. It's a powerful tool passed down through generations."

We gathered around the table as she prepared a potion, a blend of herbs and spices. "Once you drink this, you'll recite the incantation three times. It will take you back to the first encounter with the figure, so you can understand its origins and intentions."

I took the potion, feeling a sharp, fiery pain in my arm as the burn from the mark flared up again. I gritted my teeth, the anticipation of the journey making the discomfort bearable.

We were transported back to that fateful night, huddled together in the shadows of the French Quarter. The figure stood before us, a dark silhouette that stirred uneasy memories.

"That figure doesn't look like Damien," Annie said, her voice steady despite the eerie scene. "But it's close."

I studied the figure's forehead, where a dark mark marred the smooth skin. "Damien doesn't have that mark. There's something more to this."

Christian's frustration was palpable. "Maybe Damien's hiding something from us."

"No," I said firmly. "We have to consider all possibilities, but we can't jump to conclusions."

Nancy agreed, her gaze sharp. "We need more information before we make any decisions."

Ariella's voice trembled. "What if Damien's been hiding things from us? What if he's been lying?"

Gwen, ever the mediator, offered a measured response. "We shouldn't rush to judgment. Let's uncover the truth first."

The tension in the room was thick as we resolved to seek answers. We woke up from the vision, the weight of our discoveries heavy on our minds.

Damien reached out to me, his eyes filled with concern. "What did you see?" he asked, his voice gentle.

"Vampires," I said, my voice edged with panic. "We have to act before they become a threat."

Damien's confusion was evident. "Vampires? I've only ever known of myself and the elders."

"Maybe the elders are hiding things from us," I said, my mind racing. "We need to confront these vampires before it's too late."

The coven and the wolf pack agreed—Damien would remain behind. This was our fight, and his presence might complicate things.

With weapons in hand, we moved through the darkened alleyways of the French Quarter, our senses alert for the impending confrontation. The wolf pack led the way, their instincts guiding us through the shadows.

As we ventured deeper, the tension was almost tangible. The distant howls of the wolf pack mixed with the sound of our footsteps against the cobblestones.

Suddenly, a horde of vampires emerged from the darkness, their eyes gleaming with malevolence.

"Stay close!" Christian's voice rang out as he leaped into the fray, claws extended.

"Let's show them what we're made of!" Nancy shouted, lightning crackling from her fingertips.

The battle was fierce, the clash of steel and magic filling the night. We fought with everything we had, each of us driven by the urgency of our mission.

Amidst the chaos, I saw Damien watching from the shadows, his eyes conflicted but resolute. He wanted to be with us, but he understood why he couldn't be.

As we fought, our unity proved stronger than any threat. Each strike, each spell, brought us closer to victory.

When the last vampire fell, relief and triumph washed over us.

"We did it!" Ariella gasped, looking around at the fallen vampires.

"As long as we stand together, we can face anything," Grayson said, his words a testament to our shared strength.

We made our way back through the now-quiet streets of New Orleans, our victory hard-won but sweet. Damien remained unaware of the night's events, and we decided to keep it that way. Our next adventure awaited us in New York, and we needed to be ready for whatever came next.

With the promise of new challenges ahead, we prepared ourselves for the journey, the shadows of the past already beginning to fade as we looked forward to the future.

Chapter 40

The days before our New York City trip felt like a whirlwind of excitement. Every day was filled with planning and packing, and the anticipation was almost as thrilling as the trip itself.

"Alright, let's go over the checklist one more time," I said, flipping through the pages of my planner with a focused frown. "Tickets, hotel reservations, packing lists—everything's in order?"

Damien held up a stack of papers with a grin. "Check, check, and check. I even made a packing list for everyone," he said, his pride evident in the neatly organized documents.

Annie rolled her eyes playfully but with genuine affection. "Leave it to Damien to be so prepared," she teased. "But seriously, thanks for keeping us all on track."

As we gathered around the kitchen table, maps and guidebooks spread out like treasures before us, the excitement was almost tangible.

"I can't wait to see Times Square," Kaitlin said, her eyes sparkling as she flipped through a tourist brochure.

"Me too!" Paige added, practically bouncing in her seat. "And the Empire State Building! And Central Park!"

"Let's not forget about Broadway," Lucian said, his eyes alight with excitement. "I heard the shows are out of this world."

Our enthusiasm grew with every passing day, until the morning of our departure finally arrived. We stood in the airport lobby, our suitcases packed and ready for adventure.

"Are we really doing this?" I asked, my nerves buzzing with excitement as we headed through security.

Damien squeezed my hand reassuringly. "We sure are. And we're going to have the time of our lives."

As we boarded the plane, I took a deep breath and looked around. This was our first family flight, and the thrill of the journey was almost overwhelming.

"Wow, this is amazing!" Kaitlin exclaimed, pressing her face against the window as the plane began to taxi.

"It's like we're flying with dragons," Paige said, her eyes wide as she watched the ground below.

I laughed, watching their wonder with a warm heart. "It really is something, isn't it?" I said, taking in the expansive sky outside.

Damien nodded, his eyes fixed on the clouds. "It's a whole new perspective. Makes you realize just how big the world is."

Annie took my hand and gave it a gentle squeeze. "And how connected we all are in this big world."

As the plane climbed higher, the view below was a breathtaking mosaic of landscapes. I could see the patchwork of fields, winding rivers, and distant cityscapes.

"Look, you can see the Statue of Liberty!" Lucian pointed out, his excitement as evident as the landmark itself.

"It looks so small from up here," I said, feeling a swell of pride as I gazed at the symbol of freedom.

When we landed, the sight of the towering skyscrapers of New York City was even more impressive up close.

"Wow, this place is huge!" Kaitlin said, her neck craned as she looked up at the massive buildings.

"It's like something out of a movie," Paige agreed, her voice filled with wonder.

We entered the grand lobby of the hotel, where marble floors gleamed and crystal chandeliers cast a soft glow.

"Welcome to the Big Apple," Damien said with a flourish, gesturing around the opulent lobby. "Where dreams come true and adventures begin."

At the check-in desk, the receptionist handed us shiny brass keys on sleek black keycard holders.

"Here are your keys to the Royal Suite on the top floor," she said with a warm smile.

"The Royal Suite?" Annie echoed, her eyes wide with surprise.

"It's the best suite in the hotel," the receptionist said. "You'll have plenty of room to enjoy yourselves."

With eager excitement, we took the elevator to the top floor, anticipation buzzing through the air.

"Here we go," Lucian said as he pressed the button for the top floor.

"Top floor, here we come!" I added, grinning as the elevator began its ascent.

As we stepped out onto the top floor, the grandeur of the Royal Suite was even more stunning than I had imagined.

"Wow," I breathed as we unlocked the door and stepped inside. "This is incredible!"

After we settled in, Mom, Annie, the girls, and I were ready for a shopping spree. I glanced at my planner and said, "I'm thinking I could use a new outfit for the big night. Maybe something with lace, since it's colder here than in New Orleans."

The excitement was contagious as we prepared to explore the shops. "Let's find something perfect!" Kaitlin said, her eyes shining.

Meanwhile, Dad, Lucian, and Damien chose a quieter night in. "Let's order some food and catch up on American football," Lucian suggested, and Damien nodded in agreement.

We hit the vibrant streets of New York City, the crisp air and dazzling lights adding to the magic of the moment. As we entered one of the most exclusive shops in the city, the luxury of the place took my breath away.

"I found the perfect dress for you, Nana!" Kaitlin said, holding up a stunning lace gown.

"That's lovely, Kaitlin," Mom said with a smile. "But let's keep looking. We want to make sure it's just right."

Annie and I sifted through racks of elegant clothes, searching for the ideal outfits. "What do you think of this one?" Annie asked, holding up a sleek black dress with shimmering sequins.

"It's beautiful, but I'm leaning towards something with more lace," I said, gesturing to a midnight black gown nearby. "Let's try this one."

After trying on several dresses and accessories, we finally found our perfect ensembles. Mom looked radiant in a flowing emerald gown, while Annie chose a navy dress with a statement necklace and a chic leather jacket.

With our purchases in hand, we headed back to the hotel to show off our new outfits.

"I can't wait to see how you all look," Damien said, his eyes twinkling with anticipation.

"You'll love them!" I said, excitement bubbling over as we entered the room.

When we finally emerged in our dresses, Damien's eyes widened. "Wow, you all look stunning!"

"You too, Damien," I said, playfully adjusting his tie. "Looking sharp!"

Annie twirled in her gown, her fiery hair catching the light. "Thanks, Amy."

Lucian gave Damien a friendly pat. "Looking sharp, buddy."

When Mom and Dad arrived, their elegant appearance made me swell with pride. "You two look amazing," I said.

And as the girls appeared in their cute pink dresses, I gathered them into a hug. "Our two beautiful princesses," I said, smiling at them.

With everyone looking their best, we headed out for the evening, excitement and anticipation filling the air.

The awards ceremony was a glittering affair, with a sense of grandeur that took my breath away. Surrounded by fellow authors and literary enthusiasts, I took a deep breath and prepared for what would be a defining moment in my career.

"And the award for Best Selling Author Worldwide goes to... Amy Johnston!" the announcer's voice echoed through the room, and a roar of applause filled the space.

My heart raced as I walked to the stage, the applause and cheers lifting me on a wave of exhilaration. Standing before the audience, I looked out at the sea of faces and felt a profound sense of gratitude.

"I am truly humbled and honored to receive this award," I said, my voice trembling with emotion. "Writing has always been my passion, and to have my work recognized on this scale is a dream come true."

Memories of late nights spent writing, of the struggles and triumphs, flooded my mind. "To all the aspiring writers out there," I continued, my voice steadying with conviction, "never give up on your dreams. Believe in yourself and your voice, because you never know where it will take you."

With a final thank you, I stepped off the stage, my heart full of joy and anticipation for the future. This was only the beginning of a new chapter in my life, and I couldn't wait to see where the journey would lead. For now, I would savor this moment, knowing that it was a testament to hard work and the support of my incredible family.

As the evening continued, I reveled in the celebration, surrounded by those who had been with me every step of the way. And as I looked around at the glittering ballroom and my loved ones beside me, I knew this was a night I would never forget.

Chapter 41

Morning light seeped through the heavy curtains of our Royal Suite, casting a golden glow over the room. I stretched beneath the silk sheets, savoring the serenity of the moment. My thoughts drifted back to last night's awards ceremony, the thrill of my name being called, the sea of faces applauding my achievement. A smile tugged at my lips, as vivid as the champagne bubbles that had tickled my senses.

Damien stirred beside me, blinking sleep from his eyes. "Good morning," he murmured, his voice a warm rumble in the quiet room.

"Good morning," I replied, leaning over to kiss his cheek. "Last night was incredible, wasn't it?"

"It was." He smiled, brushing his hair off his forehead. "You were amazing up there. I still can't believe you won."

I chuckled, resting my head on the pillow beside him. "I had my doubts at times. The pressure, the expectations... sometimes it felt like it would crush me."

Damien took my hand, giving it a gentle squeeze. "But you did it. And it's not just for you—it's for everyone who believes in the magic of stories."

We lay there in companionable silence until the knock on the door heralded our breakfast. A hotel staff member stepped in, wheeling a silver cart laden with steaming coffee and pastries.

"This looks amazing," I said, my eyes widening at the sight of fresh croissants and perfectly brewed coffee.

Damien poured us both a cup. "Here's to celebrating new beginnings."

As I took my first sip, the rich, bold flavor of the coffee mingled with the buttery flakiness of the croissant, and I sighed in contentment. "You know, I've always loved writing. It's been my escape, my solace. And now, seeing the impact it has—it's surreal."

"You've always had that gift," Damien said softly. "It's about time the world saw it too."

"Thanks," I said, beaming at him. "I've realized that my stories can inspire others, just like mine were inspired by the greats before me. It's my turn to be that beacon."

With the first bite of pastry, I savored the moment of peace before we began our day's adventures. "So, what's on the agenda for today?" I asked, glancing at the clock.

The door to the suite opened, and the rest of the family started trickling in, each face bright with excitement.

"Good morning, everyone!" I greeted them. "Ready to explore the city?"

"Absolutely!" Dad said, adjusting his hat. "This city's got so much to offer."

Lucian pulled out a folded map from his jacket pocket, spreading it across the coffee table. "How about we start at Times Square? We can wander around, see the sights, then hop on the bus to Central Park. After that, we could catch a Broadway show."

"Perfect plan," Annie said, her eyes sparkling. "I've always wanted to ride the subway too."

"Don't forget the ferry to Liberty Island," I said, excitement bubbling. "We have to see the Statue of Liberty up close."

Mom nodded, her camera already in hand. "I'm going to take so many pictures. We'll have memories to last a lifetime."

We made our way out into the bustling streets, each of us marveling at the skyscrapers that seemed to touch the clouds. The city was alive, buzzing with energy from street vendors, yellow cabs, and the murmur of countless conversations.

Our first stop was Times Square. "Look at all the lights!" Kaitlin exclaimed, her eyes wide as she looked up at the massive digital billboards.

"It's like a carnival," Paige said, tugging on my sleeve. "I didn't expect it to be so colorful."

We wandered from one dazzling display to the next, hopping on and off buses to explore different neighborhoods. Central Park was a peaceful contrast to the city's frenetic pace. We wandered by the serene lakes and through the wooded paths, a gentle breeze rustling through the trees.

"I love this place," Lucian said, as we sat on a bench, watching people row boats on the lake. "It's like an oasis in the middle of all the chaos."

"Exactly," I agreed. "It's a perfect blend of nature and urban life."

Our next adventure was the subway. The entrance was marked with an old-fashioned sign that made it seem like a relic from another era.

"This is so exciting!" Annie said, practically bouncing on her toes as we descended into the underground.

The subway was a labyrinth of moving trains and bustling commuters. We rode the train, occasionally catching glimpses of graffiti-arted tunnels and the occasional street musician playing a soulful tune.

Finally, we boarded the ferry to Liberty Island. The Statue of Liberty grew larger as we approached, a silent sentinel against the backdrop of the Manhattan skyline.

"This is amazing," Damien said, his voice filled with awe.

"It really is," I said, looking up at the statue's outstretched torch. "It's like seeing a piece of history come to life."

We posed for photos in front of the statue, the city's skyline shimmering in the background. Laughter and joy filled the air as we captured this perfect moment.

As the sun began to set, we headed back to the hotel, our stomachs growling in anticipation of dinner.

"I'm starving," Lucian said, patting his stomach. "How about we try the restaurant downstairs? I heard it's incredible."

Annie linked her arm through his. "I'm in the mood for some gourmet food. Let's do it."

In the hotel's elegant dining room, the aroma of sizzling steaks and the clink of fine china greeted us. Kaitlin and Paige's eyes widened at the luxurious surroundings.

"It's so fancy," Kaitlin whispered, her gaze wandering over the gleaming chandeliers and velvet chairs.

"Definitely a step up from our usual spots," Paige agreed, grinning as she looked at the menu.

We ordered our meals, the anticipation of a delicious dinner making our mouths water.

"I'll have the filet mignon, medium rare," Damien said, rubbing his hands together.

"Same for me," Lucian added. "Can't resist a good steak."

"And I'll have the salmon," Annie said, her eyes twinkling at the thought of the delicate dish. "And can we get three seafood plates on the side?"

I gave a quick nod. "I'll have the same for Mom and Dad."

As we waited for our food, we relaxed in the plush seats, sharing stories of the day's adventures.

"This day has been incredible," Lucian said, reaching for Annie's hand.

"I couldn't agree more," I said, savoring the warmth of the moment. "It's been everything I hoped for and more."

The waiter returned with our meals, and we dug into the sumptuous dishes, savoring each bite. The meal was a celebration of the day's triumphs and a promise of future adventures.

As the evening wore on, we toasted to the memories we had made and to the many more to come.

"This has been the best day ever," Kaitlin said, her voice filled with excitement as she twirled around in her new dress.

"It really has," Paige agreed. "Thanks, Momma."

With satisfied bellies and happy hearts, we returned to our suite, our arms laden with shopping bags and our spirits high.

As we settled into the luxury of our room, surrounded by the trappings of our successful adventure, I felt a profound gratitude. This was more than just a trip; it was a celebration of dreams realized and new ones forged.

And as I looked around at my family, sharing laughter and stories, I knew that these moments would be the ones we cherished forever. This was just the beginning of a journey that would continue to weave its magic through our lives.

Chapter 42

Six months had drifted by since we returned to New Orleans, and life had settled into a surprising rhythm. Our new normal had woven itself into the vibrant fabric of this city—a tapestry of magic and mystery that somehow felt like home.

One evening, Damien sank into the plush couch beside me, his eyes scanning the cozy living room. "Can you believe how normal things feel now?" he asked, wrapping his hands around a mug of steaming cocoa.

I took a sip of my own cocoa and glanced around at the familiar scene—our living room was warm, lived-in, and full of the gentle hum of everyday life. "Yeah, it's almost like we never left," I said, smiling as Annie snuggled into Lucian's side on the couch.

"It's nice, isn't it?" Annie said, her fingers brushing against Lucian's arm as she flipped through a magazine. "To have a bit of normalcy after everything."

"We've built a life here," I said, my eyes falling on Kaitlin and Paige huddled over their books at the kitchen table. Their soft laughter was a comforting backdrop to the evening's calm.

Damien nodded, his gaze lingering on our daughters. "We've made a home for ourselves, and that's something to be grateful for."

I took a deep breath, the scent of the city—jazz music, spiced food, and an undercurrent of enchantment—saturating the air. "But

I can't shake the feeling that this is just a pause. We have to go back to Tridion eventually."

Annie squeezed my hand, her eyes steady. "Whatever's coming, we'll face it together. That's what families do."

"Exactly," Damien said, giving her a warm smile. "We've faced challenges before, and we're stronger for it."

Lucian, leaning against the bar in the vampire club, looked around at the eclectic crowd—vampires, witches, and fae mingling with humans under the neon lights. "Strange life we lead, huh?" he mused, swirling a glass of bourbon.

Damien chuckled, nodding. "Yeah, but it's our life. And I wouldn't trade it for anything."

The bass of the music thrummed through the floor, and I watched as a group of vampires danced with graceful abandon, their movements fluid and hypnotic. "We've carved out a place for ourselves here," I said, feeling a swell of pride.

"True," Annie said, sliding up beside me as she watched a trio of fae perform a mesmerizing aerial dance. "But I keep having this nagging feeling that something big is coming."

"We'll deal with it when it happens," Lucian said, his gaze thoughtful. "We have to stay alert and be ready for anything."

The days rolled on, and we settled further into our roles in the city. Kaitlin and Paige thrived at their new school, making friends and exploring their surroundings with the same enthusiasm they'd shown for New Orleans' hidden magic. I dove into my writing, crafting new worlds and characters while my books topped the bestseller lists. Annie's freelance articles were in high demand, and she seemed to be everywhere, from local magazines to national publications. Damien and Lucian split their time between selling cars and working as bouncers at the Midnight Veil, a vampire club where the supernatural elite mingled.

One night at the Midnight Veil, I found Damien and Lucian standing by the bar, observing the crowd of supernatural beings moving through the space. The club was alive with an eclectic mix of patrons—vampires, witches, and humans.

Lucian sipped his drink, his eyes scanning the room. "You ever get used to this?"

Damien grinned, leaning against the bar. "Not really. But it's a good life, even with the chaos."

The room pulsed with energy, and I could see fae flirting with vampires, witches casting subtle enchantments, and humans lost in the beat of the music. "It's like a never-ending carnival," I said, admiring the vibrant chaos.

"Yeah, and we're right in the middle of it," Damien said, his eyes reflecting the dance floor's colorful lights. "We're part of the story now."

Months flew by, and our lives continued to intertwine with the city's rhythm. The magic of New Orleans became a familiar comfort. Every corner of the city held memories—both recent and from our past adventures.

One evening, Kaitlin gazed out at the bustling streets from our balcony, a look of awe on her face. "Can you believe how much we've become a part of this city?"

"It does feel like home," Paige said, her eyes sparkling as she watched street performers entertain a crowd below

I stood beside them, feeling a swell of gratitude. "It's been quite the journey to get here."

But amid the sense of belonging, a shadow of unease lingered. "I can't shake the feeling that something big is coming," I said, breaking the silence as we stood on the balcony, the city's lights twinkling around us.

Annie reached for my hand, her grip steady. "Whatever it is, we'll face it together. That's what families do."

"Agreed," Damien said, squeezing my hand in return. "We've proven time and time again that we're stronger together."

Kaitlin and Paige exchanged worried looks. "I don't want to leave," Kaitlin said quietly, her voice tinged with sadness.

"Me neither," Paige added, her lower lip quivering slightly.

Annie pulled them into a comforting hug. "I know, sweethearts. But whatever we decide, we'll do it as a family."

I took a deep breath, my heart heavy with the weight of the decision we faced. "We are in this together," I said, my voice resolute. "We'll face whatever comes as one."

Lucian nodded, his face serious. "We have responsibilities in Tridion, but we've built something here too. It's a tough choice."

As the days passed, we weighed our options. We consulted with our allies—both human and supernatural—seeking wisdom and insight. Each conversation, each decision, brought us closer to understanding our path forward.

Finally, the day came for us to make our choice. We gathered around the kitchen table, the weight of our decision hanging in the air.

"We've decided," Damien said, his voice steady. "We need to return to Tridion. Our true destiny awaits there."

With a mix of anticipation and apprehension, we began preparing for our journey back. The farewell was bittersweet, filled with memories of our time in New Orleans. The city had been a refuge, a place where we had found peace and adventure.

As we left the familiar streets of New Orleans behind, I looked at my family, each face marked by hope and determination.

"This isn't the end," I said, my voice filled with resolve. "It's just the beginning of the next chapter of our story."

Together, we stepped into the unknown, ready to face the challenges and embrace the destiny that awaited us in Tridion. The road ahead was uncertain, but we were united, and that was our greatest strength.

Chapter 43

We'd barely stepped off the portal and onto the cracked streets of Tridion when the weight of our mission settled over us like a heavy fog. The city was scarred from the battles we'd missed, but there was also a flicker of hope in the rubble—the chance to rebuild and protect what we had left.

"Mom, why do we have to go back to Tridion?" Kaitlin's voice was soft, almost lost amidst the sounds of distant clashes and the murmur of the city reclaiming itself. Her eyes searched mine, trying to understand the gravity of our return.

"It's hard to explain, sweetheart," I said, crouching beside her as the cool evening air mingled with the scents of old magic and fresh earth. "There's something dangerous that's resurfaced, something from our past that threatens everyone here."

"What kind of danger?" Paige's curiosity was a gentle prod, her eyes wide as she clutched her sister's hand.

"It's an ancient threat," Damien said, stepping closer with a grave expression. "Something we thought we'd dealt with long ago. But it's back, and we can't ignore it any longer."

Annie nodded, her face set in a serious line. "We need to protect Tridion and our people. It's a responsibility we can't escape."

Lucian placed a reassuring hand on Annie's shoulder. "We face this challenge as a family," he said firmly. "And we'll stand together until it's resolved."

I looked at each of them—my family, my heart—and felt a surge of pride. "You're right," I said, my voice steady. "We can't turn our backs on Tridion. We have to fight for it."

Our decision was made. We would fight whatever shadows loomed over our homeland, united and resolute.

The days after our return were a whirlwind of activity. The city was in disrepair, the aftermath of battles and dark forces leaving their mark. But we found hope in the familiar faces of friends and allies. The echoes of our past deeds were bittersweet, reminders of what we had lost but also of what we had to fight for.

Damien stood before the gathered citizens, his crown glinting faintly in the torchlight. "It's time for me to step up as King and protector of Tridion," he said, his voice carrying the weight of responsibility. "We need to prepare for the battles ahead and show our enemies that we're not to be trifled with."

Annie squeezed my hand and smiled. "See? You're already thinking like a king."

Damien grinned back at her, a glint of determination in his eyes. "Lucian, we'll need you and Gregory to start training the soldiers. We need to see who's ready to fight and who has the makings of a dragon rider."

Lucian nodded, a fierce resolve in his eyes. "We'll start right away. We need to get everyone battle-ready."

I stepped forward, Fire's scales shimmering in the dim light. "I can help with the dragon-riding lessons. Fire and I can work with the new recruits and give them a taste of what they'll face."

Lucian and Damien exchanged a glance, then nodded. "Your skills will be invaluable," Lucian said, acknowledging my expertise.

The people watched as Lucian and Gregory began training the soldiers. I stood beside Fire, running a hand over her sleek back. She had chosen me, recognizing both my strength and my spirit.

Over the next few days, Annie and I worked with the women and children, teaching them basic combat skills and sharing what we knew. It was important that everyone could defend themselves, not just prepare for battle but also stand strong in the face of danger.

Dragons emerged from their hiding places, their majestic forms stirring awe among the citizens. I selected a few promising women—Trina, Hardy, Evelyn, Grace, and Tish—hoping they would prove themselves worthy of becoming dragon riders. The dragons chose their riders, each bond forged through trust and courage.

Training was intense, a mix of grueling exercises and strategic planning. We practiced swordplay, perfected our riding skills, and prepared for the challenges that lay ahead.

In the quiet moments between training sessions, we gathered in the study, surrounded by ancient tomes and scrolls that whispered of old secrets.

"It's a being of pure malevolence," Lucian said one evening, his eyes scanning the pages of a dusty book. "An ancient evil that's returned to enslave our world."

Annie leaned over another book, her eyes focused. "According to this, it was banished by our ancestors, but it's come back stronger and more determined."

"The necromancer," I said, a chill running down my spine. "This is the darkness we must confront."

Mayson, who had been quiet until now, met my gaze with grim determination. "We can't let this evil consume Tridion. We have to stop it."

I nodded, feeling the weight of our task. "We need to gather our allies, fortify our defenses, and prepare for battle. This fight is just beginning, but we will face it together."

Lucian's eyes were sharp as he outlined our next steps. "We'll need reinforcements from the neighboring kingdoms and to strengthen our magical defenses."

Annie's mind was already racing ahead. "We should also explore our magical reserves and see what other advantages we can uncover."

Our days were filled with intense training and strategic planning. We spoke with werewolves, Fae, and the coven, rallying them to our cause. The weight of our responsibilities was heavy, but our resolve was unwavering.

"We have our allies," I said, gathering everyone for a meeting. "The werewolves, the Fae, the coven, and the people of Tridion. With their help, and with our training and dragons, we have the strength to face this threat."

"We'll also need to work on our strategies for the battles to come," Lucian said, looking at each of us. "And make sure our defenses are as strong as possible."

Annie nodded, her mind already racing with plans. "We'll need every advantage we can get. We're facing an enemy unlike any we've encountered before."

The days blended into nights as we prepared for the conflict ahead. Our training sessions became more rigorous, our strategies more refined. The sense of urgency was palpable, but so was the hope that we could make a difference.

"The fate of Tridion, and maybe the entire world, is in our hands," I said one evening, as we reviewed our plans.

Damien, Lucian, Annie, and Mayson nodded in agreement. We had a long road ahead, but we were ready to face it together.

Our bonds were our greatest strength, and with each passing day, we prepared ourselves for the battle to come. We were determined to protect our world, to fight against the darkness that threatened to engulf everything we held dear.

Whatever came next, we would meet it with courage and unity, ready to defend Tridion and carve out our future in the heart of the storm.

Chapter 44

The campfire crackled in the still night air, casting a warm, flickering light on the faces gathered around it. I could see the weariness in my friends' eyes, but there was a determination that shone through, as bright as the flames.

"Beyond just numbers, the diversity among our allies gives us an advantage," Lucian said, his gaze sweeping over the group. He motioned to the mages chatting in low tones, the warriors sharpening their blades, and the archers testing their arrows under the moonlight. "We've got mages, warriors, and even a handful of skilled archers. Together, we've got all our bases covered."

Gregory, hunched over a map that was spread out on the ground, looked up with a serious expression. "Let's not forget the strategists," he said, tapping a finger on the map where X's and O's marked our plans. "Our tactical planning is just as crucial as the battle itself. We need to be smart about this."

Lucian nodded, his eyes reflecting the firelight. "Exactly. We've got the skill and the strategy to outthink even the most cunning adversary."

A comfortable silence settled over us as we sat around the fire. It was a brief respite from the looming threat, a moment to gather strength for the battles to come.

Grayson's eyes were sharp as he spoke, breaking the silence. "We can't afford to let our guard down," he said, his tone firm. "We need to stay vigilant. Every detail counts if we're going to win this."

Annie's voice cut through the night's quiet, carrying an edge of urgency. "The Necromancer isn't going to make this easy," she said, her fingers tapping rhythmically on the armrest of her chair. "We have to be ready for the worst."

Her words were a stark reminder of what lay ahead. I felt a chill run through me, but it was tempered by a growing sense of hope. With our allies at our side, I believed we could face whatever came our way.

"We're ready," Damien said, standing up and extending his hand to me. His eyes burned with the same fierce determination I saw in the others. "Let's show the Necromancer what we're made of."

We all stood, the firelight casting long shadows as we prepared for the final stretch of our journey. The fortress loomed ahead, a dark silhouette against the twilight sky.

Annie stepped forward, her voice strong and commanding. "We stand as one," she declared, her gaze sweeping over our group. "We fight together, and we fight to win."

Her words resonated with all of us, a rallying cry that forged a bond stronger than steel. We mounted our dragons, the familiar weight of our gear and the power of our beasts bolstering our resolve.

As we flew towards the fortress, I took a deep breath and shouted instructions over the roar of the wind and the clash of battle below. "Stay sharp! Watch for the dark energy blasts and stick to the plan!"

The battlefield below was a chaotic dance of steel and spell. Swords clashed, spells exploded, and the ground shook under the weight of our struggle. Through the chaos, Christian stood out, his dragon circling above as he prepared to face the Necromancer.

"This ends now!" Christian's voice rang out, cutting through the din of battle as he faced the dark figure before him.

The Necromancer's laughter was a chilling echo. "You dare challenge me?" he sneered, his staff glowing with dark energy. "You think you can defeat me?"

Christian met his gaze with unyielding resolve. "We may not be invincible, but we are united. That's our strength."

With a roar, Christian's dragon dove from the sky, unleashing a torrent of flames that surged towards the Necromancer. The battle raged on around us, and with every strike, with every spell cast, we pushed closer to victory.

When the dust finally settled, we stood among the remains of the fight, exhaustion and relief mingling in the cool evening air. I glanced around, looking for Damien. "Where were you, Damien? We needed you out there."

He approached with a smirk that didn't quite reach his eyes. "Sorry, I...got a bit sidetracked. I was going to join the fight, but things seemed under control." He looked around, his smile widening slightly. "But hey, you guys did great! Only lost a few soldiers—fortunately, none of our close friends. And it looks like you took care of the Necromancer. A win-win, I'd say."

I studied him, trying to decipher the glint in his eyes. "You were afraid, weren't you?" I asked quietly, my voice tinged with hurt.

Damien shrugged, his grin faltering for a moment. "Maybe a little. But you know how it is. Sometimes the fear gets to you."

I wanted to press further, but I knew Damien better than that. He had always been the bravest among us, even if he had his moments of doubt. I took a deep breath and pushed my unsettling thoughts aside.

"We did it," I said, trying to focus on the victory we had achieved. "We beat the Necromancer."

One of the dragon riders, his face smeared with dirt and blood, nodded in agreement. "We fought as one," he said, his voice full of pride and fatigue. "We couldn't have done it without each other."

I looked at my friends, my family. The bonds we'd forged through the trials of this battle were unbreakable. "Yes," I said, my voice steady despite the weariness. "We did it together. And that's what makes us strong."

We gathered around the remains of the battlefield, the shadows of the past battles giving way to a new dawn. The weight of our victory settled on us, mingled with the knowledge that there was still much to do.

As we prepared to leave the fortress behind, I knew that the challenges of the future awaited us. But for now, we had achieved something monumental. And with our allies, our dragons, and our unity, we were ready to face whatever came next.

"The fate of Tridion—and perhaps the entire world—rests in our hands," I said, looking out at the horizon where the first light of dawn began to break through the darkness.

Damien, Lucian, Annie, and Mayson stood beside me, their faces set with resolve. We had faced the darkness and emerged victorious, but the journey was far from over.

Together, we would meet the future head-on, ready to defend our world and continue our fight against the shadows that sought to consume it.

We had won this battle, but the war was far from over.

Chapter 45

"Are you sure you're up for this trip?" Damien's voice was laced with concern as he watched me fold the last of the clothes into our travel bags. His eyes flickered over me, catching the faint lines of exhaustion on my face.

I looked up from the suitcase and forced a bright smile. "I'll be fine. We all need a break from everything—just a change of scenery, you know?"

He didn't look convinced, his brow furrowing as he lightly touched my shoulder. "Promise me you'll take care of yourself?"

"I promise," I said, squeezing his hand with what I hoped was enough sincerity. "And you should take care of yourself too. We all need this."

He nodded slowly, though his eyes remained troubled. "Alright. Just... be safe."

With that, we headed out to the car. The city of Tridion, with its hum of mystical energies and hidden dangers, faded behind us as we drove toward New Orleans. Despite the scenic route and the kids' excited chatter about seeing Grandma and Grandpa, a knot of anxiety twisted in my stomach.

"Mommy, are we going to see Daddy later?" Kaitlyn asked from the back seat, her small voice filled with both curiosity and concern.

I glanced at her in the rearview mirror, trying to sound as calm as possible. "No, sweetheart. Daddy's staying behind to sort some things out. Uncle Lucian and Uncle Gregory will be there if he needs anything."

"Okay," Kaitlyn said, though she still looked a little worried. Paige, sitting next to her, was already absorbed in her favorite book, so she didn't seem too bothered.

By the time we arrived in New Orleans, the comfort of familiar faces and the warmth of home began to ease my worries. We settled into the house, and I tried to focus on something positive.

As I unloaded the last of the bags, Annie joined me, her eyes studying my face. "You've been quiet today," she said, her voice gentle.

"I'm just worried about Damien," I admitted, sitting down on the edge of the bed. "Mom and Dad keep saying to trust him and that everyone deals with grief differently. But I can't shake this feeling that something is off."

Annie sat beside me, her gaze steady and full of understanding. "It's natural to doubt when things are uncertain. But remember, Damien has always been your rock. You believe in him for a reason."

"I know," I said, letting out a heavy sigh. "But what if I've been blind to things I didn't want to see?"

Annie took my hand in hers. "You're not alone in this. Lucian and the pack trust him too. We're all in this together."

I gave a small nod, though my anxiety didn't completely fade. "I think I'll catch up with my agent while we're here. They want me to work on a follow-up to my first book. Maybe a change of pace will help."

Annie smiled. "That sounds like a good distraction. Just be careful not to let slip too much about the supernatural world. We don't need any more trouble."

I chuckled, though the nervous edge was still there. "Yeah, wouldn't want to end up on any vampire hit lists."

A few days in New Orleans did manage to help me unwind a bit. I wrote diligently and enjoyed the time with my parents. But as we prepared to return to Tridion, the unease that had been simmering underneath my calm exterior resurfaced.

When we stepped back through the portal to Tridion, the atmosphere was thick with tension, a stark contrast to the easygoing days we'd just had.

"Lucian, what's going on?" I demanded, my heart racing. "Where's Damien?"

Lucian's face was somber, his eyes reflecting the seriousness of the situation. "It's Damien," he said, his voice strained. "He's vanished."

The word "vanished" hit me like a physical blow. My stomach churned with a mix of fear and anger. "Do you think the Necromancer has him?" I asked, trying to keep my voice steady. "Maybe he's been kidnapped, or worse, under the Necromancer's influence?"

Trinity stepped forward, her eyes filled with tears. "It's possible. We must find him before it's too late."

"Then let's not waste time," I said, steeling myself. "We need a plan. We need to find Damien and figure out what's happened to him."

Annie flipped through her spell book, searching for a locator spell. "Let's see if we can track him down. We have to be prepared for anything."

As she chanted the incantation, the shadows around us seemed to pulse with a dark energy. A figure emerged from the darkness, their eyes gleaming with malevolence.

"Damien?" I stammered, my heart pounding.

The figure laughed, a cruel sound that echoed off the walls. "You fools," they said. "I've been serving the Necromancer all along."

I could barely process the betrayal. The man I loved was revealed as a pawn in the Necromancer's game. Tears stung my eyes as I tried to hold onto my resolve.

"What do I tell our children about this?" I choked out, my voice breaking.

The figure sneered. "Tell them whatever you like. I can't father children. I'm a vampire. The half-witch facade was just a spell from the Necromancer.

And then, with a flicker, he vanished, leaving us in stunned silence.

"I can't believe it," Lucian murmured, the disbelief evident in his voice. "Damien was one of us. How could he have done this?"

Trinity shook her head, her face a mask of grief. "We can't dwell on it now. We have to focus on the Necromancer."

"But who else might be working for him?" Annie's voice trembled with the weight of uncertainty.

"We can't let fear divide us," I said, taking a deep breath. "We have to trust in each other. We'll face this together."

Trinity gave a firm nod. "We have to stay vigilant. Trust our instincts and each other."

With renewed determination, we set out to confront the Necromancer. We navigated through the dense forest until we reached the entrance to his lair, the air around us thick with dark magic.

"Proceed with caution," Trinity whispered, her voice a mere breath against the oppressive silence. "The Necromancer won't be easy to defeat."

As we moved through the corridors of the lair, eerie whispers echoed off the stone walls.

"Welcome," a voice hissed, sending a chill down my spine. "I've been expecting you."

We turned the corner to find the Necromancer standing before us, his eyes blazing with a sinister fire.

"So, you've come to stop me?" he sneered. "How amusing. You thought you had defeated me before. But I had Damien deceive you all."

Nancy stepped forward, her stance resolute. "We are not here for your amusement," she said, her voice steady. "We are here to end your reign of terror."

The Necromancer laughed, a sound devoid of warmth. "You think you can defeat me? You are nothing but insects."

Nancy didn't flinch. "We may be small, but together we are strong. And we will stop you."

The Necromancer's laughter died away as he summoned dark energy to his staff. "We'll see about that," he said, his voice dripping with malice.

The battle erupted in a fury of spells and swordplay, the clash of steel and magic filling the corridors. Despite my exhaustion, a fierce determination fueled my movements. We couldn't let the Necromancer's darkness win.

The fight was intense, the Necromancer's power seemingly endless. But then, a glimmer of hope emerged—a vulnerability in his defenses.

"Now's our chance!" Gwen shouted, her voice ringing with conviction.

With renewed strength, we pressed our attack. Each spell and strike seemed to bring us closer to victory.

Finally, with a final, desperate blow, the Necromancer fell, his dark power crumbling into dust. Relief washed over me as the oppressive weight of his presence lifted.

"We did it," Annie said, awe in her voice. "We actually did it."

I nodded, my heart swelling with a mix of pride and grief. "Yes. We did it. Together."

Damien's betrayal still stung, but we had to move forward. As we faced the aftermath of our battle, the questions of Damien's true nature and our future loomed large.

"What now?" Lucian asked, his voice filled with weariness.

I took a deep breath, my mind racing through the possibilities. "We have to stay strong. We can't let the darkness win. We'll face whatever comes next, together."

As we prepared to leave the lair, the weight of our mission's success mingled with the sorrow of what we had lost. We ventured out into the world, determined to rebuild and to confront the challenges ahead. Each step was a testament to our resolve, our unity, and our hope for a brighter future.

Chapter 46

The questions gnawed at me, relentless and unforgiving. I paced the room, frustration and confusion clawing at my insides. "Was it truly Damien who did all this?" I muttered, my voice wavering as if hoping to find answers in the empty air.

Annie looked up from her spot by the window, her eyes troubled. "I don't know, Amy, but we can't ignore any possibilities. We have to look at everything."

"Maybe it wasn't him at all," I suggested, my hands clasped together as if that might stop them from trembling. "What if there's something—or someone—behind him, pulling the strings?"

Grayson rolled his eyes, clearly skeptical. "Come on, Amy. Damien's always been a bit of an oddball, but to say he's under some dark enchantment? That's a stretch."

I let out a heavy sigh, staring at the crackling fire in the hearth. "I don't even know what to believe anymore. We were blind to the danger right in front of us."

"And now we're paying the price," Lily said quietly, her gaze fixed on the flames as though they might offer some comfort.

Grayson's fists clenched at his sides. "We should've seen it coming. We let ourselves be deceived by his lies."

I closed my eyes, trying to shove away the guilt. "How could I have been so naive?" I whispered, my voice barely more than a breath.

Annie's voice was soft, but firm. "We all wanted to believe in him. Now we have to face the truth, no matter how much it hurts."

The weight of our realization pressed down on me. Damien had betrayed us, and I couldn't shake the feeling that things would never be the same. The betrayal wasn't just personal—it was a threat to everything we held dear.

I cleared my throat, trying to focus. "I've called you all together because the questions I have are too heavy for me to bear alone. I think you might have your own questions too."

The room was silent for a moment. Lucian broke the quiet with a steady voice. "We need to look at all angles, but jumping to conclusions could be dangerous."

I nodded, feeling a pang of gratitude for his level-headedness. "True, but we can't ignore the possibility of external forces. What if there's another necromancer, or something worse? Damien might have cheated death before, but maybe he's just a pawn in a bigger scheme."

Gwen looked worried. "Regardless of what's happening, we need to act fast. Damien's actions have put us all at risk."

"And what about Damien himself?" Mayson asked, his face etched with concern. "Is there any chance of saving him, or is he lost to us?"

The question hung heavy in the room, a reminder of how much was at stake. We all knew that darker days were coming, and finding Damien was just the start.

"I still can't believe Damien would betray us like this," I said, the words almost a plea. "We've known him for centuries. Could he really have had an evil twin hiding in the shadows? Or maybe Vivien, in her grief, twisted into something dark and took his place?"

Gwen shook her head, her voice cautious. "It's an interesting idea, but it seems far-fetched. We have to consider it, though."

Lucian nodded, though his brow was furrowed. "We should be careful not to let our imaginations run wild. We need evidence, not theories."

Nancy agreed. "We need to find more clues before we make any decisions. There might be something we've missed."

The idea that we were missing something crucial gnawed at me. Whether Damien was truly the villain or there was a more sinister force at work, one thing was clear: our world was on the brink of chaos.

Lucian's eyes met mine, and he spoke slowly. "Amy, what if Vivien's envy of Damien is the key? She might have wanted to take his place, manipulate the ogres, and deceive us all."

The thought hit me like a jolt. "But how could I not see it? Even when we were close, I couldn't see through her disguise. Did she steal Damien's memories, leaving him trapped somewhere, lost and forgotten?"

Lucian's gaze softened with sympathy. "It's possible. Vivien is powerful, and if she wanted to deceive us, she could have done it with magic we don't fully understand."

Gregory stepped forward, his tone resolute. "Then we need to act fast. If Vivien is pretending to be Damien, we have to stop her before she can cause more damage."

Lucian nodded gravely. "Damien had secrets, dark ones that even you didn't know, Amy. He was more vampire than we ever let on, hiding his true nature from all of us."

My heart sank as the truth of his words settled in. "So you knew all along? You let us believe he was one of us while hiding the darkness within him. Did you ever think about the consequences of your silence?"

Gregory's eyes held a mixture of sorrow and regret. "We did what we thought was best. Revealing Damien's nature would have caused more harm than good, but now I see that our silence only made things worse."

"I get why you did it," I said, trying to keep my voice steady. "But we have to face the truth now. We can't move forward until we do."

The room was heavy with unspoken regrets and hopes. We knew the path ahead was fraught with danger, but it was the only way forward.

Annie and I exchanged a look. "We need to go back to New Orleans," I said, determination sharpening my voice. "We have to talk to our parents about what's happened."

Annie nodded, her face set with resolve. "Let's get back and figure this out."

With a wave of Annie's hand, we stepped through the portal, emerging on the doorstep of our childhood home. My parents were waiting, their faces reflecting both worry and anticipation.

"Welcome home, my darlings," Mom said, her voice warm but laced with concern. "We've been expecting you."

Tears welled up in my eyes as they hugged us, their comfort a temporary balm for my aching heart. In their embrace, I felt a momentary relief from the weight of our troubles.

Dad's brow was furrowed. "Didn't the others from the coven come with you?"

"No," I said, my voice thick with emotion. "I asked them to stay and help Gregory with the archives."

The gravity of the situation was apparent in their expressions. They ushered us inside, guiding us to a quiet place where we could talk without prying eyes.

Annie looked at me, wide-eyed. "How do our parents always know what's happening before we even tell them?"

I managed a weak smile. "They're Elders. They have knowledge and intuition that's beyond us."

Annie chuckled softly, a brief moment of levity. "It's a little spooky, but kind of amazing too."

Mom began preparing lunch and brewing coffee. Meanwhile, the girls settled in front of the TV, finding a brief escape from our harsh reality in a Netflix show.

Dad watched them, his worry evident. "That should keep them busy for a while," he murmured, his eyes betraying the anxiety he felt for us.

As we sat around the table, the weight of our mission pressed on us. The danger we faced was immense, and Damien's betrayal had shattered our world.

Mom broke the silence, her voice steady and strong. "We mustn't underestimate the danger ahead. We need to stay united to protect ourselves and the coven."

I nodded, feeling the weight of our responsibility. "We'll face this together," I said, determination lining my voice.

Mom's eyes shone with a mix of hope and resolve. "I know someone who might help us. An Oracle with great knowledge."

The mention of the Oracle sparked a flicker of hope in me. Seeking her wisdom might be our only chance.

"Do you think she'll agree to help us?" Annie asked, her voice a blend of hope and hesitation.

Mom smiled reassuringly. "I believe she will. She understands the gravity of our situation."

With that hope guiding us, we prepared to meet the Oracle. As Mom chanted the incantation, the room filled with a shimmering light, and Gilda appeared.

Gilda was a vision of ethereal grace, her presence both commanding and comforting. Her silver hair and piercing blue eyes seemed to hold the wisdom of ages.

"Michelle," she said with a warm smile. "You still radiate the same strength and light."

Mom returned the smile. "And you, Gilda, always have a way of making an entrance."

Gilda's eyes turned to us. "And you must be Amy and Annie. You look so much like your mother."

Her gaze was kind but intense, her presence a beacon of hope. "The answers we seek are hidden in our history," she advised. "We must search through the archives for clues and remember that courage and unity will see us through."

Her words resonated deeply. We knew our path forward would be fraught with challenges, but Gilda's wisdom offered a glimmer of hope.

"Thank you, Gilda," I said, gratitude filling my voice. "We'll follow your advice."

With a final, reassuring nod, Gilda vanished, leaving us with a renewed sense of purpose.

As we poured over the archives, we uncovered forgotten knowledge and ancient spells. During our research, inspiration struck. "We can call upon the dragons," I said, a spark of excitement in my eyes. "Their power

might be the key to finding Damien and restoring balance."

Annie's eyes lit up. "That's brilliant! They have been guardians of our realm for centuries. Their aid could be crucial."

With this new hope guiding us, we prepared to seek out the dragons. The weight of our mission was heavy, but the prospect of hope and the wisdom of the Oracle were our guiding lights in the darkness.

Chapter 47

The journey to find the dragons took us through ancient forests and across forgotten lands. The path was treacherous, filled with obstacles that tested our resolve and strength.

Each step brought us closer to our goal, and with every challenge we overcame, we grew more determined. The dragons' lairs were hidden away in places both beautiful and dangerous, and we had to navigate through trials that tested our courage and unity.

Finally, we arrived at the entrance to the dragons' domain. It was a magnificent cavern, filled with glistening crystals and an aura of ancient magic.

As we stepped into the cavern, the air was charged with energy. The dragons emerged from the shadows, their majestic forms a testament to the power and beauty of their kind.

One dragon, larger than the rest, approached us. His scales gleamed like molten gold, and his eyes held a depth of ancient wisdom.

"Welcome, seekers of truth," he said, his voice a deep rumble that reverberated through the cavern. "I am Pyros, the Elder Dragon."

I stepped forward, trying to steady my nerves. "Great Pyros, we come to seek your aid. Our world is in peril, and we need your wisdom and strength to restore balance."

Pyros's eyes studied us with a keen interest. "I have heard of your trials and your quest. Why should we aid you, and what do you offer in return?"

I took a deep breath, knowing that our plea was urgent. "We offer our loyalty and our commitment to protect the realms we inhabit. We seek only to restore what was lost and to prevent further darkness from spreading."

Pyros regarded us with a thoughtful gaze. "Very well. If you are to receive our aid, you must first prove your worth through a test of courage and unity. Only those who can stand together against great adversity will be deemed worthy."

With that, Pyros led us to a great arena within the cavern. The test was grueling, challenging us physically, mentally, and emotionally. We faced trials that tested our strength, courage, and loyalty to one another.

Through the challenges, we supported each other, overcoming the obstacles that came our way. Our unity and determination shone through, proving our worth to the dragons.

At the end of the trials, Pyros approached us with a solemn nod. "You have proven yourselves worthy. We will aid you in your quest. But remember, the path you walk is fraught with danger, and you must face it with strength and resolve."

We bowed deeply in gratitude. "Thank you, Great Pyros. We will not fail."

With the dragons' support, we began our preparations for the battle ahead. We knew the road was long and the challenges were great, but with the dragons at our side, we had hope.

Our next step was clear: we had to find Damien and confront him. The knowledge we had gained and the strength we had gathered would guide us in our quest...

As we set out on our journey, the weight of our mission pressed on us, but we faced it with a newfound determination. Together, we would confront the darkness and strive to restore the balance that had been lost.

The path ahead was uncertain, but with hope and courage, we were ready to face whatever challenges lay in our way.

"Where the heck did they summon that kind of power from? Who are these people?" Gregory exclaimed, frustration evident in his voice.

"Honestly, I'm starting to think Damien might be the necromancer," I replied, feeling the weight of my words.

"Damn it, Amy, do you think so? It makes sense. Damien used weird magic when we thought he was just half witch, half vampire. He could have been playing us all this time, acting innocent when he might be the necromancer," Lucian added, his tone a mix of disbelief and realization.

A sense of shock rippled through the group as we exchanged glances. "That could be it, the bloody bastard. Son of a gun," Annie muttered in agreement.

I felt tainted and betrayed by the person who was supposed to share their life with me and our children. Was this indeed how it was all meant to conclude? We managed to reach the age of twenty-six this time, but I doubt I will see my next birthday next Friday.

"This lifetime has been the most fulfilling one I can remember among all the others we've lived through. It cannot simply end like this. I am an author, and a damn good one at that. I have two daughters and an incredible family, both blood-related and chosen. I refuse to let history repeat itself with another death. Not with the understanding I now hold," I declared, my voice unwavering.

"The audacity of Damien, playing his twisted games for centuries, likely orchestrating my demise at the age of twenty-three, along with everyone else following the same grim pattern every twenty-three years. Does he think he can subject me to that fate again? Not a chance. This time, I'll be the one to end him. He underestimates who he's dealing with now. I am Amy Johnston, the mighty witch and leader of the New Orleans coven. That's my claim, and I won't yield an inch," I finished, a wicked grin creeping across my face, leaving those around me to wonder what thoughts lurked behind it.

"Care to share, sis?" Annie finally ventured, curiosity evident in her tone.

I burst into laughter. "I was just quietly contemplating Damien's audacity to believe he can bring about our downfall again, especially now that we have this incredible life. As the supreme witch of our New Orleans coven, he won't prevail in this battle. I'll be the one to end him," I declared, frustration seeping into my words.

"He's pushed it too far this time. He won't be the end of us," Christian said from the back, his voice unwavering.

We decided this would mark the final confrontation with Damien and his minions. Now, it was time to devise Plan C. We settled on returning to New Orleans, where Damien and his cohorts could only cross with our knowledge. Our next step is to seek more information from the oracle, Gilda.

Upon our return to New Orleans, my mom effortlessly summoned her friend with a snap of her fingers, showcasing the immense power of the Elders. Gilda scrutinized us all with a curious gaze. "What happened? Did you not emerge victorious?" she inquired.

"No, Damien had minions—Ogres and bloodthirsty vampires. And something else, something incredibly potent," I replied. "We even suspected he might be the necromancer. What are your thoughts, Gilda?"

The shock mirrored on my parents' faces matched Gilda's astonishment. "No way," my mom interjected. "Why do you believe that, Amy?"

"The powers he wielded. None of our attacks affected him, not even the dragons' might. They vanished without a scratch. That's the only explanation. We desperately need a Plan C—I have to end him. He won't claim my life or the coven's. We never know when it's our last, and I refuse to find out. Please, Gilda, lend us your aid. What do you truly know about Damien that you haven't shared before?" I implored.

My mom's suspicion was palpable. "Could they be right about Damien, Gilda?" she questioned.

Gilda appeared just as taken aback. "I believe your daughter may be onto something. Given Amy's supremacy, I sensed a greater power earlier but attributed it to the coven. However, it could indeed be the necromancer. Give me a few days, and I'll return with a spell to obliterate him for eternity. No return, no minions."

With that promise, she vanished in a flash of light. "Can we trust Gilda, Mom?" Annie voiced her concern.

"Something is unsettling about her," my mom mused. "Could she be in league with Damien? And if so, now he'll be aware of our suspicions."

"So let's all come to a consensus: Gilda can't be trusted," I asserted. "We'll have to devise our spell. Perhaps we can lure them here to New Orleans, in our territory, to bind them."

"Alternatively, we could summon them to Tridion, the old house, and seal them in for eternity. That would serve as punishment enough," Annie suggested with amusement.

"Sounds like a plan, but then we'd need to summon Zakariya and the other fallen angels to keep watch over them to maintain balance," I added.

"All your plans sound solid, though they might need some refinement. Let's brainstorm together and decide on a few options. If one fails, we move to the next. I lean more towards the last one,

Amy, but we can't trust Zakariya either. What if he sets them free in exchange for his freedom?" Mom raised a valid concern.

After a few hours of brainstorming, we settled on my final plan: summoning Zakariya and the other fallen angels. However, we recognized the need for a robust spell that could not be overpowered or refused. Thus, we concluded that we needed two summoning spells: one for Damien and his minions and another for Zachariah and the fallen angels. We had our work cut out for us. But first, we needed to rest. It was well past midnight, and exhaustion hung heavy after the day's excitement.

"Alright, let's call it a night," Mom tiredly suggested, rubbing her eyes. "We'll reconvene tomorrow morning with fresh minds and renewed energy."

"Agreed," I replied, stifling a yawn. "We've made progress today but still have a long way to go."

As we prepared to retire for the night, Annie said, "Despite the setbacks, I feel good about our plan. Damien won't see this coming."

"We just need to keep it under wraps," Gregory added. "We can't afford any leaks."

With nods of agreement, we dispersed to our respective chambers, each carrying a sense of determination and purpose. Damien may think he's outsmarted us, but our cunning surpasses his. We might have the advantage this time.

The pack gathered downstairs, their presence a comforting reassurance of strength and unity. Meanwhile, the coven and elders delved into their research upstairs, determined to craft the spells that would shape the fate of our confrontation with Damien and Zachariah.

"Having the packs with us gives us a significant advantage," Lucian remarked, echoing through the room. "Their strength and loyalty will bolster our efforts."

"I agree," Mom added. "But let's remember the importance of our dragons. They've been invaluable allies in our past battles."

With a nod of agreement, we settled into our tasks, the weight of responsibility heavy upon our shoulders. We knew the spells we crafted would be crucial in tipping the scales in our favor.

After a restful night's sleep, we reconvened the following day, refreshed and determined to make progress. As we gathered around the table, plates of breakfast before us, excitement and anticipation filled the air.

"I think I've found the perfect spell," I announced, drawing everyone's attention. With eager eyes, they leaned in, ready to hear the details of our next move.

"The incantation was discovered in the forbidden spell book," I continued, my voice steady despite the gravity of our discovery. "Its warnings are ominously written in red, but I believe it holds the key to our success."

As I recited the incantation, a solemn hush fell over the room. Each word carried the weight of our impending confrontation with Damien and his minions. The air seemed to hum with anticipation, charged with the spell's energy.

As the final words echoed through the room, a sense of expectancy hung in the air, mingled with a tinge of apprehension. We knew we had set a chain of events to lead to the ultimate confrontation.

"I've found a spell to shield our minds," Annie announced eagerly, breaking the tense silence. "Are you ready to have your minds blown?"

Her words sparked a ripple of curiosity and excitement among us. We eagerly awaited her revelation, knowing that it would be a crucial defense against the formidable foes we were about to face.

Annie's voice resonated with power as she chanted the protective spell, weaving a barrier of magic around us with each repetition of the chant.

"Now we just need to find our final spell for Zachariah and the fallen angels," Mom declared, her tone brimming with determination.

After a brief search, Mom's excitement bubbled over. "Found one! Are you all ready to hear it? Don't worry; it won't summon them until we're ready. But listen closely as I've added my unique twists."

With anticipation thick in the air, Mom began to chant the spell:

I couldn't help but acknowledge my mom's multitude of talents. "Well done, Mom. That's the perfect spell," I praised. "I aspire to be as skilled as you one day," I insisted earnestly.

"We forgot about Gilda," Annie panicked.

"Don't worry about her. The spell you cast protects us. She can't interfere or break it without us knowing," Mom reassured, exhaling with relief.

Finally, we gathered all the necessary ingredients for the spells and planned to perform the chants on Saturday during the full moon, just in case we needed the pack in their fierce, hungry wolf forms. It would add a classic touch to the occasion.

I stared at the chaos before us, trying to make sense of the situation. Gregory's frustration was evident as he paced back and forth, his hands clenched into fists.

“Where the heck did they summon that kind of power from? Who are these people?” he demanded, his voice rough with anger.

I took a deep breath, fighting to keep my own emotions in check. “Honestly, I'm starting to think Damien might be the necromancer,” I said, feeling the weight of my realization.

Lucian's eyes widened, the gears turning in his head. "Damn it, Amy, do you really think so? It makes sense. Damien's been messing with dark magic for ages. We thought he was just some half-witch, half-vampire freak, but he could've been hiding his true nature all this time."

Annie nodded slowly, her face twisted in a mix of anger and sadness. "That bastard. He's been toying with us. It's like he's playing a twisted game where the stakes are our lives."

A bitter laugh escaped me. "Yeah, it feels like he's been orchestrating this entire mess, all to end our lives every twenty-three years. He's not just a petty villain; he's a mastermind of darkness. But I refuse to let him have another victory."

I looked around at my friends, my family. "This lifetime has been the most fulfilling one I can remember. I'm a successful author, I have two amazing daughters, and a family that's fought by my side. I won't let Damien drag us into the same tragic end. I won't be a victim of history's cruel joke."

Annie's eyes met mine, full of concern. "What are you planning, Amy?"

I grinned, a hint of madness in my smile. "I'm planning to make sure Damien faces justice. He's underestimated us, thinking he could break us like he's done in the past. But this time, we're going to end him. I'm Amy Johnston, the supreme witch of the New Orleans coven, and I'm not backing down."

Christian stepped forward, his expression resolute. "He's gone too far. We're not going to let him win."

With our minds made up, we started formulating a Plan C. The answer lay in returning to New Orleans, where Damien and his minions had no idea what awaited them. Our next move was to seek out Gilda, the Oracle, for guidance.

Back in New Orleans, we gathered in the familiar surroundings of the coven's old meeting room. My mom raised her hand and snapped her fingers, summoning Gilda with effortless power. The Oracle appeared in a swirl of shimmering light, her eyes sharp and inquisitive.

"What happened? Did you not emerge victorious?" Gilda asked, her gaze sweeping over us.

I met her eyes, steeling myself. "No. Damien had an army of ogres and bloodthirsty vampires at his command, and something even more dangerous. We suspect he might be the necromancer."

Gilda's eyes widened slightly. "The necromancer? You're serious?"

Mom's frown deepened. "Amy, why do you believe Damien is the necromancer?"

"The powers he wielded were unlike anything we've faced before. We threw everything we had at him, including the dragons, and still, he remained untouched. There's only one explanation for that kind of power," I said, frustration creeping into my tone. "We need a new plan, one that will finally put an end to him. Can you help us, Gilda?"

Mom's gaze was intense. "Gilda, do you think Damien really is the necromancer?"

Gilda took a deep breath, her eyes serious. "You might be onto something, Amy. I sensed a dark, overwhelming power, but I attributed it to your coven's strength. It could indeed be the necromancer. I'll need a few days to find a spell that will destroy him for good."

With a flash of light, Gilda vanished, leaving us in a tense silence.

"Can we trust Gilda, Mom?" Annie asked, her voice barely above a whisper.

Mom bit her lip. "There's something about her that doesn't sit right with me. If she's in league with Damien, she'll know we suspect her."

I took a deep breath, trying to push away my doubts. "For now, we have to assume that Gilda will do her part. But we also need a backup plan. We can't rely on anyone but ourselves. We need to come up with a strategy to draw Damien and his minions into our territory. Maybe we can use Tridion for that."

Annie's eyes lit up with a hint of mischief. "Or we could summon them to Tridion and trap them there for good. It would be a fitting punishment."

I nodded. "That's a solid idea, but we'd need to summon Zakariya and the other fallen angels to keep watch over them. We'd need strong spells to ensure they can't escape or be freed."

Mom raised an eyebrow. "We have to be careful with Zakariya. What if he betrays us for his freedom?"

"We need to prepare two spells then," I said firmly. "One for Damien and his minions, and another to bind Zakariya and the fallen angels. We've got a lot of work ahead of us, but first, we need to rest."

Mom rubbed her eyes, looking exhausted. "Let's call it a night. We'll regroup tomorrow with fresh minds."

"Agreed," I said, stifling a yawn. "We've made good progress, but there's still a lot to do."

As we headed to our rooms, Annie's voice carried a note of optimism. "Despite the setbacks, I feel good about our plan. Damien won't see this coming."

Gregory nodded, a determined glint in his eyes. "Let's keep this under wraps. We can't afford any leaks."

The pack gathered downstairs, their presence a solid anchor of strength. Meanwhile, the coven and elders took to their research upstairs, diving into the spells that would shape our confrontation with Damien.

The next morning, after a restful sleep, we gathered around the table for breakfast, a renewed sense of purpose in the air.

"I think I've found the perfect spell," I announced, a sense of excitement in my voice.

Everyone leaned in, eager for details. "It's from a forbidden spell book," I explained. "The warnings are written in red, but I believe it's exactly what we need."

As I recited the incantation, the room fell silent, each of us feeling the weight of the upcoming battle. The spell's energy seemed to pulse through the room, thick with anticipation.

When I finished, Annie broke the silence. "I've found a spell to shield our minds from Damien's influence. Ready to be amazed?"

Her enthusiasm was contagious. We watched as she chanted the spell, weaving a protective barrier around us.

Mom's eyes sparkled with renewed excitement. "I've found a spell for summoning Zakariya and the fallen angels. It won't activate until we're ready, but it's got my unique touches."

With bated breath, we listened as Mom recited the spell, her voice steady and powerful.

"Nice work, Mom. I hope to be as skilled as you one day," I said, genuinely impressed.

Annie's eyes widened. "We forgot about Gilda."

Mom waved off the concern. "The spells you've cast will keep us safe from her. She won't be able to interfere.

We gathered the ingredients for the spells and planned to perform them on Saturday during the full moon. The pack would be at their strongest then, ready to fight alongside us if needed.

"Having the packs with us will be a big advantage," Lucian said, his voice filled with determination. "Their strength and loyalty will bolster our efforts."

Mom nodded. "Let's not forget the dragons. They've been crucial in our battles before."

With that, we settled into our tasks, knowing the spells we crafted would decide the fate of our fight against Damien and Zakariya.

Saturday night arrived, we gathered under the full moon, the air charged with the weight of our task. We were ready.

"I'm ready to begin the spells," I said, taking a deep breath.

Annie and Mom exchanged a look, and then Mom began the chant for Zakariya and the fallen angels, her voice carrying the weight of the magic we needed.

As the last words of the incantation faded into the night, we felt a surge of hope. We had done everything we could to prepare for the final battle.

With the full moon overhead and the pack at our side, we stood united, ready to face whatever came next. Damien might have thought he had outsmarted us, but we had a plan and the resolve to see it through.

Our future was uncertain, but with determination in our hearts, we were ready to fight for our world and for each other.

The stage was set. The final battle awaited us, and we were prepared to meet it head-on. The spells were cast, the plans made, and the resolve was unbreakable.

We just had to see it through.

Chapter 48

As I settled into a moment of respite amidst the chaos of our preparations, a nagging weight bore down on me, urging me to seek solace in rest and contemplation. It had been a tumultuous journey marked by fleeting triumphs and profound losses. Damien's betrayal, in particular, had left me grappling with a profound sense of betrayal and disbelief, a wound that festered unhealed within me.

As I allowed my thoughts to drift back, a troubling pattern emerged, hinting at a recurring theme in my tumultuous existence. Damien's deceit had been a constant, a specter haunting my path in every iteration of my life. Despite the clarity of my memories upon each awakening, I had failed to pre-empt his betrayal, and the consequences had always been dire.

Could my awareness of his betrayal have been my undoing in past lives? Had my pursuit of truth and justice repeatedly led me to my demise? The thought gnawed at my conscience, stirring a mix of frustration and determination within me.

But this time would be different. Armed with the knowledge of my past and a newfound resolve, I was determined to unravel the mysteries that had eluded me for so long. This was my moment to confront the uncomfortable truths that lurked beneath the surface, to forge a path forward unburdened by the shadows of the past.

"I need you right beside me, Annie," I implored, my voice tinged with urgency as I turned to my twin. "Keep watch over me, ready to pull me back if things get too intense."

Annie's response was immediate, her commitment unwavering. "You got it, Amy," she affirmed, her eyes reflecting the moment's gravity. "I'll be right here every step of the way. We're in this together."

Her words were a lifeline, a reminder of our unbreakable bond. "Thank you, Annie," I expressed, my voice soft with gratitude. Having you by my side means everything to me."

"That's what sisters are for, silly. Now, try to get some rest, and I'll watch you closely. Would you like me to perform a little spell? It won't bring back all your memories at once, but it'll help them come back as you're ready," Annie offered, her voice soothing with sisterly concern.

"Yes, please. That would be appreciated. Thank you, sis," I replied, grateful for her support.

"You're welcome. Let me grab the grimoire, and I'll cast a spell for you," Annie responded, moving to retrieve the ancient book of spells.

Annie fetched the grimoire and began to chant the spell, her words weaving a sense of tranquillity around me as I settled into a peaceful slumber, ready to embrace whatever memories awaited.

And so, I drifted into a deep slumber, my mind open to the whispers of the past, eager to uncover the truths hidden within my memories of lives long past, including the reasons behind Damien's betrayal.

As the memories trickled in, a vivid picture emerged: Damien and I, once a content family with our two daughters, were disrupted by the arrival of his sinister allies. They plotted my demise, hoping it would cement Damien's grip on both worlds—Tridion and Earth. But I uncovered his treachery, nearly ending him in the process. My strike narrowly missed his heart; instead, I held oak wood, a weapon foreign to vampire slaying. It was an unprecedented challenge.

"It's staggering to realize that someone orchestrated this, deliberately obstructing my memories, including the crucial moments when I uncovered Damien's true identity as the necromancer... and the involvement of the oracle, Gilda... of course," I murmured; the pieces of the puzzle slowly falling into place.

Annie, who had been watching me, leaned in with concern. "What is it, Amy? Are you remembering something important?" she asked, her voice filled with curiosity and worry.

I can't help but wonder how long she served Damien and how deep this betrayal runs. It's unsettling to think that my parents trusted her; she was their friend, a longstanding member of our coven for centuries. Yet all this time, her loyalties lay with Damien, not us. If we rid ourselves of her influence, it could bring my mother some peace.

In the following memories, the horror intensified as Damien attacked me relentlessly. He struck me, pierced my heart with a sword, poisoned me, threw me off a mountain, humiliated me, and tore me apart. With each assault, I felt the pain, the betrayal, the tears streaming down my face. The rage surged within me once I discovered his true nature and the atrocities he had committed.

It was as though I was trapped in a never-ending nightmare, forced to relive each moment in agonizing detail. The constant threat of danger loomed over me, leaving me perpetually vulnerable. It seemed as though I was trapped in a nightmare, forced to endure each agonizing moment repeatedly. Perpetually at risk, our love was forbidden, like a dagger through the heart; each betrayal cut me to the core. He continually transgressed against me, treating me as nothing but a servant. I once believed our fates intertwined in the celestial tapestry, yet reality revealed a harsh truth: we were adversaries. Exploiting my powers for his selfish ends, he betrayed me, ultimately orchestrating my demise at the hands of witch hunters, condemning me to the flames.

As I emerged from the depths of my memories, a familiar yet altered face greeted me, its features casting a spell of puzzlement over my senses. His touch was gentle against my cheek, a silent reassurance in the darkness of my room. Who was he? Though his face carried a semblance of recognition, time had woven unfamiliar threads into its fabric. I knew this visage, its contours etched in the recesses of my mind: blue eyes, dark hair cascading like shadows, a sturdy frame. Was he a wolf, an alpha perhaps? No, he was Liam, Lucian and Gregory's cousin. But did I know him from another time? Suddenly, I jolted awake, startled by the abrupt return to reality. Annie stood before me, her expression a mixture of concern and disbelief.

"Are you alright, Amy? I've been trying to pull you out of your memories for the past hour," she asked, her voice laced with worry.

Looking around, I noticed Lucian, Gregory, and Liam standing behind her, their faces mirroring her concern.

"She's awake," Lucian called out, beckoning my mother over.

"Are you alright?" Mom's voice quivered with concern, her eyes betraying the fear she felt for me.

Tears streamed down my face as Mom and Annie enveloped me in their comforting embrace.

"It's alright. You're here now, safe. He can't harm you anymore," Mom reassured me softly, soothing my troubled soul.

In the background, the low growls of the wolves echoed in the room.

I locked eyes with Liam, sensing the depth of emotion in his gaze as he peered into the recesses of my soul. Our gazes collided, and in that moment, it felt as though I was truly seeing him for the very first time.

"It's you?" I questioned, a mix of curiosity and disbelief coloring my voice.

"Yes, it's me," he responded with his gentle smile, a beacon of warmth amongst the shadows.

My mother and Annie exchanged perplexed glances, their brows furrowing in confusion, while Lucian and Gregory maintained their composure, seemingly unsurprised by my revelation. Their calm demeanor only fueled my growing frustration. How could they keep such a significant truth from me?

"Why didn't you inform me about Liam?" I questioned, my voice laced with a mixture of confusion and irritation.

Lucian stepped forward, his expression earnest. "Liam insisted that we allow you to discover the truth in your own time," he explained, his tone measured.

I struggled to process his words. "While I was entangled in Damien's web of deception, I harbored feelings for Liam without even realizing it?" I mused aloud, the pieces of the puzzle slowly falling into place. "It's all so convoluted. I need your help to unravel this," I implored, my voice tinged with desperation as I sought clarity amidst the chaos of my emotions.

"I understand," I replied, though the weight of Liam's revelations left me reeling. "But why keep it all hidden from me? Why let me suffer through Damien's deceit?"

Liam's gaze softened with empathy. "It had to unfold this way," he explained solemnly. "You needed to confront Damien's malevolence firsthand, to see through his facade. Our memories from our past lives remained intact, as we never truly died. However, we are bound by the laws of the coven, forbidden from direct interference."

His words struck a chord, mingling with a sense of resignation. "So, everything was orchestrated to maintain balance?"

Liam nodded. "Yes. Certain memories were selectively erased to allow events to unfold naturally, for you to uncover the truth and determine your path. Lucian and Gregory knew my connection to you, but the same constraints bound them."

A surge of emotion welled within me as I grappled with the enormity of his words. "And our children?" I questioned, my voice trembling with emotion.

Liam's expression softened, reflecting the pain we both shared. "Even my memories of them were destined to be erased," he admitted, his voice heavy with sorrow.

The revelation left me staggering, grasping for solid ground amidst a whirlwind of emotions. Liam's bombshell about being the father of Kaitlin and Paige felt like a punch to the gut, shattering the fragile semblance of stability I had clung to.

"You? The father of Kaitlin and Paige?" Disbelief tinged my words, echoing the chaos in my mind. "I barely remember anything about you, Liam. How could you drop this bombshell on me now?"

Liam's frustration mirrored my own, evident in his brow furrow. "Amy, I'm still grappling with the idea of being a father myself, and—" He hesitated, his words trailing off.

"My husband? This feels like a cruel joke," I scoffed, my voice laced with bitterness. "What else have you all been hiding from me?"

Sensing the tension, my mom and Annie discreetly withdrew, leaving Liam and me alone in the silence. He reached for my arm, his touch gentle yet laden with significance. But I recoiled instinctively, a reflex honed by years of betrayal.

"I need some space, Liam. Time to process all of this," I muttered, shooting him a glare.

"Of course, I understand," he replied with unexpected calmness.

"Thank you. Right now, I can't afford distractions. We have to focus on gearing up for the fight with Damien," I asserted, my tone sharper than intended. "This revelation only complicates things further."

"Agreed. Let's keep it under wraps for now and concentrate on the task at hand," Liam suggested, his voice tinged with regret.

"Perfect," I retorted with unintended sarcasm, immediately regretting my harshness. "Listen, I'm sorry for my tone. I'm just reeling from all of this. I thought I had a life with Damien, and he tore that away from me. You've appeared out of nowhere, and I can't ignore my feelings. And please, let's hold off on telling Kaitlin and Paige. Let's figure things out before involving our kids."

The atmosphere grew heavy with unresolved tension as Liam, Lucian, and Gregory silently exited the room, leaving me with conflicting emotions.

"Amy, you need to sit down and talk with him. I didn't raise you to be so stubborn and unkind," Mom admonished, her tone firm yet laced with concern. "Consider how you treated Liam just now. Remember, he's also in the dark about you and the kids. Pushing him away isn't fair. You both need to communicate and figure out where you stand. But Amy, you can't keep him from his daughters either." Mom's frustration was evident, but her advice was sound.

I understood that my mom was speaking the truth, but it was overwhelming.

"I promise I'll talk to him, Mom, but there's another issue. Gilda has been collaborating with Damien all this time," I revealed, my voice tinged with apprehension.

Mom's expression turned to one of disbelief. "It can't be. Are you sure?"

"Yes, Mom. One of the visions hit me like a punch to the gut. And considering all the ways Damien tried to get rid of me and the cruelty he inflicted upon me, it's clear. I know Liam isn't Damien, but I must address this betrayal first and seek vengeance. Right now, all I feel is anger," I confessed, my voice heavy with emotion.

"Take a moment to step back and breathe. That's a lot of painful information to process, especially about Gilda. I'm genuinely shocked. She's been our friend for centuries. How long has she been working with Damien?" Mom asked, her concern evident.

"Since the beginning of time," I admitted solemnly.

It was undoubtedly a rough day for all of us. However, returning to my bed and city brought inner comfort. After Mom left the room to prepare supper, Annie and I were alone.

"Honestly, I think we need a treat. What do you think?" Annie suggested a mischievous glint in her eyes.

"I think that's a fantastic idea. What do you have in mind?" I asked, intrigued by her proposal.

"What about a girls' night? The guys can stay home and look after everyone," Annie proposed.

"A girls' night? That sounds amazing. We haven't had one in ages. Are you talking about a slumber party?" I inquired, a smile tugging at the corners of my lips.

"No, I mean going to a club, having drinks, dancing... Just letting go of everything for one night," Annie clarified, her eyes sparkling excitedly.

"That sounds like a fantastic idea. Let's go see what the other girls are up to and tell them to get ready for the adventure of their lives," I exclaimed eagerly, already picturing the fun night ahead.

Chapter 49

I needed to escape from the hustle and bustle to spend time with my girlfriends. These past few days have been hell, and dealing with the situation with Liam will have to wait. I don't have the time for that right now.

Bourbon Street was pulsating with music, laughter, and dancing. We were primed for a fantastic evening away. Dressed to the nines, we joined the crowd, mirroring their dance moves.

"This was a brilliant idea, Annie. Amy needed to get out of the house after everything. A night on the town," Gwen commented politely.

"Yes, the guys promised not to follow us. I told them we could handle ourselves. Lucian didn't seem thrilled about being left with Liam, sulking a bit. But they need to step up for the battle. We need this. It's a way to recharge," Annie replied, her voice barely audible over the music.

I found myself drinking far too much just to stay steady on my feet, but I managed, tossing back one tequila shot after another.

As I watched my girlfriends dancing, some guys suddenly appeared out of nowhere, getting far too touchy. Gwen and Nancy stepped aside while Arielle and Gabriella pushed them away, even throwing some punches. I couldn't control myself; I leaped off the bar stool and joined the fray, swinging but missing one guy by an inch.

"Let's kick their asses!" Meghan exclaimed. "If they want to start something, we'll finish it here and now."

As people stopped what they were doing and watched us in awe, they probably wondered how we thought we could take on those massive guys. We had no idea if they had their powers, but we weren't about to reveal ours to them or anyone in the crowd. We relied on our fists and words and literally kicked our way out the door. Our strength was palpable, more than we realized, even without magic.

We felt brave, untouchable. But before I could land another punch, someone grabbed my arm and pulled me in. Damien... The breath was knocked out of me. I was outnumbered. The coven recognized my danger and knew they had to intervene.

"Hey, I'm not here to cause trouble. Just wanted to get out for a bit, let loose, have a few drinks with my fellow vampires," Damien said, trying to ease the tension.

I locked eyes with him, my gaze burning with fury as if I could eradicate him with a look.

Surrounded by bloodthirsty vampires, all intent on draining the life out of us, we found ourselves utterly unprepared. Panic surged through us. We needed a plan, fast.

"We have to get out of here!" Gwen yelled.

"We're surrounded!" Annie exclaimed, her voice trembling with fear.

"What should we do, Amy?" Nancy cried out, desperation lacing her words.

Then, I remembered the gift I shared with Christian. I reached out to him with focused intensity.

"Christian, we're in danger. Surrounded by vampires, Damien, and his crew," I urgently transmitted.

His response was swift. "We're almost there. Hang on."

With a quick wink at the girls, I unleashed fiery energy towards our assailants. It was a signal. The girls knew the guys were on their way.

The next moment, Liam, Lucian, Gregory, Christian, Grayson, Milo, Mason, Dylan, and Richard appeared determinedly, pulling us away from the danger.

"How did you know?" I questioned Liam, feeling his protective embrace around me.

"I just did. I sensed it," he replied, keeping me close to his chest. "I knew exactly where you ladies were. I felt your presence. And Christian's urgent message confirmed it. We have a connection, Amy. I feel what you feel. I see what you see, especially when I focus on you. I can read you."

"But you're an alpha. Doesn't that connection only apply to your pack?" I inquired.

"I'll explain later. For now, let's deal with these bloodsuckers," Liam said, unveiling a few weapons. We began eliminating the vampires individually, although Damien and a few others managed to escape. After clearing the area, we hastily departed before humans could realize what had occurred.

"How did Damien know we were here?" Annie asked.

"He probably followed you. That's why I didn't want you girls going out alone," Lucian responded, his voice tinged with concern.

"But you arrived so quickly to our rescue. Come on, spill the beans, Liam. How did you know we were in danger?" I pressed for answers.

"Alright, here's the thing," Liam began. "As I mentioned, I feel you and see what you see. It's because we're intertwined, destined. Our souls are connected. We're not separate entities."

"Okay, what does that mean?" I inquired, trying to grasp the concept.

"After our earlier discussion, I delved into the mystery of us. Why, I only had a few memories of you. Then it hit me. I've been journaling for years, documenting our connection to each other, our love," Liam explained.

"So, are you saying we're connected in every possible way? You're my other half?" I asked, seeking clarification.

"Yes, exactly. Just like Annie is Lucian's other half," Liam affirmed.

"But how did you know we were in trouble so quickly? Come on, Liam, spill the beans," I pressed him for answers.

"Alright, here's the deal," Liam began. "Like I said, I feel and see what you see. It's because we're intertwined, destined. Our souls are connected. We're not separate beings."

"Okay, but what does that mean?" I probed further, trying to wrap my head around it.

"After our earlier conversation, I started digging into the mystery of us. Why did I only have fragments of memories of you? Then it dawned on me. I've been keeping journals for years, documenting our connection, our love," Liam explained.

"So, you're saying we're connected in every possible way? You're my other half?" I sought clarification.

"Yes, exactly. Just like Annie is Lucian's other half," Liam confirmed.

"Wow, that was something," Liam said, his cheeks flushed crimson as he gazed deeply into my eyes.

"Yes, a kiss between soulmates," I replied, giving him a playful wink.

"So, does this mean you're accepting and dealing with everything?" he inquired.

"Yes, but I'm taking it slow. One step at a time," I assured him with a smile.

He took my hand, our fingers intertwining. At that moment, I felt an overwhelming sense of safety. With him by my side, I knew I was protected and that no one could ever hurt me again. I could draw strength and energy from him; he was my soulmate, the one I was destined to be with. It was time to accept it and move forward.

Does this mean you're ready to meet your daughters properly? I asked, a smile spreading across my face.

"If you're sure you're ready for all of this, then yes, please," Liam replied, his face lighting up joyfully.

Once we arrived home, the moment was upon us. As soon as we stepped through the door, Mom and Dad panicked.

"Are you girls alright? Did Damien and his crew harm you?" Dad fretted.

"We're fine, Dad, I promise. We took care of a few of them, and thankfully, Liam was there to rescue me," I reassured him with a smile. "So we're good. Where are the girls?"

"They're upstairs, why?" Mom inquired.

"It's time for them to know who their dad is," I declared.

"Wow, that's progress and quick. Are you sure about this?" Mom asked, her concern etched on her face.

"Yes, tonight Liam showed me just how connected we are. I never felt anything like this with Damien. Kaitlin and Paige need to know their dad," I affirmed.

"I'll go get them," Annie insisted.

"Thanks, sis," I said gratefully.

"Are you ready to be introduced as their Daddy?" Annie asked Liam.

"As ready as I'll ever be, although I'm feeling nervous, as I was called Uncle Liam about two hours ago," he admitted with a smile.

"I assure you, everything will be fine. They've been through a lot, and they deserve to know their father, especially after what their so-called father put us through with his lies. They're old enough to understand and soon see the connection. Trust me, they'll welcome you with open arms," I promised.

Liam chuckled, "Just like you welcomed me when you first found out, huh?"

"I'm sorry for being so harsh, Liam. But I'm confident the girls will handle it better," I smiled.

Annie and the girls had just come downstairs a few minutes ago. They smiled at Liam, instantly showing their love. Rushing to him, Kaitlin and Paige both leaped into his arms, and he was strong enough to hold them both at once.

"See, I told you," I said.

Liam's face lit up with joy and love for his daughters. The twins seemed to peer into his soul, recognizing the goodness within his heart.

"Daddy," they both exclaimed simultaneously, knowing the truth.

A surge of happiness and tears overwhelmed me. We were becoming a family once more. Adjusting to Liam would take some time, but I hoped it would be quick.

He smiled as if he had heard my thoughts and replied, speaking through his mind, "You'll get used to it in no time, I promise."

Chapter 50

"We spent a few days together as a family, just the four of us, which was a bit of an adjustment, but I have to admit, I had a great time. We explored the vibrant streets of New Orleans before Liam suggested a trip to Disney Land in Orlando. Despite having some ongoing planning for the upcoming battle, Mom and the coven assured us they had everything in hand, with Lucian and Gregory in agreement. We were only away for five days. Upon returning to New Orleans, we planned to head back to Tridion to spend time with our dragons and strengthen our bond. I missed my dragon, eager to reunite with her again."

Annie assisted me in packing both the twins' necessities and my clothes, while Liam tended to matters outside with the pack and the girls. Meanwhile, Lucian took charge of grilling for my parents as a token of appreciation for all their support—a truly touching gesture.

"Are you feeling excited?" Annie suddenly broke the silence as we organized our belongings.

"Excited isn't quite the word. Nervous probably sums up how I'm feeling right now," I confessed, my expression betraying my unease.

Observing my every movement as I nervously played with my hair, Annie tilted her head to the side.

"You realize you're not sharing a bed with him now. He can't rush you or pressure you into anything you're uncomfortable with.

Despite being an Alpha, Lucian assured us his cousin is a true gentleman," she remarked with a sly smile.

I returned her smile with a hint of mockery. "I know he seems like a gentleman, but then again, so did Damien. I went there, comparing Liam to Damien, which I know is unfair. But I can't shake this feeling. I don't know how to move forward with Liam; he feels like a stranger. He's attractive and charming, but I can't recall truly being with him. It all feels so awkward. I know I should give him a chance, but honestly, Annie, it's tough."

A knock on the door interrupted our conversation; it was Mom.

"I came to offer my assistance and couldn't help but overhear your concerns, Amy. Remember, no one can compel you to do anything against your will. I understand that was your unfortunate experience with Damien. But Liam seems genuinely kind and deeply cares for you and the girls. You can sense it, feel it in his presence. I never felt that connection with Damien, which should have raised red flags for me. I've always been perceptive of people's intentions. He deceived us, too, and your dad and I feel immense guilt for not intervening. We knew vampires couldn't be trusted, and we all made that mistake."

"Mom, it's nobody's fault. We all placed our trust in Damien. But honestly, as far as I'm concerned, he's history. I want to leave him behind, and once we deal with him, he'll be gone for good, never able to harm any of us again. I get that vibe from Liam, too. His aura radiates positivity, nothing destructive unless it's for self-defence. I felt it the other evening when he came to my rescue. And the fact that we can communicate through our minds adds an extra layer of connection. We don't always need words, which is cool, considering I only share that with Christian and Annie. So that makes me trust him more. But seeing him as more than a husband figure, a lover, and everything beyond that will take time. And there's no guarantee I'll feel like he does."

Mom reached out and grasped my hand firmly. "You're powerful, Amy, and your dad and I are so proud of you. You've grown with each phase of your life, overcoming numerous obstacles. Damien won't be your last challenge; there will be more, but you'll overcome them all. You're the ultimate witch—never forget that."

"Thank you, Mom. That means a lot to me."

"Hey, Mom, I'm almost done packing. Just a few more things for me and the twins," I called out from my room.

Mom poked her head through the doorway, a warm smile on her face. "Great, sweetie. Once you're finished, come downstairs so we can all eat together."

I grinned back, already feeling the excitement bubbling inside me. "Absolutely, can't wait. This trip to Disneyland will be amazing—I can already picture the twins' faces when we arrive."

As I zipped up the last suitcase, my friend Annie appeared, her eyes sparkling with mischief. "Amy, listen to me. You're a strong witch and an even stronger mother. You and Liam are meant to be together, trust me. Keep that heart open, and share your thoughts and feelings with him. He's probably already tuned into your wavelength anyway."

Her words hit me like a bolt of lightning, stirring up emotions. "Annie, I... I understand. Maybe I've been a bit stubborn. I'll embrace whatever destiny has in store for me. I won't let my insecurities get in the way of my happiness. I'll open up to Liam and make sure he knows where he stands with me. I'll start now. Are you happy?"

Annie grinned, giving me a playful nudge. "Ecstatic, Amy. Now let's go make some memories at Disneyland."

"Yes, very. I want to see you happy, sis. You deserve it. And Liam will give you that and much more if you catch my drift," Annie winked, and I understood exactly what she meant. But I knew I wasn't ready to give myself to him entirely; it would have to wait.

After finally finishing our packing, we made our way downstairs. This was it—the night before our family trip. It felt strange to leave everyone behind and not return to Tridion to practice how we would take out Damien and his minions. I longed to hunt down more vampires.

"Finally, you girls decided to come down and have some food. Amy, you do know you're only going away for five days. Did you pack some sexy lingerie for Liam to admire you in?" Lucian teased.

I blushed furiously, feeling my face turn as red as a tomato. "Lucian, I did no such thing."

Annie's expression turned angry at Lucian's comment. "Lucian, that was very inappropriate. You know Amy isn't ready to get intimate with Liam yet. Liam, no offense, but I'm sure you understand?"

Liam stood there, utterly taken aback. This conversation hadn't unfolded the way he had imagined. He could see my embarrassment, and this time, it was his cousin who had caused it. "Lucian, please stop picking on Amy. When she's ready, I'll know, and right now, she's far from ready even to stand two inches close to me. Cut her some slack, please."

"I'm sorry, Amy. I didn't mean it; it was just a joke," Lucian said unapologetically.

Annie scoffed at Lucian and delivered a punch to his gut. "You seriously need to think before you speak, my love. Stop embarrassing my sister."

"I'm sorry. It won't happen again. I'm sorry, Amy. I'm sorry, Liam," Lucian said sincerely.

We gathered around the table for dinner, the entire family relishing a tranquil meal together. With the calm, the girls, fueled by the anticipation of the trip, dashed back and forth along the hallway, unable to contain their excitement. I never inquired, but they inherited their father's wolfish energy. It explained a lot. As a witch, one often finds oneself drained by the constant exertion of powers, even unknowingly.

Given the day's excitement, it seemed wise to promptly prepare the girls for bed to ensure an early start tomorrow. Exhaustion was creeping over me as well. Before the trip, I had intended to draft a few more chapters for my book, yet I still needed more energy to make much progress. After confronting Damien, inspiration will reignite within me, allowing me to resume writing and bring our lives back into alignment.

"Alright, everyone, I'm heading to bed. I'm wiped out, especially with our early flight tomorrow. Girls, come on, let's say goodnight to everyone so we can get some rest," I announced, feeling the weight of exhaustion settle in.

"Can I handle bedtime tonight and read them a story?" Liam offered.

"That would be wonderful. I'd love to soak in a hot bath before turning in," I replied.

"Come on, girls, let's bid goodnight to Grandma and Grandpa. Mommy will help tuck you in," Liam said, ushering them toward their grandparents.

Watching Liam effortlessly connect with the girls, I couldn't help but think that Mom was right—he was a natural.

After ensuring the girls were snug in bed and ready for a bedtime tale, I bid them all goodnight and indulged in a soothing soak before retiring.

"Sweet dreams, Kaitlin, sweet dreams, Paige, sweet dreams, Liam. Mommy will wake you up in the morning," I whispered, receiving enthusiastic bear hugs from Kaitlin and Paige.

"Goodnight, Mom," they chorused.

"Sleep tight, Amy," Liam added.

Turning on my heel, I returned to my room, where Annie was patiently perched on my bed.

"And now?" I inquired, sinking onto the mattress beside her.

"So, any feelings for Liam yet?" Annie probed as if I was expected to have developed some sentiment. Had I overlooked something that Annie had picked up on?

"What do you mean?" I asked, puzzled.

"I sensed some tension between you two while putting the girls to bed," she clarified.

"Tension? You've got quite the imagination, sis. It's just exhaustion," I dismissed.

"Maybe, but you two seem to be hitting it off," Annie persisted.

"I'm not sure I see what you do, and frankly, I don't have the time to dwell on it right now. I need some time, Annie. I need to unwind with a bath and get some rest. It's late," I explained, feeling the weight of fatigue settling in.

Annie glanced at her watch, revealing it was only six in the evening.

"You look exhausted, sis. Alright, I'll let you get to your bath and sleep. Goodnight, see you in the morning."

"Goodnight, sis. Sleep tight."

Chapter 51

The morning had arrived, signaling the need to rouse me, prepare the girls, and head to the airport. A half-hour flight awaited us, a manageable journey that promised a semblance of normalcy.

After dressing and taking my luggage downstairs, I was surprised to find the girls awake and dressed.

"Good morning, Mommy!" they chimed from the kitchen table. Liam sat beside them, and Mom was busy preparing an irresistible breakfast. I found myself ravenous once more.

"Good morning! What a surprise to see you all up and ready before me," I greeted, pleasantly taken aback.

"We couldn't sleep, mommy. We went to your room to check if you were awake but fast asleep. So, we came to the kitchen, and Daddy was here with Grandma, preparing breakfast," they explained.

"The excitement must have woken you both up early. Did you sleep okay?" I inquired of Kaitlin and Paige.

"Yes, mommy, we slept like babies. But we were too excited," they replied.

"We should finish up. Lucian and Annie said we're leaving at six am. Are you ready for our holiday, girls?" Liam asked.

"Yes, Daddy, we are," they chorused.

As the girls finished breakfast, I sipped my coffee while Liam joined me.

"Did you sleep alright?" he asked, sounding slightly suspicious.

"I think so, why?" I queried.

"Just... I woke up feeling like you were in my head," he admitted.

"What? In your head, how?" I asked, puzzled.

"I'm not sure. You were talking to me, but I knew you were asleep, so I blocked it out. If you don't remember, it probably wasn't important," he shrugged.

"Yeah, sorry, I don't recall," I replied.

"No worries. Are you ready for the trip? Are you taking your laptop to do some writing while we're away?" he inquired.

"Yes, I've got it. I must pour my feelings into my book to prepare for this battle. I can't sit with unresolved emotions when we face him," I explained.

"I understand," Liam nodded.

Annie and Lucian descended from their room.

"Morning, are you guys ready?" Annie asked.

I looked at them and nodded. "Yes, we are."

Lucian and Liam loaded our bags into the car, bid farewell to my parents, and set off for the airport.

Upon arrival, Annie and Lucian treated us to coffee before our flight. A strange sensation lingered within me—why was I in Liam's head without realizing it? It was a new experience altogether.

Sensing something amiss, Annie leaned in when we were alone at the table. "Where's your head at?" she asked, concern evident.

"Honestly, I'm not sure. Liam asked me why I was in his head this morning, and I couldn't even recall being aware of doing that," I admitted, my confusion evident.

"What do you mean, 'in his head'?" Annie inquired.

"I mean, like, drifting away and talking to him?" I attempted to explain.

"Not sure. It seems like I might have entered his subconscious, as he seemed a bit confused," I concluded.

"See, you have a strong connection with Liam; I told you so," Annie remarked.

"Yes, I know that Annie, but it's not making things easier. I'll have to channel all these emotions into my book. Just imagine what an incredible story I'll be able to write," I mused.

"Very true, with a lot of lust and lovemaking." Annie giggled.

I couldn't help but blush at that accusation.

"I can't even get close to him without blushing; it's awkward. And then I find myself in his mind while I'm sleeping. I need to get control of myself. I can't keep doing this."

"You might like him, like really like him... if you get my drift," Annie laughed, clearly amused.

"This isn't funny, Annie. It's a big problem. How can I be attracted to Liam already?" I expressed, feeling frustrated.

Before I could finish my sentence, Liam, Lucian, and the girls approached us and placed our coffee in front of us.

"What are you girls talking about? You both look so serious and Amy, you're blushing again," Lucian inquired.

"Ah, nothing that concerns you guys," Annie replied quickly, glaring at me.

I knew I was more into Liam than I cared to admit. But I couldn't tear my eyes away from his. He gazed at me intensely with those blue eyes as if I were under his spell. I blushed once more at the thought.

"Are you okay, Amy?" Liam asked, sounding nervous.

"I'm fine; we were just having a serious twin talk, that's all. We have a few things to figure out," I replied.

"I hope it's not about me?" Liam asked, sounding curious.

I found myself gazing at Liam, lost in his eyes. His striking face and muscular physique overwhelmed me. He wasn't just a man but an alpha, a god among men.

He maintained his gaze on mine, clearly perplexed by my behaviour. Annie swiftly interrupted my train of thought. "No, not about you, Liam. We were discussing Amy's book and all her ideas for a few chapters," Annie quickly clarified.

"Oh, okay. Well, that sounds promising, right?" Liam responded, looking slightly disappointed as he glanced in my direction.

Lucian interrupted, "So, are you guys excited? Annie and I wanted to come with you, but we thought you would need time alone."

Without hesitation, I interjected, "That's a brilliant idea! You guys can get two tickets, and we have clothes. You could rush through, pack a bag, and come straight back. Liam, isn't that a brilliant idea? I won't be much company, but at least you'll have Annie and Lucian to help you with the girls."

Liam looked confused momentarily, then nodded, "Sure, that sounds like a brilliant idea, guys. Yes, please do join us."

Lucian purchased two tickets for him and Annie and packed their bags.

I felt saved. Being alone with Liam and grappling with these impure thoughts would have been awkward. With Annie and Lucian joining us, I could channel my energy into my book and focus on the monumental task ahead without distraction. This was perfect.

Lucian arrived just before our flight, and we departed for Disneyland. Upon arrival, I was delighted to discover that I had my room while the girls were sleeping with their dad, and Annie and Lucian would share a room. Being on my own meant I could write without any interruptions.

After unpacking, we decided to take a tour of the area. The girls were bouncing with excitement, practically hysterical with joy. Liam kept up with them effortlessly, and his fitness and experience of running with his pack came in handy.

"Isn't it amazing how quickly the girls accepted Liam as their dad? He's a natural," Lucian exclaimed, giving me a knowing look.

"Yes, it is. I'm happy that the girls are happy. They've forgotten all about Damien and his betrayal. It's good. I'm happy for the girls. They needed a dad, and Liam has stepped into that role perfectly. Hey, thanks for deciding to come with me, guys. I'm glad Liam will have some help with the girls while I focus," I expressed gratefully.

"No problem, sis. We're always here to help with our godchildren," Annie smiled warmly.

"Well, yes, you both are like their second parents. You helped me so much when they first came into our lives. Thank you for that," I acknowledged sincerely.

"It's incredible to think about how much our lives have changed since our eighteenth birthday. It's been a whirlwind. And I'm so grateful to have such a massive extended family now. Not just our coven, but the packs, the dragons, the Fae. Everyone has been so good to me and my girls, fighting my battles with me and helping me with the girls. We've been through so much together. And Lucian, you changed everything. You piqued our curiosity when you first emerged from the other side of the door. That's where it all began," I reflected.

"So true; we are blessed in so many ways," Lucian agreed, his voice filled with appreciation.

"Let's have some fun now before you go back to writing. Spend a day with us, sis," Annie exclaimed, her eyes sparkling excitedly.

And so, we embraced the opportunity to immerse ourselves in the enchanting world of Disneyland. From the moment we stepped foot in the park, we were transported to a realm of fantasy and adventure. The girls practically bounced excitedly, their laughter echoing as we walked through the bustling streets.

Our first stop was the iconic Sleeping Beauty Castle, its towering spires beckoning us to explore its magical interior. We marvelled at the intricate details of the castle's design before venturing into Fantasyland, where we embarked on whimsical rides and encountered beloved Disney characters.

Next, we journeyed to Tomorrowland, where we experienced thrilling attractions that whisked us away on exhilarating adventures through space and time. Liam was a natural at navigating the crowds, effortlessly keeping pace with the girls as they dashed from one ride to the next.

With all the excitement, we took breaks to indulge in delicious treats, from freshly baked churros to decadent Mickey-shaped ice cream. The joy on the girls' faces as they savoured these delights was genuinely heartwarming.

As the day progressed, we continued exploring Disneyland's wonders, from Main Street, U.S.A.'s bustling streets, to the enchanting sights and sounds of Adventureland and Frontierland. Everywhere we turned, there was something new and exciting to discover.

As the sun set, we were in awe of the dazzling fireworks display that illuminated the night sky above the castle. The girls' eyes sparkled with delight, and we couldn't help but feel a sense of wonder and awe as we watched the colorful explosions burst forth in a symphony of light and sound.

Back at our hotel, drained yet invigorated by the day's escapades, we reminisced about the unforgettable moments we shared, laughter and smiles abounding. As hunger gnawed at us, we realized it was time for supper, and we were all famished. Making our way to the hotel restaurant, we eagerly perused the menu and ordered various dishes, from succulent meats to fresh fish. With drinks in hand and appetites voracious, we savoured every bite, delighting in the Flavors and the company of loved ones.

As bedtime approached, I ascended the stairs to Liam's room to assist with tucking the girls in.

"Good night, my loves. I hope you have amazing dreams of today's adventures," I whispered as I leaned down to kiss each of them goodnight. "Good night, mommy. Good night, Daddy," they murmured sleepily in response.

"Good night, my beauties," Liam replied softly before closing the door to their room.

Turning to leave, I headed towards the front door. However, as I turned around, I found Liam standing behind me, so close that I could almost feel his presence. Instinctively, I stepped back, but he continued to advance towards me.

I gazed at him, his face as captivating as ever. Unsure if it was the effect of the drinks or simply his undeniable beauty, I couldn't deny the pull I felt towards him. He locked eyes with me, his touch gentle as he traced his fingers along my cheek.

"Amy, I don't want you to fear me. I need you to understand that I'm in love with you and willing to give you all the time you need to reciprocate those feelings. You and the girls mean everything to me, and I promise to always protect and care for you. I need you to open up to me when you're ready," he confessed earnestly.

"Liam, I do love you. I feel it deep down, but it scares me," I admitted, trembling slightly. "I just need time to adjust to all of this. It's new, and I don't want to rush into anything. I know you understand, and I appreciate everything you do for me and the girls."

"You do love me?" Liam asked, his eyes searching mine.

"Yes, I do, Liam," I affirmed, meeting his gaze with sincerity.

A smile spread across his face as he leaned in, his lips meeting mine in a tender kiss that ignited a passionate explosion of emotions between us.

Before anything else could transpire, I instinctively stepped back once more. I recognized that things would escalate if I remained in that moment, and I wasn't prepared yet.

Liam gently grasped my arm, his expression puzzled. "Where are you going?" he inquired softly.

I met his gaze, feeling torn. "Liam, you know if I stay, things will escalate. I'm just not ready for that right now," I explained gently.

His eyes remained fixed on mine. "Please, stay the night with me. Please, I need to hold you, Amy. I need to feel you," he pleaded earnestly.

"I can't, Liam. I am still waiting. Please understand, it's not you, it's me," I whispered, my voice filled with remorse.

He released my arm, shaking his head in understanding. But I could see the pain reflected in his eyes, the longing he felt to be with me at that moment. It was clear that I needed to overcome my fears and allow him into my heart.

"Okay," I murmured.

Liam smiled, a sense of relief evident in his expression. Taking my hand, he guided me to his room, conveniently located next door to the girls'. Gently, he removed my shoes and helped me settle into bed. Then, he climbed in beside me, wrapping his arm around me protectively. And with that, we drifted to sleep, finding peace in each other's embrace.

Chapter 52

"Guys, I've written down a list of techniques for you to learn. After lunch, we'll start practicing," I announced to the group gathered in the training area. "We're going to train with our dragons and swords, combining both elements to catch Damien off guard."

Liam raised an eyebrow, concern evident in his expression. "Are you sure you're okay, Amy? You've been avoiding me since Disney, especially when it comes to... well, you know."

I sighed, feeling the weight of the unspoken conversation pressing down on me. "It's not personal, Liam. I just... I don't know how to talk about it yet."

Thankfully, Lucian chimed in, offering his support. "She's right, mate. Amy's got a lot on her plate right now. Our priority is ending Damien's reign of terror. Once that's done, we can focus on everything else."

Returning to Tridion had brought a sense of urgency. There would be no rest, no time for hesitation. It was time to train, to prepare for the inevitable showdown with Damien.

"I've devised a series of innovative fighting techniques that incorporate both swords and dragons," I continued, trying to shift the focus back to our mission. "We need to catch Damien off guard, and this combination will do just that. After we've honed our skills, we'll activate plan C: getting him to the house and calling upon Zachariah to keep Damien there, locked away forever."

"I've outlined a set of techniques for us to work on," I said, flipping through the pages of my notebook and listing them off.

"First up, we have the Dragon Tail Swipe," I explained, gesturing to the diagram on the page. "This relies on the sheer strength of a dragon's tail to knock opponents off balance with a single, sweeping motion."

"Next, we've got the Flaming Sword Thrust," I continued, pointing to the illustration. "This one's all about adding a fiery punch to our sword strikes, courtesy of our dragon friends."

Annie and Lucian exchanged impressed glances as I moved on to the following technique.

"Then, there's the Dragon Wing Shield," I said, tapping the page. "Think of it as using our swords to mimic the protective stance of a dragon's wings, deflecting incoming attacks."

"Following that, we've got the Dragon Fang Strike," I explained, tracing the pattern of slashes depicted. "This one's all about speed and precision, like the swift bite of a dragon."

As I continued to detail each technique, Gregory chimed in with encouragement. "You guys will be able to master all of these," he reassured the group, instilling confidence in our abilities.

"Absolutely," Lucian agreed, nodding in determination. "Damien won't stand a chance with these moves in our arsenal."

"For the past ten days, we've been hitting the training hard," I announced to the group, gathered around a table covered in maps and diagrams. "Thanks to the support of the Fae, the coven, the elders, and the three packs, we're as ready as we'll ever be for Damien and his crew."

I glanced around the room, meeting the determined gazes of my companions. "With our dragons by our side, we're prepared for whatever they throw at us."

"Speaking of threats," I continued, my tone growing serious, "we can't overlook the danger posed by the vampires. That's why I've made sure everyone's armed with Oakwood stakes. We need to defend ourselves if they come knocking at our doors."

"But Damien..." I trailed off, the weight of his name hanging heavy in the air. "He's a different story altogether. We need a plan to take him down and ensure he stays down for good."

Pooling our knowledge and brainstorming strategies, we came up with eight potential ways to deal with Damien, though none were guaranteed:

"First, we considered exploiting his vulnerabilities," I explained, pointing to the list of options. "With him being both a vampire and a necromancer, we thought about traditional weaknesses like sunlight, silver, garlic, and holy symbols, as well as anything specific to his control over the undead and dark magic."

"Sunlight might weaken him," I suggested, "so we could try to lure him into a daylight ambush. Or we could arm ourselves with silver weapons, use holy water, or find a way to resist his dark magic."

"Diversion tactics could buy us time," I added, "and building alliances with other supernatural beings who have a bone to pick with him might tip the scales in our favor."

"Of course," I concluded, "we can always resort to the classics: decapitation or staking through the heart. It's all about finding what works best against him."

"As we went through each strategy, it became clear that we needed a comprehensive plan," I said, studying the list of options with a furrowed brow. "Flexibility will be key when facing Damien. We might need to blend a few approaches to finish the job."

Annie nodded in agreement. "Yeah, we can't afford any slip-ups. We'll likely have to utilize all eight possibilities to ensure Damien doesn't slip through our fingers."

"And dealing with regular vampires should be a breeze with those oakwood stakes," Lucian chimed in, a confident smirk on his lips.

With our strategy outlined, it was time to gather supplies and make our final preparations. "It'll take us about five more days to get everything sorted," I estimated, glancing around at the determined faces of my friends. "But once we're ready, Damien won't know what hit him."

Thanks to our dragons' swift assistance, the journey to our old house was quicker than expected, taking only half a day instead of the usual trek. As we arrived, we took a moment to steel ourselves for what lay ahead.

"We summon Zakariah and the fallen angels first," I instructed, going over the plan with the group. "Then, we summon Damien and his minions once they're on board. We fight off the vampires and capture Damien, sealing him away in the house for all eternity."

After a few deep breaths, Annie stepped forward, her voice steady as she began to conjure the spell. The rest of the coven joined in, their voices blending in a powerful chant:

A burst of light filled the room as Zakariah and his fallen angels appeared before us, immediately drawing attention.

"What's going on here?" Zakariah demanded, his irritation palpable.

"We called upon you to fulfill your duties to the coven," I replied tersely, annoyance coloring my tone. "You owe us for what happened during our last encounter."

Zakariah's gaze darted around the room, his frustration evident as he realized their situation—the combined forces of the coven, elders, wolves, and dragons surrounded them.

"What exactly do you mean, witch?" he asked mockingly, his demeanor attempting to conceal his unease.

"You know perfectly well what I mean," I retorted, my voice firm. "Your deception led to chaos with the demons and lost souls. We had to rectify your mess. You tricked us, and now it's time to settle the score."

"What's your demand?" Zakariah asked, his tone tinged with scepticism.

"I command you and your fallen angels to ensure Damien and his remaining minions are confined to the house," I declared firmly. "If they escape, it'll spell the end for you. This will put an end to everything once and for all."

"Is that so witch? And what makes you think that I am scared of you?"

"I can see it in your face and feel your feelings. Your emotions, you are terrified of me. As you know, I have grown into my full powers; I am the supreme Zakariah; I can end you in a flash; do not underestimate me." I said annoyingly.

"So what, now, I must obey a witch and her coven? Is that it?"

"Is that so, witch? And what makes you think that I am scared of you?"

"I can see it in your face and feel your feelings. Your emotions. You are terrified of me. As you know, I have grown into my full powers. I am the supreme Zakariah. I can end you in a flash. Do not underestimate me," I said annoyingly.

"So what, now, I must obey a witch and her coven? Is that it?"

"Yes, Zakariah, you will obey me or face the consequences," I asserted firmly, my tone leaving no room for negotiation. "Damien is a necromancer who has betrayed our coven, broken our trust, and attempted to kill us multiple times. I refuse to let him harm me or my family any longer. So you and your fallen angels will comply. Considering the spell we've cast on you, you don't have much choice. If you break it, there will be dire consequences. I can promise you that."

Zakariah's expression shifted, a mixture of resignation and understanding crossing his features. He knew I wasn't making idle threats. It was clear: either he obeyed, or they faced destruction.

"Fine," he relented. "What do you need us to do?"

"You'll be responsible for keeping them under constant watch, ensuring they never escape," I instructed, my voice firm. "No communication with them whatsoever. Damien will try to deceive you, and it could lead to your downfall. So, tread very carefully. Trust me, he's extremely dangerous and won't hesitate to take advantage of any opportunity."

Zakariah's expression turned grim as he absorbed my words, knowing the gravity of the situation.

"Now that's settled, we'll summon Damien and his minions, neutralize a few, and then lock him up," I continued, addressing the group.

"Everyone, take your positions. Annie, lead us in the summoning spell," I directed, receiving a nod of understanding from Annie.

She began the summoning spell, and we all followed along, repeating after her ten times.

Damien and his minions materialized before us, caught off guard by their sudden appearance at our old house. The shock on his face was priceless—he hadn't anticipated our move. We had successfully deceived the oracle, feeding him false information through Gilda. This was a triumph, and I was fueled by a simmering anger, ready to unleash the pain he had inflicted upon me back onto him. It was time for revenge.

"What's going on, Amy? What's the meaning of this?" Damien demanded, his voice tinged with uncertainty.

I met his gaze, and my expression hardened. "We're here to put an end to this, once and for all."

His minions surged forward, but we were prepared. With the skills we honed during training, we dispatched them individually. The oakwood stakes proved invaluable in finishing them off, reducing them to dust. Now, only Damien remained, stripped of his protectors.

Zakariah and his angels appeared, further sealing Damien's fate. He attempted to plead with them, promising them a better deal, claiming to be their master.

"Zachariah, whatever promises she's made you, I can offer more. Don't do this. I am your true master," Damien pleaded desperately.

"Sorry, Damien. We are now bound to Amy and her coven. We cannot help you this time," Zachariah responded firmly.

Damien's frustration was palpable, his realization sinking that this was his end.

Annie began the spell, and the coven followed suit. This was the moment, the final confrontation with that bastard. And soon, we would finally be rid of him. We repeated the incantation ten times, sealing Damien's fate once and for all.

As Damien began to vanish, I levelled a final gaze at him. "Goodbye, Damien. Hope you rot."

"Noooo!!!" Damien's desperate cry echoed through the room as he disappeared in a flash.

"Now we have to seal the house, hide it away where no one can find it," I declared, a sense of finality settling over us.

Annie delved into the grimoire again, flipping through its pages with determination. "Found it. This should do the trick. Repeat after me," she instructed, her voice steady.

We exerted all our energy, pouring it into locking the house securely.

"Zachariah, it's now your responsibility to keep Damien hidden and contained," I instructed, my tone unwavering. "Don't fail."

"We'll keep him locked away for eternity," Zachariah affirmed.

"And don't think we won't check in unexpectedly," I warned, my gaze piercing. "We can return any moment to ensure you're holding up your end of the deal. Remember not to cross me."

"I promise, ma'am. We'll keep him confined. No one will release him. If they try, they'll have to deal with me," Zachariah vowed solemnly.

Chapter 53

After the battle, with Damien neutralized, we returned to Tridion with a sense of liberation and newfound freedom. Determined to rebuild our community, we committed to establishing a sanctuary for our fellow fighters, ensuring they had a place to call their own with all the necessary amenities.

Under the guidance of Liam, Lucian, and Gregory, renovation plans took shape. Sketches were meticulously drawn, and blueprints were carefully laid out. Our once-modest dwelling underwent a remarkable transformation, emerging as a towering masterpiece that reached proudly toward the heavens. Its commanding height symbolized our resilience and provided a strategic vantage point for our dragons, safeguarding us from potential threats.

As construction progressed, our home began to materialize, offering comfort and security to all who sought shelter within its walls. Each passing day saw Tridion evolve from a simple refuge to a true sanctuary, where our bonds deepened, and our spirits soared.

While New Orleans held a cherished place in our hearts, Tridion had become our true sanctuary, a beacon of hope and resilience. Though we acknowledged the possibility of returning to the city for necessary meetings and discussions, our priority lay in forging a brighter future within the comforting confines of our newfound home.

Our parents chose to return to New Orleans, finding solace in their familiar routines. Their contentment brought us all peace, reaffirming the choices we had made. With their departure, I had ample time to dedicate to completing my novel.

I immersed myself in my writing for a week, tirelessly shaping, revising, and perfecting each word. My room's seclusion provided the ideal setting for my creativity to flourish. Once I completed the manuscript, I sought the coven's feedback to ensure no crucial secrets were accidentally revealed. Their input was invaluable in maintaining the integrity of my story.

"Remarkable work, Amy," Christian and Milo exclaimed, clearly impressed. "You've captured our journey perfectly, encompassing every twist and turn. Your talent truly shines. You've kept our secrets safe and made the story flow seamlessly."

"Fantastic job, Amy," Nancy and Arielle chimed in enthusiastically. "This manuscript completely immersed us in your story, and that ending—wow! Are you planning to continue our journey with more books?"

"It's truly incredible, sis," Annie added, brimming with happiness. "You've done such a fantastic job. I'm so proud of you."

A knock on my door interrupted us, and I sensed Liam's nervousness from the other side.

"Come in, Liam," I called out, bracing myself for his entrance.

The coven exchanged knowing looks, understanding the significance of Liam and me needing a private conversation. "We'll give you two some space," Annie said calmly, sensing our tension. "Just be nice," she added gently before ushering the others out of the room.

Since our trip to Disneyland, Liam and I hadn't had much time together. I had deliberately avoided him, needing time to clear my head and sort out my feelings.

His unshaven face added to his rugged charm as he entered the room. Despite my efforts to deny it, he stirred emotions within me that I wasn't prepared to confront.

Liam offered a soft smile. "Amy, it's time we talked about where we stand or where we're going, if anywhere. You've been avoiding me since our kiss and the night we spent together. I want you to know that I promised never to take advantage of you. I sense that you're pushing me away, and I'm not entirely sure why," Liam confessed, his voice tinged with concern.

I held his gaze, seeing the pain reflected in his eyes. "Liam, I'm truly sorry. I never meant to make things complicated for you. I haven't been myself lately; I've been consumed by the need to defeat Damien and finish my book. Now that both are accomplished, you have my full attention."

"Is that what you truly believe?" Liam's frustration was evident in his tone. "Or are you going to continue avoiding the issue? I can't keep living in this uncertainty. It's a simple question, Amy. Do you want us to be together or not? You admitted that you love me. Right, or has that changed?"

I looked at him, feeling a sense of disbelief. "Liam, I had no idea I was affecting you like this, and I'm genuinely sorry. I never meant to cause you pain. Yes, I do love you. But I need time for intimacy and fully embracing the idea of being in a relationship with you. Having you as the father of our girls has been the best thing that ever happened to them, and I have to admit, I was relieved it was you and not someone else. But the truth is, I can't remember everything about our past lives together. It was always with Damien, and that is what I remember. I hope you can understand that. Yes, I want to be with you, and only you, but we must take things one step at a time. Cuddling and kissing are fine, but for now, I need to set a boundary where kissing doesn't lead to intimacy."

"I completely understand, Amy," Liam replied, his voice tinged with shyness. "All I want is to be close to you, spend time together, maybe even share the same bed?"

"Fine, if that's all," I relented. "You can move in with me. Just know there will be times when I need my space, whether for writing or simply needing time alone."

"Understood," Liam affirmed, his expression reflecting gratitude.

"So, can we start tonight?" Liam asked eagerly.

"Yes, but you have to shower first," I replied with a smile.

"Sorry, the building has been hectic," Liam explained. "But we want to finish as soon as possible. We want it to feel more homey, especially for the girls to invite their friends over eventually."

"That's sweet of you, Daddy, but they don't have friends here, only in New Orleans, at one of the schools there."

"Oh no, well then, we need to make a plan," Liam said thoughtfully. "Well, we could give them a sibling," Liam suggested with a mischievous grin.

"Oh, hell no, we're not there yet, Liam!" I exclaimed, feeling my face flush.

"I'm joking; I was hoping you would change your mind," Liam said, chuckling.

"But who knows, Annie and Lucian have been very cozy. Maybe soon they'll have a little wolf witch of their own," I said enthusiastically.

"Indeed, who knows," Liam agreed. "The girls need playmates, but then they'd be too big to play with their cousins."

"Jasper and Trinity already have children, and so do the other Fae couples. And the whole of Tridion is no exception. We must invite their parents and them over once everything is in order, and have a big celebration. We haven't had a good party in ages. I feel like dancing, drinking, and being merry. We deserve this," I exclaimed enthusiastically.

"That's the spirit, Amy! Where have you been hiding, loka?" Liam asked.

I gave Liam a quizzical look. "Who are you calling Loka? What does that even mean?"

"It doesn't mean much, just like the entire world. But I've heard the term used by other mundane in New Orleans and thought it was catchy. It's just a playful term of affection," Liam explained.

"Please don't call me that, Liam. It sounds like you're calling me crazy, as 'loka' means crazy woman," I said firmly.

"Sorry, Amy, I don't mean you're crazy. I know you're not. Okay, let me gather my things. Is there space for my stuff?" Liam asked.

I looked around. "Sure, you can find space. You probably don't have as many clothes and stuff as I do. Please don't take up too much space, as I am still trying to sort out my makeup and shoes. You know, a girl can never have enough."

"I think I might have to build a bigger closet for you before I move my things in. May I?" Liam asked.

"Sure, I will leave you to it," I replied.

Liam pressed on and built a big closet in the corner of the room, his own space, also making my space bigger. My room looked much more significant when he knocked down a few walls.

After he had completed his complete makeover of my room, which only took him a few hours, he called me in.

I was amazed at how incredible it looked. Liam had many talents and knew how to work with his hands. Those big hands of his.

"Come in, what do you think, Amy? Big enough for you? I even added a study with shelves, a desk, and a few other things I thought you might need. Do you like it?" Liam asked.

"I love it, Liam, thank you. It's beautiful. How did you know I eventually wanted a study of my own?" I asked, genuinely surprised.

"You can spend your time writing in your new study. Away from everything and everyone, right next to your bathroom and room.

You deserve only the best, and I want to give you everything your heart desires. As to your question, you know I know everything, right?" Liam replied with a grin.

"That's sweet of you, Liam. Thank you for this; it means so much," I said, grateful as I stepped forward and hugged him.

He looked into my eyes, and his hand moved to my cheek. "Can I kiss you?" he asked gently.

I couldn't breathe, swept up in this moment. "Yes," I finally managed to say.

His lips touched mine, holding me so close to him. I felt like I was drifting, looking at us from the outside. We looked so good together. The passion, the romance, everything was there. He was my soulmate, and it finally hit me.

Before things heated, he let go, a look of bewilderment crossing his face. I mirrored his expression, wondering why he stopped.

"Because if I continue, I might end up making love to you, Amy. I need you. I ache for you. But I know you're not ready. And I'm not pushing you," he explained softly.

"I want you too," I managed to say.

"Are you sure?"

"Yes," I replied firmly.

Liam carried me to our bed, and that was it. The world faded away. It was only us—passion, love, and joy. Happiness poured out of my heart into his. The emotions I felt while he was making love to me, the tenderness he showed, the emotion—it all came together. The wait was over. I was his and mine as long as we both shall live. Right there, I gave my heart to him, my soul.

Chapter Fifty-five: Embracing New Beginnings

Annie and I were catching up over coffee when I couldn't contain my excitement. "Annie, things have heated up between Liam and me. Are you thrilled now that we've finally found our way back to each other?"

Annie's grin mirrored my bubbling joy. "Absolutely! It's about time, Amy."

Relief washed over me as I nodded. "And my writing has been improving too. Everything feels so normal now; there are no threats or danger. At this moment, our house is just filled with love."

Annie took a thoughtful sip of her coffee before chiming in, "We've come a long way since Damien was locked away."

"Yeah, it's been quite a journey," I agreed, feeling a pang of nostalgia. "Can you believe Kaitlin and Paige will be sixteen soon? Time flies."

Annie chuckled. "Tell me about it. It feels like just yesterday they were little girls running around."

"And it's been fun," I remarked, a smile spreading across my face. "Life couldn't be better in so many ways. Looking back, this life at twenty-four surpassed any expectations."

Annie's eyes widened with disbelief. "We haven't even celebrated yet. It's high time we all went out and had a big event like we always talked about. It's the first time in so many lifetimes we've passed twenty-three. We should be thrilled. Hopefully, we don't grow old."

I laughed, sharing in Annie's infectious excitement. "I know. It's like a dream come true."

"Well, let's make sure to celebrate properly," Annie suggested, her grin widening. "Who knows when we'll get another chance like this?"

"Agreed," I said, already brainstorming party plans. "Let's make it unforgettable."

And unforgettable it would be. "I think we need a spa day," I suggested, picturing the relaxation.

Annie's eyes lit up with enthusiasm. "Yes, that sounds perfect! Massages, facials, the whole nine yards."

"Absolutely," I agreed, feeling the anticipation building. "We deserve to pamper ourselves for reaching this milestone."

Annie nodded eagerly. "Let's book it right away before we get caught up in our busy lives.

"Great idea," I replied, realizing the practicalities. "We'll have to head back to New Orleans to make bookings since cell phones don't work in Tridion. This is going to be amazing."

Liam and Lucian interrupted our conversation, their presence casting a shadow over our plans for our twenty-fourth birthday.

"What are you two up to?" Liam's voice carried a note of caution while Lucian's gaze held a hint of concern.

Caught off guard, I glanced at Annie before responding, "Oh, we're discussing our birthday plans. No wars or danger involved, I promise."

Lucian raised an eyebrow sceptically. "Are you sure about that? Knowing you two, trouble seems to follow wherever you go."

I chuckled, shaking my head. "No trouble this time, Lucian. Just a celebration with friends and family."

Liam relaxed slightly, a smile tugging at the corners of his lips. "Well, count us in then. We could all use a reason to celebrate."

Annie grinned, relieved by their reaction. "Great! We'll make sure it's a birthday to remember."

With Liam and Lucian on board, our birthday plans took on a new energy, infused with the promise of laughter and joy.

"We just have to run a few errands in New Orleans," I insisted.

"For how long?" Liam asked, his brow furrowing with concern.

"Maybe a day or two. Annie and I want to go to a spa and have a few things done, plus we need outfits. The girls will also come with us to decide what they want to wear for their sixteenth. After all they have been through, our daughters need some normalcy," I explained, hoping he would understand.

Liam nodded, his expression softening with understanding. "Okay, Amy, take a few days. We'll start decorating. Let Lucian and me know what you want, and we will put the packs and the coven to work. To make it the best celebration. After all, this is the first time you turn twenty-four, and our girls are sixteen. It's still hard to believe; they were smaller a few months ago. Their aging seems to be infected with my wolf genes, that they grow up so quickly."

I smiled gratefully at Liam's support, relieved that he understood the importance of giving our daughters a special celebration. With his reassurance, I felt confident that our birthday festivities would be unforgettable.

"And with the girls proliferating, that will be another day's problems," I remarked with a wry smile, acknowledging the inevitable challenges of parenthood.

Liam chuckled softly, his eyes twinkling with affection. "True, but we'll tackle those challenges together like always."

Liam held my hand gently, his thumb tracing small circles on my palm. "I am going to miss you, sleeping alone," he admitted softly, his voice tinged with a hint of longing.

I smiled, squeezing his hand reassuringly. "You will be fine, and I will be home soon. Plus, we have a lifetime together, Liam. I am yours, and you are mine," I reassured him, my words filled with love and conviction.

With a lingering gaze, we shared a silent understanding, finding solace in the promise of a future filled with endless moments together.

We packed the girls up, ensuring they had everything they needed for the trip. Then, after giving Liam and Lucian detailed instructions on what we wanted done while we were away, we made our way to the portal once more, ready to return to New Orleans.

As we stepped through the shimmering gateway, I couldn't help but feel a sense of anticipation for the adventures that awaited us on the other side. With Annie by my side and my daughters in tow, I knew this would be a fun time with my sister.

We emerged onto our parents' porch, greeted by the familiar sight of Mom and Dad waiting for us. Their smiles warmed my heart, filling me with a sense of homecoming and belonging.

"Welcome back, girls!" Mom exclaimed, enveloping us warmly as Dad stood beside her, his eyes twinkling with joy.

"It's so good to see you both," Dad added, his voice filled with affection.

I hugged them tightly, feeling grateful for their unwavering love and support. Our family was reunited once more.

"Where are Liam and Lucian?" Dad inquired, curiosity dancing in his eyes.

Annie chuckled, her laughter light and infectious. "We left them in charge of our party decorations."

Mom let out a sceptical scoff. "Really? You trust the men to decorate?"

"Yes, we did tell them what to do," I interjected, reassuringly smiling.

Dad laughed heartily, the sound echoing across the porch. "This will be good."

"They do have direction and the coven and packs. So they should be okay," I reasoned, hoping to ease any lingering doubts.

With a collective nod of agreement, we settled into the familiarity of family banter. Our next task was to make appointments for the spa, hair, and makeup and find outfits for ourselves and the girls. It promised to be a hectic day or two, but the excitement of preparing for the celebration made it all worthwhile.

As we stepped into the house, ready to embark on our whirlwind of preparations, I couldn't help but feel anticipation for the festivities ahead.

"Alright, ladies, we're all set for the day spa," Mom announced, holding up her phone with the confirmation email. "We'll have a relaxing morning before the big day."

"Thanks, Mom," Annie chimed in. "And Dad, you're the best for caring for the girls," I said.

Dad grinned. "It's my pleasure. You ladies enjoy yourselves."

After our indulgent spa session, feeling utterly relaxed and rejuvenated, we headed to the hairdresser for our next round of pampering.

As I settled into the plush chair, I discussed hair options with the stylist. "I'm thinking just a few subtle highlights," I suggested. "Something to add a bit of dimension and brightness."

Annie, always one for bold choices, had different plans. "I want big, blonde streaks," she declared, eagerly flipping through a magazine for inspiration. "I want heads to turn when we walk into that party tonight.

The stylists got to work, their skilled hands weaving magic with scissors and dye. As they worked their magic, I reflected on the swift passage of time. "It's crazy to think about bringing Kaitlin and Paige here one day," I remarked to Annie. "They're growing up so fast."

Annie nodded in agreement, her eyes shining with excitement. "Yeah, it's wild. But for now, let's soak up this moment of luxury."

Mom's eyes widened pleasantly as she took in our new looks. "You two look amazing. Your hair, wow." She then turned her attention to the array of makeup products on display. "Now, let's check out these makeup options. You girls will be shocked at the variety, and it's my treat. Take whatever you need. I know you don't have shops like these in Tridion."

"Thanks, Mom. We appreciate it," Annie and I said in unison, grateful for her generosity.

As we perused through the vast selection of makeup, we were thrilled to find the perfect shades and products to suit our preferences. Access to such a variety was a rare treat, and we took full advantage of it.

Once we had finished our spa treatments, makeovers, and shopping spree, Mom treated us to a delicious lunch at one of the cozy cafes in New Orleans. After our busy day, we were famished, so we indulged in various delectable treats.

"We'll have chocolate croissants, please," I requested eagerly, knowing how much I enjoyed them.

Annie added, "Let's get some ice cream, a seafood platter, and some sushi for variety. It's a rare combination, but I'm feeling adventurous today."

Mom nodded with a smile, placing our orders with the waiter. "And a bottle of sweet red wine to accompany our meal," she added, ensuring that our day of pampering would end ideally.

As we savored our delicious meal, I couldn't help but feel grateful for this particular time spent with Mom and Annie. Moments like these make life genuinely remarkable.

"Thank you for such a wonderful day, Mom," I said, truly blessed by her generosity.

Annie chimed in, echoing my sentiments. "Yes, thank you, Mom. It's been amazing spending this time together."

Mom smiled warmly at us, her eyes reflecting pride and love. "It's my pleasure, my girls. It's not every day my daughters turn twenty-four, and I wanted to make it special for both of you. I'm so grateful you've survived this lifetime and have such strong, caring men to look after you."

She turned her attention to me. "How's your novel coming along, Amy? And Annie, any new stories or gossip to share from your journalism adventures?" she asked, always curious about our pursuits.

“My novel is nearly done; I only have five chapters left of this book two.”

"That's fantastic, Amy!" Mom exclaimed, her eyes lighting up with pride. "I'm so proud of you for nearly finishing your novel. It sounds like it's going to be a real page-turner. And to think, you've managed to weave in all those supernatural elements without giving too much away. Your readers are going to be in for a treat."

I nodded, feeling a sense of accomplishment. "Thanks, Mom. It's been quite the journey, but I'm excited to see it all come together. Writing about our experiences has been challenging and rewarding, but I wouldn't have it any other way."

Mom smiled, her expression filled with warmth. "I'm sure it's going to be amazing, Amy. You've always had a way with words, and I do not doubt your book will be a bestseller."

With a renewed sense of confidence, I looked forward to the final chapters of my novel, eager to see where the story would take me next.

“And you, Annie?”

“Not so much is going on in journalism, but sure, it will get interesting soon. For now, I am relaxing and spending more time with Lucian. Getting to know him has been a blast. We have so much in common. He has mentioned marriage to me. But I said that I needed time.”

Mom's eyes widened with surprise. "Lucian wants to get married? That's so sweet, Annie! And, of course, you'll be a bridesmaid. I can already picture how beautiful the wedding will be."

Annie nodded, a hint of uncertainty in her expression. "Yeah, it was unexpected, but we've talked about it. Our relationship has much to explore, especially with his pack and everything. We're taking it slow for now."

Mom smiled reassuringly. "That sounds like a wise approach, Annie. It's important to take the time to truly understand each other before taking such a big step. And if anyone can navigate the complexities of the wolf world, it's you."

Annie returned the smile, grateful for Mom's understanding. "Thanks, Mom. It means a lot to have your support."

As we continued our conversation, I couldn't help but feel excited about Annie and Lucian's future together. I wondered if that would be Liam and me one-day discussing marriage.

Mom smiled, her eyes twinkling with pride. "You two are my greatest blessings," she said softly. "I am so proud of the woman you have become, and I know that you will continue to achieve great things in life. Remember, no matter where life takes you, you will always have a home with us."

Tears welled in my eyes as Mom spoke, touching me deeply. "Thank you, Mom," I said, my voice filled with emotion. "I couldn't have done it without your love and support."

Annie nodded in agreement, her eyes shining with gratitude. "Yes, Mom, thank you for always being there for us, guiding and believing in us."

With tears of happiness streaming down our cheeks, we hugged Mom tightly, grateful for her unwavering love and support.

As we stepped out of the café, the afternoon sun casting a warm glow around us, I couldn't help but feel rejuvenated after our pampering session. The tension and stress of the day seemed to melt away, replaced by a sense of peace and contentment.

Dad and the girls were bustling around the kitchen when Mom's voice interrupted our thoughts. "What are the three of you up to?" she asked, her tone laced with surprise.

Dad looked up from the stove, a proud smile on his face. "We're helping Grandpa, Nana," Kaitlin chimed in, her eyes shining with excitement as she stirred a pot on the stove with Paige by her side, carefully following their grandad's instructions.

"What a sight this is." Mom looked amazed.

I chuckled at Kaitlin's incredulous expression. "Well, I'm sure Uncle Lucian could use some extra help in the kitchen, too," I replied with a playful grin, glancing at Dad, who nodded in agreement.

Paige's playful jab elicited a laugh from all of us. "Hey, I do not burn everything," Kaitlin retorted with mock offense, her eyes sparkling with mischief.

With nods of agreement, we wrapped up our meal preparations, eager to rest before our busy shopping day and returning home.

We rose with renewed energy the following day, eager to embark on our shopping adventure. "Alright, girls, let's get ready," I announced, excited about the day ahead. We've got a lot to do before heading home for the party. Hopefully, everything will be sorted out by then."

Annie and the girls nodded in agreement, already buzzing with anticipation for the day ahead. "I can't wait to find the perfect outfits," Annie exclaimed, her eyes excitedly shining.

Kaitlin and Paige exchanged excited glances, eager to join the fun. "Me too! I hope we find something amazing," Kaitlin chimed in.

With our spirits high and our minds set on our mission, we set out to make the most of our shopping day.

The streets of New Orleans were buzzing with people. Everyone seemed to have somewhere to go, and the shops were packed. Thankfully, the clothing store we were eager to visit first was empty. Mom took Kaitlin and Paige while Annie and I went to look for some sexy dresses.

"I hope we find something amazing," Annie said as we entered the store.

"Me too," I replied, scanning the racks. "It's so nice that it's not crowded in here."

"Yeah, we can take our time and try things on without a rush," Annie agreed.

"Do you think this would look good on me?" I asked, holding up a red dress.

Annie gave me a once-over and smiled. "Absolutely. You should try it on."

I tried it on but wasn't too fond of this particular cut. I needed something unique.

"How does it look?" I asked, stepping out of the dressing room.

Annie tilted her head, considering. "It's nice, but I think you can find something better. Maybe something shorter and with a heart-shaped top?"

"Exactly what I was thinking," I said, relieved she understood.

Annie then held up a blue dress she had found. "What do you think of this one?"

"You always look great in blue," I said, admiring the dress. "You should try it on."

"Annie, you look beautiful. It's perfect. Lucian will go gaga over your new look," I said, admiring her. "The blue blends so perfectly with your blonde highlights. You look stunning, sis. You're almost unrecognizable."

Just then, the lady in the store approached us with a smile. "You look amazing in that dress," she remarked to Annie. "It brings out your eyes."

"Thank you," Annie remarked, smiling at the lady.

She then turned to me. "What type of dress are you looking for?"

I looked at her and explained, "I'm looking for something short with a heart-shaped neckline, preferably red or black. And I need shoes to match, too."

Annie nodded thoughtfully. "Got it. Let's see what we can find."

Annie went with the lady to look for shoes to match her dress. A moment later, the lady returned and stood next to me, holding up two beautiful dresses, just as I had imagined—one in red and one in black.

I couldn't take my eyes off them. "These are perfect," I whispered, awestruck.

Annie returned with matching shoes for both dresses and a pair of gold high heels. "Look what I found!" she said excitedly. "These will look amazing with either dress."

I smiled, feeling a rush of excitement. "Annie, you're the best. Let's try everything on!"

I couldn't decide which dress to take—they were both excellent. "I'll take both," I said, beaming. "And all the shoes here, plus these three bags."

The lady rang up my items, and I paid in cash.

Annie went to the counter and paid for her dress. She then chose another dress, a few pairs of shoes, and a couple of handbags.

Mom returned from the teen section with the twins, Kaitlin and Paige. They both wore beautiful baby pink dresses, matching shoes, and tiaras.

"That's what we forgot!" Annie yelled, suddenly remembering.

Paige ran back and grabbed three more tiaras, one for each of us. The lady at the counter who helped us earlier rang everything up, and Mom paid for the additional items.

"Looks like we're all set," Mom said, smiling at the pile of shopping bags.

"Definitely," I agreed, feeling a thrill of excitement. "This is going to be amazing."

"Now, that was the most fun we've had in a long time," Kaitlin exclaimed. "Shopping is so much fun!"

"You're just like the rest of our Johnston family," Mom said with a chuckle. "We ladies love shopping, especially for clothes."

"What time is it?" Annie asked.

Mom checked her watch. "Time for a quick lunch, and then we need to go home and get ready before we head to Tridion."

"Sounds like a plan," I said, gathering my bags. "Let's find a good place to eat."

We decided to go to the same little café around the corner. We ordered a bottle of wine for the adults while the girls had strawberry milkshakes and burgers. Mom, Annie, and I opted for steak and fries.

"How spoiled are we?" I asked, taking a sip of wine. "This is the life. Gosh, I miss this."

"Me too," Annie admitted. "We must return to New Orleans more often to do things like this. The last two days have been glorious."

Mom nodded in agreement. "Absolutely. It's been wonderful spending time together like this."

We finished our lunch and headed back home.

"We need to get ready," Dad said eagerly, already dressed in his suit.

"You look so handsome, Daddy," Annie and I exclaimed in unison.

"Thank you, girls. You better get a move on," Dad replied with a smile. Liam and Lucian were here earlier to check how far along you were. They said everything was ready, and the guests arrived about an hour ago. I told them you went shopping, so they surely understand how much you love shopping."

"Alright, let's not keep them waiting any longer," I said, grabbing my bags and heading to my room.

"Time to get glamorous!" Annie added, hurrying after me.

We finished getting ready and walked downstairs. Everyone looked so glamorous.

"Oh wow, we've outdone ourselves," Mom said, beaming with pride.

"We all look amazing," I added, admiring our reflections in the hallway mirror.

"The guys will be shocked when they see us," Annie said, grinning from ear to ear.

"Let's go show them what they're in for," I said, excited, as we headed back to the party in Tridion.

We arrived at the sound of pumping music. People were dancing, laughter filling the air. Liam and Lucian were acting as DJs, techno music blaring in the background.

As the music stopped, it was evident that they knew we had arrived. The expressions on their faces were priceless.

"Oh, wow," that was all they could manage, both staring at us.

"Hey, boys, we're back. Did you miss us?" I teased.

They approached us, and one of them exclaimed, "You both look extraordinary, exquisite. You're so beautiful."

"Of course, we missed you. Liam couldn't take his eyes off you," one of them replied. Then Kaitlin and Paige came running up.

"Hey, Dad, what do you think of our outfits?" they asked eagerly.

Liam got choked up. "You both look like your mother. You're beautiful. I got fortunate," he said, watching my expression closely.

Then, leaning in, he whispered, "I love you, and I'm so thankful you're mine. I still don't know how I got so lucky. But I did."

"I'm the lucky one, Liam. You saved me and our family. Now, we have a chance to live a full life, to do what makes us happy. You make me and the girls so happy. We're grateful for you, too," I said gratefully.

With that, Liam kissed me, and in that moment, I knew this would be our forever...?

Chapter 54

Annie and I were catching up over coffee when I couldn't contain my excitement. "Annie, things have heated up between Liam and me. Are you thrilled now that we've finally found our way back to each other?"

Annie's grin mirrored my bubbling joy. "Absolutely! It's about time, Amy."

Relief washed over me as I nodded. "And my writing has been improving too. Everything feels so normal now; there are no threats or danger. At this moment, our house is just filled with love."

Annie took a thoughtful sip of her coffee before chiming in, "We've come a long way since Damien was locked away."

"Yeah, it's been quite a journey," I agreed, feeling a pang of nostalgia. "Can you believe Kaitlin and Paige will be sixteen soon? Time flies."

Annie chuckled. "Tell me about it. It feels like just yesterday they were little girls running around."

"And it's been fun," I remarked, a smile spreading across my face. "Life couldn't be better in so many ways. Looking back, this life at twenty-four surpassed any expectations."

Annie's eyes widened with disbelief. "We haven't even celebrated yet. It's high time we all went out and had a big event like we always talked about. It's the first time in so many lifetimes we've passed twenty-three. We should be thrilled. Hopefully, we don't grow old."

I laughed, sharing in Annie's infectious excitement. "I know. It's like a dream come true."

"Well, let's make sure to celebrate properly," Annie suggested, her grin widening. "Who knows when we'll get another chance like this?"

"Agreed," I said, already brainstorming party plans. "Let's make it unforgettable."

And unforgettable it would be. "I think we need a spa day," I suggested, picturing the relaxation.

Annie's eyes lit up with enthusiasm. "Yes, that sounds perfect! Massages, facials, the whole nine yards."

"Absolutely," I agreed, feeling the anticipation building. "We deserve to pamper ourselves for reaching this milestone."

Annie nodded eagerly. "Let's book it right away before we get caught up in our busy lives.

"Great idea," I replied, realizing the practicalities. "We'll have to head back to New Orleans to make bookings since cell phones don't work in Tridion. This is going to be amazing."

Liam and Lucian interrupted our conversation, their presence casting a shadow over our plans for our twenty-fourth birthday.

"What are you two up to?" Liam's voice carried a note of caution while Lucian's gaze held a hint of concern.

Caught off guard, I glanced at Annie before responding, "Oh, we're discussing our birthday plans. No wars or danger involved, I promise."

Lucian raised an eyebrow skeptically. "Are you sure about that? Knowing you two, trouble seems to follow wherever you go."

I chuckled, shaking my head. "No trouble this time, Lucian. Just a celebration with friends and family."

Liam relaxed slightly, a smile tugging at the corners of his lips. "Well, count us in then. We could all use a reason to celebrate."

Annie grinned, relieved by their reaction. "Great! We'll make sure it's a birthday to remember."

With Liam and Lucian on board, our birthday plans took on a new energy, infused with the promise of laughter and joy.

"We just have to run a few errands in New Orleans," I insisted.

"For how long?" Liam asked, his brow furrowing with concern.

"Maybe a day or two. Annie and I want to go to a spa and have a few things done, plus we need outfits. The girls will also come with us to decide what they want to wear for their sixteenth. After all they have been through, our daughters need some normalcy," I explained, hoping he would understand.

Liam nodded, his expression softening with understanding. "Okay, Amy, take a few days. We'll start decorating. Let Lucian and me know what you want, and we will put the packs and the coven to work. To make it the best celebration. After all, this is the first time you turn twenty-four, and our girls are sixteen. It's still hard to believe; they were smaller a few months ago. Their aging seems to be infected with my wolf genes, that they grow up so quickly."

I smiled gratefully at Liam's support, relieved that he understood the importance of giving our daughters a special celebration. With his reassurance, I felt confident that our birthday festivities would be unforgettable.

"And with the girls proliferating, that will be another day's problems," I remarked with a wry smile, acknowledging the inevitable challenges of parenthood.

Liam chuckled softly, his eyes twinkling with affection. "True, but we'll tackle those challenges together like always."

Liam held my hand gently, his thumb tracing small circles on my palm. "I am going to miss you, sleeping alone," he admitted softly, his voice tinged with a hint of longing.

I smiled, squeezing his hand reassuringly. "You will be fine, and I will be home soon. Plus, we have a lifetime together, Liam. I am yours, and you are mine," I reassured him, my words filled with love and conviction.

With a lingering gaze, we shared a silent understanding, finding solace in the promise of a future filled with endless moments together.

We packed the girls up, ensuring they had everything they needed for the trip. Then, after giving Liam and Lucian detailed instructions on what we wanted done while we were away, we made our way to the portal once more, ready to return to New Orleans.

As we stepped through the shimmering gateway, I couldn't help but feel a sense of anticipation for the adventures that awaited us on the other side. With Annie by my side and my daughters in tow, I knew this would be a fun time with my sister.

We emerged onto our parents' porch, greeted by the familiar sight of Mom and Dad waiting for us. Their smiles warmed my heart, filling me with a sense of homecoming and belonging.

"Welcome back, girls!" Mom exclaimed, enveloping us warmly as Dad stood beside her, his eyes twinkling with joy.

"It's so good to see you both," Dad added, his voice filled with affection.

I hugged them tightly, feeling grateful for their unwavering love and support. Our family was reunited once more.

"Where are Liam and Lucian?" Dad inquired, curiosity dancing in his eyes.

Annie chuckled, her laughter light and infectious. "We left them in charge of our party decorations."

Mom let out a skeptical scoff. "Really? You trust the men to decorate?"

"Yes, we did tell them what to do," I interjected, reassuringly smiling.

Dad laughed heartily, the sound echoing across the porch. "This will be good."

"They do have direction and the coven and packs. So they should be okay," I reasoned, hoping to ease any lingering doubts.

With a collective nod of agreement, we settled into the familiarity of family banter. Our next task was to make appointments for the spa, hair, and makeup and find outfits for ourselves and the girls. It promised to be a hectic day or two, but the excitement of preparing for the celebration made it all worthwhile.

As we stepped into the house, ready to embark on our whirlwind of preparations, I couldn't help but feel anticipation for the festivities ahead.

"Alright, ladies, we're all set for the day spa," Mom announced, holding up her phone with the confirmation email. "We'll have a relaxing morning before the big day."

"Thanks, Mom," Annie chimed in. "And Dad, you're the best for caring for the girls," I said.

Dad grinned. "It's my pleasure. You ladies enjoy yourselves."

After our indulgent spa session, feeling utterly relaxed and rejuvenated, we headed to the hairdresser for our next round of pampering.

As I settled into the plush chair, I discussed hair options with the stylist. "I'm thinking just a few subtle highlights," I suggested. "Something to add a bit of dimension and brightness."

Annie, always one for bold choices, had different plans. "I want big, blonde streaks," she declared, eagerly flipping through a magazine for inspiration. "I want heads to turn when we walk into that party tonight.

The stylists got to work, their skilled hands weaving magic with scissors and dye. As they worked their magic, I reflected on the swift passage of time. "It's crazy to think about bringing Kaitlin and Paige here one day," I remarked to Annie. "They're growing up so fast."

Annie nodded in agreement, her eyes shining with excitement. "Yeah, it's wild. But for now, let's soak up this moment of luxury."

Mom's eyes widened pleasantly as she took in our new looks. "You two look amazing. Your hair, wow." She then turned her attention to the array of makeup products on display. "Now, let's check out these makeup options. You girls will be shocked at the variety, and it's my treat. Take whatever you need. I know you don't have shops like these in Tridion."

"Thanks, Mom. We appreciate it," Annie and I said in unison, grateful for her generosity.

As we perused through the vast selection of makeup, we were thrilled to find the perfect shades and products to suit our preferences. Access to such a variety was a rare treat, and we took full advantage of it.

Once we had finished our spa treatments, makeovers, and shopping spree, Mom treated us to a delicious lunch at one of the cozy cafes in New Orleans. After our busy day, we were famished, so we indulged in various delectable treats.

"We'll have chocolate croissants, please," I requested eagerly, knowing how much I enjoyed them.

Annie added, "Let's get some ice cream, a seafood platter, and some sushi for variety. It's a rare combination, but I'm feeling adventurous today."

Mom nodded with a smile, placing our orders with the waiter. "And a bottle of sweet red wine to accompany our meal," she added, ensuring that our day of pampering would end ideally.

As we savored our delicious meal, I couldn't help but feel grateful for this particular time spent with Mom and Annie. Moments like these make life genuinely remarkable.

"Thank you for such a wonderful day, Mom," I said, truly blessed by her generosity.

Annie chimed in, echoing my sentiments. "Yes, thank you, Mom. It's been amazing spending this time together."

Mom smiled warmly at us, her eyes reflecting pride and love. "It's my pleasure, my girls. It's not every day my daughters turn twenty-four, and I wanted to make it special for both of you. I'm so grateful you've survived this lifetime and have such strong, caring men to look after you."

She turned her attention to me. "How's your novel coming along, Amy? And Annie, any new stories or gossip to share from your journalism adventures?" she asked, always curious about our pursuits.

"My novel is nearly done; I only have five chapters left of this book two."

"That's fantastic, Amy!" Mom exclaimed, her eyes lighting up with pride. "I'm so proud of you for nearly finishing your novel. It sounds like it's going to be a real page-turner. And to think, you've managed to weave in all those supernatural elements without giving too much away. Your readers are going to be in for a treat."

I nodded, feeling a sense of accomplishment. "Thanks, Mom. It's been quite the journey, but I'm excited to see it all come together. Writing about our experiences has been challenging and rewarding, but I wouldn't have it any other way."

Mom smiled, her expression filled with warmth. "I'm sure it's going to be amazing, Amy. You've always had a way with words, and I do not doubt your book will be a bestseller."

With a renewed sense of confidence, I looked forward to the final chapters of my novel, eager to see where the story would take me next.

"And you, Annie?"

"Not so much is going on in journalism, but sure, it will get interesting soon. For now, I am relaxing and spending more time with Lucian. Getting to know him has been a blast. We have so much in common. He has mentioned marriage to me. But I said that I needed time."

Mom's eyes widened with surprise. "Lucian wants to get married? That's so sweet, Annie! And, of course, you'll be a bridesmaid. I can already picture how beautiful the wedding will be."

Annie nodded, a hint of uncertainty in her expression. "Yeah, it was unexpected, but we've talked about it. Our relationship has much to explore, especially with his pack and everything. We're taking it slow for now."

Mom smiled reassuringly. "That sounds like a wise approach, Annie. It's important to take the time to truly understand each other before taking such a big step. And if anyone can navigate the complexities of the wolf world, it's you."

Annie returned the smile, grateful for Mom's understanding. "Thanks, Mom. It means a lot to have your support."

As we continued our conversation, I couldn't help but feel excited about Annie and Lucian's future together. I wondered if that would be Liam and me one-day discussing marriage.

Mom smiled, her eyes twinkling with pride. "You two are my greatest blessings," she said softly. "I am so proud of the woman you have become, and I know that you will continue to achieve great things in life. Remember, no matter where life takes you, you will always have a home with us."

Tears welled in my eyes as Mom spoke, touching me deeply. "Thank you, Mom," I said, my voice filled with emotion. "I couldn't have done it without your love and support."

Annie nodded in agreement, her eyes shining with gratitude. "Yes, Mom, thank you for always being there for us, guiding and believing in us."

With tears of happiness streaming down our cheeks, we hugged Mom tightly, grateful for her unwavering love and support.

As we stepped out of the café, the afternoon sun casting a warm glow around us, I couldn't help but feel rejuvenated after our pampering session. The tension and stress of the day seemed to melt away, replaced by a sense of peace and contentment.

Dad and the girls were bustling around the kitchen when Mom's voice interrupted our thoughts. "What are the three of you up to?" she asked, her tone laced with surprise.

Dad looked up from the stove, a proud smile on his face. "We're helping Grandpa, Nana," Kaitlin chimed in, her eyes shining with excitement as she stirred a pot on the stove with Paige by her side, carefully following their grandad's instructions.

"What a sight this is." Mom looked amazed.

I chuckled at Kaitlin's incredulous expression. "Well, I'm sure Uncle Lucian could use some extra help in the kitchen, too," I replied with a playful grin, glancing at Dad, who nodded in agreement.

Paige's playful jab elicited a laugh from all of us. "Hey, I do not burn everything," Kaitlin retorted with mock offense, her eyes sparkling with mischief.

With nods of agreement, we wrapped up our meal preparations, eager to rest before our busy shopping day and returning home.

We rose with renewed energy the following day, eager to embark on our shopping adventure. "Alright, girls, let's get ready," I announced, excited about the day ahead. We've got a lot to do before heading home for the party. Hopefully, everything will be sorted out by then."

Annie and the girls nodded in agreement, already buzzing with anticipation for the day ahead. "I can't wait to find the perfect outfits," Annie exclaimed, her eyes excitedly shining.

Kaitlin and Paige exchanged excited glances, eager to join the fun. "Me too! I hope we find something amazing," Kaitlin chimed in.

With our spirits high and our minds set on our mission, we set out to make the most of our shopping day.

The streets of New Orleans were buzzing with people. Everyone seemed to have somewhere to go, and the shops were packed.

Thankfully, the clothing store we were eager to visit first was empty. Mom took Kaitlin and Paige while Annie and I went to look for some sexy dresses.

"I hope we find something amazing," Annie said as we entered the store.

"Me too," I replied, scanning the racks. "It's so nice that it's not crowded in here."

"Yeah, we can take our time and try things on without a rush," Annie agreed.

"Do you think this would look good on me?" I asked, holding up a red dress.

Annie gave me a once-over and smiled. "Absolutely. You should try it on."

I tried it on but wasn't too fond of this particular cut. I needed something unique.

"How does it look?" I asked, stepping out of the dressing room.

Annie tilted her head, considering. "It's nice, but I think you can find something better. Maybe something shorter and with a heart-shaped top?"

"Exactly what I was thinking," I said, relieved she understood.

Annie then held up a blue dress she had found. "What do you think of this one?"

"You always look great in blue," I said, admiring the dress. "You should try it on."

"Annie, you look beautiful. It's perfect. Lucian will go gaga over your new look," I said, admiring her. "The blue blends so perfectly with your blonde highlights. You look stunning, sis. You're almost unrecognizable."

Just then, the lady in the store approached us with a smile. "You look amazing in that dress," she remarked to Annie. "It brings out your eyes."

"Thank you," Annie remarked, smiling at the lady.

She then turned to me. "What type of dress are you looking for?"

I looked at her and explained, "I'm looking for something short with a heart-shaped neckline, preferably red or black. And I need shoes to match, too."

Annie nodded thoughtfully. "Got it. Let's see what we can find."

Annie went with the lady to look for shoes to match her dress. A moment later, the lady returned and stood next to me, holding up two beautiful dresses, just as I had imagined—one in red and one in black.

I couldn't take my eyes off them. "These are perfect," I whispered, awestruck.

Annie returned with matching shoes for both dresses and a pair of gold high heels. "Look what I found!" she said excitedly. "These will look amazing with either dress."

I smiled, feeling a rush of excitement. "Annie, you're the best. Let's try everything on!"

I couldn't decide which dress to take—they were both excellent. "I'll take both," I said, beaming. "And all the shoes here, plus these three bags."

The lady rang up my items, and I paid in cash.

Annie went to the counter and paid for her dress. She then chose another dress, a few pairs of shoes, and a couple of handbags.

Mom returned from the teen section with the twins, Kaitlin and Paige. They both wore beautiful baby pink dresses, matching shoes, and tiaras.

"That's what we forgot!" Annie yelled, suddenly remembering.

Paige ran back and grabbed three more tiaras, one for each of us. The lady at the counter who helped us earlier rang everything up, and Mom paid for the additional items.

"Looks like we're all set," Mom said, smiling at the pile of shopping bags.

"Definitely," I agreed, feeling a thrill of excitement. "This is going to be amazing."

"Now, that was the most fun we've had in a long time," Kaitlin exclaimed. "Shopping is so much fun!"

"You're just like the rest of our Johnston family," Mom said with a chuckle. "We ladies love shopping, especially for clothes."

"What time is it?" Annie asked.

Mom checked her watch. "Time for a quick lunch, and then we need to go home and get ready before we head to Tridion."

"Sounds like a plan," I said, gathering my bags. "Let's find a good place to eat."

We decided to go to the same little café around the corner. We ordered a bottle of wine for the adults while the girls had strawberry milkshakes and burgers. Mom, Annie, and I opted for steak and fries.

"How spoiled are we?" I asked, taking a sip of wine. "This is the life. Gosh, I miss this."

"Me too," Annie admitted. "We must return to New Orleans more often to do things like this. The last two days have been glorious."

Mom nodded in agreement. "Absolutely. It's been wonderful spending time together like this."

We finished our lunch and headed back home.

"We need to get ready," Dad said eagerly, already dressed in his suit.

"You look so handsome, Daddy," Annie and I exclaimed in unison.

"Thank you, girls. You better get a move on," Dad replied with a smile. Liam and Lucian were here earlier to check how far along you were. They said everything was ready, and the guests arrived about an hour ago. I told them you went shopping, so they surely understand how much you love shopping."

"Alright, let's not keep them waiting any longer," I said, grabbing my bags and heading to my room.

"Time to get glamorous!" Annie added, hurrying after me.

We finished getting ready and walked downstairs. Everyone looked so glamorous.

"Oh wow, we've outdone ourselves," Mom said, beaming with pride.

"We all look amazing," I added, admiring our reflections in the hallway mirror.

"The guys will be shocked when they see us," Annie said, grinning from ear to ear.

"Let's go show them what they're in for," I said, excited, as we headed back to the party in Tridion.

We arrived at the sound of pumping music. People were dancing, laughter filling the air. Liam and Lucian were acting as DJs, techno music blaring in the background.

As the music stopped, it was evident that they knew we had arrived. The expressions on their faces were priceless.

"Oh, wow," that was all they could manage, both staring at us.

"Hey, boys, we're back. Did you miss us?" I teased.

They approached us, and one of them exclaimed, "You both look extraordinary, exquisite. You're so beautiful."

"Of course, we missed you. Liam couldn't take his eyes off you," one of them replied. Then Kaitlin and Paige came running up.

"Hey, Dad, what do you think of our outfits?" they asked eagerly.

Liam got choked up. "You both look like your mother. You're beautiful. I got fortunate," he said, watching my expression closely.

Then, leaning in, he whispered, "I love you, and I'm so thankful you're mine. I still don't know how I got so lucky. But I did."

"I'm the lucky one, Liam. You saved me and our family. Now, we have a chance to live a full life, to do what makes us happy. You make me and the girls so happy. We're grateful for you, too," I said gratefully.

With that, Liam kissed me, and in that moment, I knew this would be our forever...?

Epilogue

Together, Liam and I weave our love and laughter through the maze of our sanctuary, our bond growing stronger with each step. One question lingers as we reflect on our incredible journey: are we soulmates?

Within the comforting embrace of our home, we are surrounded by our close-knit community, a new era dawns. Liam, Lucian, and Gregory rise as Tridion's new kings, leading our world into an era of peace where supernatural creatures live in harmony. No longer enemies or fearful, they become the guardians of our realm.

With Annie and me by their side, we support Lucian and Liam while Gregory begins his quest for a soulmate. Although our coven offers a few possibilities, many are already paired. Undeterred, we set out to find Gregory's perfect match, careful not to disrupt fate. Alongside us, my magnificent dragon, Stormfire, soars through the skies, her fiery breath and formidable presence a symbol of our might and unity.

Our community stands united through every challenge, a beacon of strength amongst change. Our journey is one of growth and discovery, reflecting our shared dreams and aspirations. Through highs and lows, our commitment to each other remains unwavering.

Our adventures continue as we delve deeper into the mysteries of Tridion. One day, a dark omen appears in the sky, a harbinger of an ancient evil stirring beneath the mountains. Stormfire senses the danger first, her mighty wings beating urgently as she guides us toward the looming threat. Together, we embark on a perilous journey to uncover the source of this malignancy.

Along the way, we encounter forgotten ruins and cryptic prophecies, each clue leading us closer to the heart of the darkness. Liam's leadership and Lucian's wisdom guide our steps, while Gregory's strength and Annie's cunning prove invaluable. We face trials that test our limits: treacherous ravines, enchanted forests, and spectral guardians. Yet, our bond strengthens through every obstacle, and our resolve hardens.

As we traverse these lands, we encounter allies—supernatural beings long hidden in the shadows. A reclusive fae queen, Trinity, a noble centaur chieftain, and a mysterious shapeshifter join our cause, each bringing unique strengths to our fellowship. Together, we form a diverse alliance, united against the encroaching darkness.

One fateful night, we reach the entrance to an ancient cavern rumored to house the essence of the evil threatening our land. With Stormfire lighting our path, we descend into the depths, ready to confront whatever lies ahead. The air is tense as we venture further; ancient spells and protective wards crack around us.

In the cavern's heart, we face an entity of pure malevolence, a dark sorcerer long thought defeated. His power is immense, his hatred palpable. A fierce battle ensues, with Stormfire unleashing torrents of flame and our combined might clashing against his dark magic. The fight is arduous, but our unity and determination prevail. The sorcerer is defeated, his essence sealed away, restoring peace to Tridion.

Emerging from the cavern, we are greeted by the dawn of a new day. Once dark and foreboding, the sky now shines with the promise of hope and renewal. Our community, strengthened by our trials, celebrates our victory. Inspired by our journey, Gregory finds his soulmate in one of our newfound allies, a fierce and noble warrior who stood beside us in our darkest hour.

As love, growth, and community intertwine, a tapestry of hope and possibility emerges. With new beginnings on the horizon, we eagerly anticipate more adventures and surprises in Tridion. This is not the end but the thrilling start of our reign as Kings and Queens, shaping the kingdom with love and unity.

We look forward to a future brimming with peace, love, and prosperity, united as one kingdom to face any threat. As Tridion's supreme witch and protector, I vow to defend both realms against the encroaching darkness. Whenever evil dares to invade, I will stand firm and fight for what is right...

Don't miss out!

Visit the website below and you can sign up to receive emails whenever Andrea A James publishes a new book. There's no charge and no obligation.

https://books2read.com/r/B-A-QCVVC-HGTIF

BOOKS 2 READ

Connecting independent readers to independent writers.

About the Author

Born and raised in the vibrant city of Johannesburg, South Africa, I've been captivated by the magic of storytelling since childhood. As a devoted bookworm, my love for literature has been a constant companion, fueling my dreams of becoming a full-time writer.

For years, the idea of pursuing my passion seemed like a distant fantasy, overshadowed by the pressures of daily life. However, everything changed four years ago when I crossed paths with extraordinary individuals—my dear friends Iris, Cibele, and Colin—who saw the storyteller within me and encouraged me to embrace my calling.

As a creative Pisces, I discovered that crafting stories wasn't just a hobby; it was a calling that resonated deep within my soul. Despite the demands of being a single mother to my son and maintaining a full-time job in procurement, I carve out precious moments in the evenings and weekends to nurture my true passion: writing.

The delicate balance between motherhood, career, and writing is a testament to my unwavering determination and dedication to my craft. With dreams of becoming a renowned, traditionally published author, I am driven by the desire to make a meaningful impact through my storytelling.

Beyond the pages of my books, I envision creating an animal shelter to provide sanctuary and care for countless needy animals. This melding of my love for animals and passion for writing represents my commitment to leaving a lasting legacy of compassion and creativity.

Every day, I draw strength from the memory of my late brother, whose unwavering belief in me continues to inspire my journey. Supported by my loving parents, sister, and friends, I am reminded of the power of love and encouragement in achieving one's dreams.

In my literary endeavors, my debut novel "Hearts Entwined" received praise, earning several five-star reviews. Encouraged by its success, I am currently busy with twenty other books that you won't be able to put down.

All my Love xoxo

Milton Keynes UK
Ingram Content Group UK Ltd.
UKHW030147051224
452010UK00001B/80

9 798230 480655